Country Girls 2:

Carl Weber Presents

Country Girls 2:

Carl Weber Presents

Blake Karrington

www.urbanbooks.net

Urban Books, LLC
97 N18th Street
Wyandanch, NY 11798

ISBN 13: 978-1-62286-937-4
ISBN 10: 1-62286-937-0

First Trade Paperback Printing November 2015
Printed in the United States of America

10 9 8 7 6 5 4 3 2 1

This is a work of fiction. Any references or similarities to actual events, real people, living or dead, or to real locales are intended to give the novel a sense of reality. Any similarity in other names, characters, places, and incidents is entirely coincidental.

Distributed by Kensington Publishing Corp.
Submit orders to:
Customer Service
400 Hahn Road
Westminster, MD 21157-4627
Phone: 1-800-733-3000
Fax: 1-800-659-2436

Country Girls 2:

Carl Weber Presents

Blake Karrington

Prologue

The car was completely silent as Diamond drove down the dark highway. Alexus sat in the back seat holding Dink at gunpoint, not once taking her eyes off him. She was more than willing to open up his chest in the event that he tried to act stupid.

"Y'all can let a nigga out right here," Dink said, breaking the silence in the car. "I'll walk."

"Nah, you still too close to my city. You have to learn ya lesson, and if I let you go now, you can just walk back to ya ride," Alexus told him, lying with a straight face. She just wanted him to shut up.

They did not intend to let him go. This was their second time catching Dink selling large amounts of dope on the west side of Charlotte. The crew had given him a pass the last time. Since he wasn't from the city, he was given a stern warning, and it was reiterated that Charlotte belonged to MHB. But just like a nigga, instead of taking heed to the advice, as he should have, Dink didn't take them seriously and continued to do his own thing. That's what brought him to his current situation.

"It's coming up," Alexus told Diamond as she read the signs on the side of the road.

A couple of minutes later, Diamond merged off the exit and proceeded down the empty street.

"Motor Trend," Dink said to himself, trying to remember his location.

When the car came to a complete stop, Diamond turned off the engine. Except for the single light shining over the dirt bike trail about a quarter mile away, the area was pitch black.

"Damn, y'all gonna make a nigga walk from here? I don't even know where the fuck I'm at," Dink said, trying his best to look out the tinted windows of the truck.

"Nigga, shut up and get out!" Alexus said, shoving the gun into his side.

Diamond grabbed the 9 mm that was sitting on her lap then exited the car with Dink and Alexus.

"Walk," Diamond told him, nodding toward the dirt trails.

Dink started to walk, but his gut told him that they weren't going to let him just walk out of there. Alexus and Diamond took small strides behind him with their guns aimed at his back. It wasn't until Dink saw where they were taking him that he realized for sure that the two women were about to kill him. The narrow dirt road kept getting darker and darker. Dink's flight instincts kicked in and he took off.

Alexus let off two shots as she took off behind him. Diamond joined the chase, firing several more shots as she ran. Dink was fast. He was starting to put a nice distance between him and the girls. He ran toward the dirt bike trail, ducking the bullets that whizzed right over his head. In the distance, he could hear the sound of a dirt bike going through the course, and the only thing that stood between him and the bike course was a twelve-foot wall of dirt that stretched the length of the track. The gunfire had ceased.

He scurried up the mountain of dirt as fast as he could, then tossed himself over once he got to the top. His body tumbled down the other side. He got up and was about to continue running when he looked up and saw Gwen standing directly in front of him with her gun pointed at his head.

"Don't shoot me," he managed to utter right before Gwen squeezed the trigger, sending a single bullet through the front of his head.

Hearing the shot, Diamond and Alexus hastily climbed to the top of the dirt hill. They paused when they saw that Dink was laid out flat and Gwen was standing over him. Tired as hell, they were short of breath as they slid down the other side of the dirt hill on their butts.

Gwen shook her head and smiled. Diamond and Alexus looked beat. Their clothes were dirty and their hair looked a mess.

"Damn, that muthafucka was fast," Diamond said. She walked over and fired another bullet into Dink's head. "That's for making a bitch run and sweating out my new perm."

The dirt bike rider in the distance caught everyone's attention. He was on the other side of the track, but he was on his way over to where the girls were.

"Let's get outta here," Gwen said and began to climb up the dirt hill.

Diamond and Alexus made their way back up and over the dirt hill, still tired from climbing the first time. The three women vanished into the night like cat burglars, leaving Dink's body behind for the lonely rider to find him on his final turn around the track.

Chapter 1

The visiting room was nearly empty when Gwen stepped in. She went straight to the vending machines and grabbed a couple of sodas. Almost four months had passed since her last visit with Niya, and that was mainly due to how far the feds had shipped her out. No one could figure out why Niya was sent all the way to Tucson, Arizona, but it was the government, and they could do what they pleased once you belonged to them.

Gwen did manage to make the trip on a couple of occasions, but as time went on, business on the streets took up a lot of her attention. Niya understood; she knew what it was like to have all the pressure of the team on her back.

"You look good, girl," Gwen said, greeting Niya with a hug and a kiss on the cheek.

"You like my khakis?" Niya playfully joked, stepping back and posing in her inmate uniform.

Gwen just shook her head. Even under these circumstances, Niya kept her sense of humor.

"Girl, you crazy." Gwen smiled then sat down. "Did you get the pictures of the twins I sent you two weeks ago?"

"Yeah, thanks. I can't believe how big they're getting," Niya replied. "I know they bad as hell." She chuckled.

Gwen couldn't argue with that. The twins had been living with her for the past seven months, and she had come to know them very well. Bad wasn't the word for those kids. They were terrorists. Even so, Gwen loved them as if they were her own. Having them around led to her decision to finally remove Zion from life support. She knew he was in heaven now, cutting up with all the other children, and that warmed her heart.

"I still don't know why you won't let me bring them up here," Gwen said, taking a swig of her soda.

"Nah. I don't want them to see me like this. Then after the visit is over, I know they are gonna cry 'cause I can't leave with them. I just can't do that right now. I'll be home in a couple of months anyway," Niya replied.

November 19th was Niya's release date. She had to go to a halfway house, but that would only be for about a month, or at least until her probation officer approved her home plan.

"So how is he?" Niya asked, inquiring about Chad.

She really hadn't heard from him much. Even though they weren't together, she still cared about his well-being. Plus, she knew how much losing Zion had affected him.

"He's doing okay." Gwen lied. "Chillin' wit' the twins."

Chad wasn't doing well at all, and hadn't been since the day they buried their son. He stopped going to work, which cost him his job, and the couple of rental houses he owned were becoming worthless in the housing market due to him letting them fall apart. Not only that, but he had also picked up a bad drinking habit. He was drunk every day. On several occasions, he had to be taken to the hospital for near alcohol poisoning.

Gwen didn't want to tell Niya all of that. She didn't want to stress her with outside problems. The main focus right now was preparing for Niya's return to the streets.

"What about the girls? Is everybody all right?" she asked, missing her MHB sisters.

"Everybody's good. We miss the hell out of you. Everybody sends their love, and MHB is growing larger than ever. Last I checked, we were over five hundred members, scattered throughout Charlotte, Durham,

Raleigh, and Greensboro. We growin' at a nice rate, and it's all love out there.

"Wow!" Niya said with a big smile on her face.

She was excited to hear how much MHB had grown. With over five hundred members, they pretty much had Charlotte on lockdown. They controlled the drug trade and now were about to expand into a different market, one that would take them to a completely new level.

Gwen and Niya sat for the remainder of the visit, catching up on old times. Gwen had made plans to stay in Tucson for the weekend, so they were going to have a few days to talk. She definitely had some power moves for MHB, but before she could put anything into motion, she had to run it by Niya. Even while in prison, Niya was the boss. Nothing went on in the streets without her knowledge.

Mayo sat in the prison yard with his celly, Lucky. They were talking smack about how they used to get down when they were out in the world. That was typical for most inmates to do. They shared war stories and bragged about how many females they'd slept with. Most of the time it was all lies, but Mayo was known in the streets and could back up every story he told and prove that he had sex with every female he talked about.

"Inmate Harper, report back to your housing unit!" the correctional officer yelled over the intercom.

Mayo looked at his celly and raised an eyebrow. He had no idea why he was being called.

Once he got back to the block, the unit officer informed him that he had a legal visit. He was given a pass then sent on his way. The whole way to the visiting room, he thought about his upcoming trial. The last he had heard, the government was ready to take another shot at a jury trial.

"I hope you got some good news," Mayo said to his attorney when he entered the lawyer's room.

"In fact, I believe I do," Robert Graham, Mayo's lawyer responded. "I just came from the district attorney's office. They are willing to drop the first degree murder charge and allow you to plead guilty to conspiracy to commit murder," he said, pulling the paperwork out of his briefcase.

"And how much time does that hold?" Mayo asked.

"The D.A. said they would go as low as ten years for the conspiracy count. I think it's a hell of a deal, since you're facing life without the chance of parole if you get convicted on the murder one charge," the lawyer explained.

The state had a case, but the chances of winning it were fifty-fifty. Obviously, the jury couldn't come together and agree on a verdict at his last trial. That's what caused the hung jury. When the government knows that their case really isn't that strong, they normally offer a deal just so they can at least walk away with a conviction. Many times, it's a deal one would be stupid to refuse.

"So you telling me I'ma get ten years if I sign these papers?" Mayo asked as he sifted through the paperwork.

"Yeah! You can be a free man within the next eight years," the lawyer said.

Ten years compared to a life sentence was a no brainer, and Mayo wasn't stupid at all. Ten years was nothing; it was spending the rest of his life in prison that would kill him.

Mayo finished looking through the documents then looked up at his lawyer. His choice had been made the moment Graham told him the number of years.

"Let me see ya ink pen," Mayo said, more than willing to sign off on the deal.

Chad walked into the gas station and approached the counter. Without a word, he pulled out a large .44 Magnum and pointed it at the cashier's head. No mask covered his face; he looked at the cashier dead on, as if he wanted to be remembered. The strong scent of alcohol radiated from his pores, tickling the cashier's nose.

"Take whatever you want. Please, just don't shoot me," the scared man pled, placing both hands in the air.

Several customers darted out of the store when they realized what was happening. To the surprise of the cashier, Chad made no move to stop them. He actually seemed to be pleased.

Another employee came from the back and walked right into the robbery. "Oh, shit!" he said as he stepped back with his hands up.

Chad still didn't say anything. He nodded toward the cash register while keeping his gun on the two men. Then he pointed with his free hand to the boxes of cigarettes behind the counter, and finally to the candy bar section.

The cashier looked at him curiously, wondering what he was thinking. Snapping out of his thoughts, he quickly did what he was told and threw everything in the bag.

The tension in the air was thick as the employees waited anxiously for Chad's next move. The bag sat on the counter, but Chad just kept his gun pointed at the two cashiers.

"Please don't shoot," one of the men pled, feeling that this was more than just a simple robbery.

Chad didn't budge. He didn't say a word. He just kept the two men at gunpoint and waited.

Within minutes, Charlotte police were on the scene. One of the customers had immediately called the cops once they were safely out of the store.

"Drop the gun and get down on your knees!" one officer yelled as he burst through the door. "I'm not gonna tell you again!" the cop threatened, inching his way toward Chad.

The young rookie cop swore for a moment that he was going to have to shoot Chad, but as he walked right up behind him, Chad began to lower his weapon. He didn't put up a fight or a struggle; he complied by dropping to his knees. As the officer was patting Chad down to see if he had any more weapons, Chad looked up at the two scared employees and he silently mouthed the words, "I'm sorry."

Diamond walked into the condo and jumped slightly at the sight of people standing in the living room. She was about to reach for her weapon, until Tiffany pushed her way through the crowd and began clapping. Everybody else in the room joined her. They were celebrating the fact that Diamond had received her realtor's license that morning after completing a three-month program. It didn't seem like much to the average person, but for MHB, it was a huge step. Diamond was just the first. Tiffany, Gwen, Alexus, April, and Portia would get their licenses too.

"Congratulations!" Tiffany said, leaning in and giving Diamond a hug. "We 'bout to turn dis shit up!"

Diamond looked around the room and smiled. Everyone there was an MHB member, and it had to be at least fifty girls present. Diamond could feel the love. It was a feeling she could never get tired of. The support and loyalty MHB members showed to each other was beyond anything any of the girls had ever seen in their lives.

***

Chad was taken to the police station and charged with robbery, reckless endangerment, and about twenty other offenses. Chad didn't mind at all. He needed this case to be violent. This was the only way he could heighten his chances of being put in one of the most violent housing units down at county lockup. Two main blocks in that jail housed violent offenders. It was a fifty-fifty chance he would land on his intended cellblock, but Chad was willing to take that chance.

"Chad?" Detective Rose said as she passed the holding cells.

Chad tried to turn away before she could see him, but it was too late. She was standing right in front of the cell, looking directly at him.

"What are you in here for?" she asked, tucking her folder under her arm.

Chad shook his head in frustration. It wasn't because he didn't want to answer her, but more so because he knew that Rose was still an active member of MHB. The last thing he wanted her to do was try to help out, which he knew she was going to do anyway.

"Drunk in public, and disorderly conduct," he lied, hoping she wouldn't investigate any further after hearing the non-serious charges. "I'll be out when I sober up."

She could see that he was drunk, but she knew that wasn't the reason he was there. The cell he was in gave it away. Drunk and disorderly conduct inmates were placed in the tank on the other side of the cellblock. Where Chad was, only violent offenders were housed. Rose went ahead and played along for the time being.

"A'ight, Chad. Let me know if you need anything," she said, tapping on the cell door before walking off.

Rose didn't hesitate to go straight to the logs to find out what Chad was in for. She was a cop, but her loyalty remained with MHB, so whether Chad liked it or not, he was still an extended part of the family.

"Damn, Chad!" Rose said, looking at the long list of charges stemming from the robbery. "What in da hell did you do?"

She was perplexed. This wasn't like Chad. As Rose thought about it, she realized what Chad was attempting to do. She grabbed his paperwork and stormed back down to the holding cells. She slammed the papers on the window of the cell's door.

"Are you serious, Chad?" Rose snapped. "You actually think this shit is gonna work?"

Chad didn't say a word. He just looked at Rose.

"Are you forgetting that you got a set of twins out there, you asshole?" Rose spazzed.

She wasn't just MHB; she was personally connected to Niya. Her family was Rose's family. The twins were like her niece and nephew, and she had mad love for them. Chad was being selfish, and he wasn't thinking about the lives of his other two kids. All he wanted to do was kill Mayo, and he was risking his life just to get next to him for the opportunity to do so. Anything could have happened. The rookie cop that arrested him could have blown his head off at the gas station. Chad wasn't thinking about stuff like that, and that was what made Rose so angry.

She walked away from the door without saying another word. As she walked down the cellblock, she reached into her back pocket and pulled out her cell. She didn't know what Gwen was going to say about it, but she definitely was going to let her know what was going on.

"What's the matter?" Tiffany asked Diamond as she joined her on the balcony.

Diamond leaned over the rail with a glass of Moscato in her hand, looking out into the city.

"What? You thinkin' about Ni?" Tiffany asked.

"Yeah. I wish she was here right now. I miss da hell out of her," Diamond confessed.

"Well, it won't be that much longer. Two more months." Tiffany smiled, leaning over the rail next to her.

Everyone was anticipating the boss's return to the streets. She was like the missing link, and although MHB was still running strong, it would have been a lot stronger with Niya leading the pack. Her presence was missed and needed.

"Oh, yeah, I set up the meeting with the Hearst Tower for next week. We have to bring proof of our business license along with our checkbook. A floor just opened up, so we gotta be on point," Tiffany advised.

Hearst Tower was one of the tallest office buildings in downtown Charlotte, and MHB was trying to set up shop among some of the most lucrative companies in North Carolina. This was all part of the plan to expand MHB. It would put the crew in a position to launder millions of dollars in drug money through their very own realty company. Houses, storefronts, and open land were a hot commodity and the perfect cover to clean large amounts of money at one time. After getting the right office space, the next thing to do was start buying properties. That wasn't going to be easy, especially in the cutthroat business of real estate.

Other companies were like wolves when it came to buying and selling properties. If MHB was going to have a chance, they were going to have to do what they did best: roll up their sleeves and get their hands a little dirty. It was something neither Diamond, nor the rest of the crew had a problem doing.

Chapter 2

Chad spent the night at the police station and then was shipped down to the county jail after not being able to post the fifty-thousand-dollar bail. He could easily pay it. All it would have taken was one phone call, but he was on another mission. So far, everything was going according to plan.

"All right, look, guys. The faster we get this process out the way, the faster I can get y'all to ya assigned housing unit," the correctional officer said as he walked over to the fifteen men, including Chad, standing against the wall.

The receiving room procedures took Chad and the rest of the men at least five hours to complete the process. Now, they were waiting to find out what block they were assigned to.

"Yo, you gonna eat that?" a dopefiend asked, seeing that Chad wasn't touching his bag lunch.

Chad gave it to him. He really didn't have an appetite for food. He was only hungry to kill, and Mayo was the only thing on the menu. He just hoped that once he made it to the cellblock, he would have enough time to do what he had to do before the police interview. Chad planned to kill Mayo with his bare hands. There was no question in his mind that he could do it. He had enough anger built up inside him to break every bone in Mayo's body.

"Everett!" one of the guards called out, motioning with his hands for Chad to come up to the front desk.

He walked out of the holding cell with his bedroll and cup right up to the front desk. The officer looked into the computer screen then back up at Chad before speaking.

"You can toss the bed roll in the hamper over there. It seems that you have made bail," the guard informed him.

"Bail? What do you mean I made bail?" Chad shot back with a bit of an attitude.

"Look, you wanna go home or what?" the guard questioned.

Chad wasn't trying to go anywhere except to where Mayo was, and that wasn't on the streets. He wanted to do what he had set out to do. "I'm refusing bail," he told the guard, determined to get to the cellblocks.

"Hey, you can refuse bail, but for your safety, we're gonna have to put you in the hole or protective custody until you go back to court," the guard told him.

Chad was frustrated, irritated, and downright mad as hell. Going to the hole would defeat the purpose. He would never be able to get to Mayo that way. He had no other choice but to toss his bedroll in the hamper and prepare for discharge.

Niya walked back to her housing unit from the visiting room, happy and thankful for Gwen coming out and staying for the weekend. She enjoyed the time they had to talk. It took her back to the better days when she and Gwen were best friends. They hadn't laughed and gossiped like that in a minute. Friday and Saturday were all about fun, but when Sunday came around, it was all about business.

Gwen broke down the status of the drug game and where MHB was concerning cleaning the money. She gave Niya the whole rundown about the realty company and the plan to wash the money through businesses and the housing market. Gwen went into specific details about the laundering process, all of which was approved by Niya. In that aspect, everything was a go.

"What da hell?" Niya mumbled to herself as she walked into the unit.

The tension in the air was thick, and females were huddled up like it was about to be a riot. It didn't help that all eyes were on Niya as she walked toward her cell. All the girls that were from Charlotte were standing in front of Niya's unit. It was only five of them, including Melissa, Niya's celly from North Philly.

"What's goin on?" Niya asked as she walked up to the cell.

"One of dese dirty bitches stole my fuckin' radio!" Melissa shouted as she stepped out of the cell so everybody could hear her.

Melissa had her hair wrapped up and her boots tied up tight. She was amped up and ready to fight.

"All this shit for a radio?" Niya asked, looking around the unit at the many girls from different cities, standing around, also ready to fight. "Come here, Mel," Niya said, grabbing her by the arm and pulling her into the cell.

Big Trina and the rest of the North Carolina girls remained posted out in front of the cell door.

"How much longer until you go home?" Niya asked.

"Come on, Ni. Don't do—"

"How much fucking longer?" Niya asked again, stepping in front of Melissa.

"Six weeks," she answered, putting her head down in shame. "But, Ni, I can't let these bitches try—"

"Stop!" Niya cut her off. "Yo, I fucks wit' you, Melissa, and I'd be less of a friend if I didn't tell you that dis shit here ain't worth it. You know these miserable bitches be running around here tryin' to snatch release dates. You about to fall into a trap, girl," Niya told her. "You got six weeks left, and I got eight weeks to go. Let's finish up this time and get the hell out of here," Niya said, sticking her fist out for a pound.

Melissa needed that. She needed to be snapped back to the reality of her situation. As bad as she hated being in jail, it wouldn't make any sense for her to mess up her release date now . . . especially over a twenty-eight-dollar Walkman. The math just didn't add up, and now Melissa was starting to see the wisdom in Niya's words.

"You right, Ni. I'ma leave dat shit alone," Melissa said, giving Niya a pound. "You like a sister to me. I don't know what I'd do if you wasn't here."

Melissa didn't know the half of it. Everything Niya did had a purpose, and even when she was thousands of miles away from home, she continued to display her boss pedigree. Niya had bigger plans for Melissa, and she'd be damned if she was going to let a petty-ass radio get in the way. Niya always had been, and always would be, smarter than that.

Chad walked into the lobby of the police station with his things in his hand. He immediately copped an attitude when he saw Diamond standing at the front door with an obvious attitude of her own. When Rose couldn't get in contact with Gwen, she gave Diamond a call, who in turn went and paid Chad's bail. She still had some hate in her heart for him because of the way he had done Niya. He had been the originator of the beef between her two girls in the first place. Diamond had a good mind to leave his ass in jail. However, she also knew both of her girls still had love for him, so she went ahead and posted the bond.

"You're welcome, nigga," she said with an attitude when Chad brushed by her on his way out the door.

"I didn't ask for your help!" he shot back.

"You know you don't have to go about it like this. Gwen is taking care of that situation. You need to let her handle it, Chad," Diamond said, following him outside.

He stopped at the edge of the pavement and turned around with an angry look on his face that made Diamond stop in her tracks.

"Y'all bitches stay out my fuckin' business!" Chad said through clenched teeth.

Diamond threw both of her hands up and backed away from him. This whole situation was a little too deep for her to understand. Gwen was the only person who could talk to him, so Diamond did the most logical thing and stayed in her lane.

Gwen walked through Charlotte Douglas Airport with her luggage and nothing but relaxation on her mind. Today, all she wanted was a nice hot bath and a couple hours of sleep in her own bed to rejuvenate.

As she walked through the double doors out onto the curb, Gwen could tell by the way Rose was leaning against the car and looking at her that the hot bath and the long nap were going to be put on hold.

"How was your flight?" Rose asked as she walked up and grabbed one of Gwen's suitcases.

"It was long, and I'm tired as hell," Gwen responded.

"Well, I hate to make things worse, but I thought I should let you know that Chad got himself arrested last night. Robbery!" Rose said, tossing the suitcase into her back seat.

"Robbery?" Gwen asked with a confused look. "Who da hell was he tryin' to rob?"

"See, that's the thing. He was faking like he was robbing a gas station, just so he could go to county and hopefully end up on the same block as Mayo. He was going to try and kill him, I'm guessing," Rose told her.

Gwen exhaled loudly as she leaned against the car. Sometimes she really didn't understand the things Chad did. She could understand how he felt about losing their son, but to put his own life in danger trying to get revenge didn't make any sense.

"So where is he now?" Gwen asked, jumping into the passenger's side of Rose's car.

Rose followed and got into the driver's side.

"Well, last night I tried to call you, but ya phone was off. I called Diamond and she went to pay his bail a few hours ago," Rose said, pulling out her cell.

Rose called Diamond, but Diamond didn't know where Chad had gone after he left the police station. The only thing she knew was that he was very upset by the fact that she had posted his bail.

"Tell Diamond to get the girls together and meet me at the condo in two . . . make it three hours." Gwen instructed Rose while she was still on the phone.

Chad was on some other shit, but Gwen still had some business to take care of along with a few messages from Niya. It was time to take MHB to the next level of play, but before that happened, everyone had to be fully on board.

"Can I get you something?" the bartender asked Chad when he walked in and took a seat at the bar.

Chad kept his hand in his jacket pocket, clutching a P.80 Ruger, debating if he should pull the gun, shoot the bartender, and then wait for the cops.

He gripped the gun tighter, knowing that after he did this, there wouldn't be a bail set. Ten times out of ten, the judge would reject administering any bail after already letting him out on one previously violent bond. It was a guaranteed one-way ticket to the county jail, and more than likely, a bed on the same violent housing unit as the enemy who Chad so desperately wanted to kill. He had to make his choice soon.

The bartender was becoming a little suspicious, and he was packing a .357 snub nose himself. He didn't care what Chad was going through. If he got stupid, the bartender wouldn't hesitate to use his weapon.

"Can I help you?" the bartender asked again, reaching under the counter and placing his hand on the revolver.

In a split second, Chad thought about his twins and what Rose had said to him while he was sitting in the cell. He loved his twins, and the more he thought about them, the more he eased up off the gun in his pocket. He wanted revenge, but going about it this way was going to land him in a worse situation than the one he was already in.

"Let me get a couple shots of brandy," Chad said, reaching into his pants pocket and pulling out his money.

The bartender eased up off his gun as well. He could see the stress in Chad's eyes, so instead of pouring the Crown Royal into the shot glass, he simply left the whole bottle on the bar for Chad to pour his own shots.

"Just let me know if you need me to call you a cab," the bartender told him.

Chad nodded his head in agreement and then began to throw back shot after shot.

Diamond, Tiffany, Portia, April, and Alexus were all seated at the large marble round table, waiting for Gwen to show up. They chatted amongst themselves for a few minutes before Gwen walked through the door. She had her new protégé, Kea, with her, a girl she had taken a liking to over the past few months. Hell, the whole crew took a liking to her when they witnessed her struggle, along with her display of loyalty to MHB. She was family now, a spot she had very well earned.

"Hey, y'all!" Gwen said, coming into the kitchen.

Kea greeted everyone before pulling a chair up to the table. Another brief conversation took place before Gwen brought the meeting to order.

"All right, look, y'all. As you already know, I just came back from seeing Niya, and first and foremost, she sends her love to every one of y'all. I'll get with everybody on an individual basis to relay her personal comments." Gwen smiled.

Diamond wanted to cry from just hearing that Niya had sent her love. She was really missing her friend. Out of everyone at the table, she probably missed Niya most. She just couldn't understand why Niya chose not to contact her or send her a visiting form so she could go see her. It ate at her every day, so at times, she was jealous of Gwen for being Niya's only contact.

"A'ight, listen, y'all. We got the green light from Ni to move forward with this realty company. I did some research, and the only way we're going to wash this dope money under the radar is by moving it through businesses. Buying and flipping houses won't be enough. We need storefronts, places that generate thousands of dollars regularly," Gwen explained.

"And how do you suggest we go about doing that?" Tiffany asked, wanting more clarity.

Pretty much everybody at the table was wondering how they were going to start businesses that would generate the type of money Gwen was talking about.

"We gotta start buying businesses that are already up and running: pizza stores, corner stores, hair salons, meat markets, clothing stores, and any other small businesses that are doing good. Niya gave us a budget of three million dollars to work with, so we gotta buy as many businesses and properties as we can at the cheapest price," Gwen explained.

"What makes you think that these people are going to just up and sell us their businesses?" April intervened.

Gwen looked over at Diamond, who had already concluded what had to be done.

"So we about to be on some mob shit?" Diamond said, intrigued by the idea.

"Yeah, we gotta make them offers they can't refuse," Gwen replied, looking around the room for everyone's reaction.

From the looks of things, they were all with it. No one objected to it, which meant that everybody agreed and understood. Just to be sure, Gwen went around the room and gave everyone the chance to voice their opinions, but nobody did. Nothing else needed to be said. Everything was a go.

"Oh, I almost forgot. You know I had to bail Chad out of jail today," Diamond said.

"Yeah, I heard. That man is going through some shit I can't help him with. We don't even talk anymore."

"What about Mayo?" Rose asked. "Word down at the station is he supposed to be pleading guilty. I don't know to how much time, but I do know his court date is in a couple of weeks," Rose spoke.

Gwen didn't want to say anything, but she already had something in motion for Mayo. She kept her plan low key for now, only because she didn't want to mess things up.

"It's being handled." It was all Gwen decided to reveal about the subject. It was better this way, and the whole crew would have to respect her decision.

Chapter 3

"Nigga, what da fuck did I tell you about playin' wit' my money?" Terrence yelled, pointing a metal baseball bat at one of his workers.

"I'm not playin' wit' ya money, homie. Shit just slowed up real crazy right now," the worker responded.

Terrence chuckled and looked over at Randy, who was sitting on the hood of his car, smoking a blunt. "Damn, da nigga said shit slowed up around here." Terrence laughed.

The laughter only lasted for a hot second. Terrence gripped the bat tightly in both of his hands, turned around, and swung it. He hit the worker clean across the jaw, breaking it instantly. Teeth, blood, spit, and anything else he had in his mouth flew out.

The one thing Terrence didn't play around with was his money. That was the easiest way to bring out his violent side, a side he really didn't like to show. Not only did the worker not have Terrence's money, but he was also short on the product, which meant that he was using the dope himself, or he was simply fuckin' up the little money he did make. Either way, he was going to pay for it one way or another. In this instance, he paid for it with his blood.

"Now get dis muthafucka off my corner before I fuck one of y'all up too!" Terrence threatened the other workers, pointing at them with the same bat.

None of them wanted to be next, so they quickly helped the guy up to his feet then walked him down the street.

"Dat shit ain't funny!" Terrence snapped at Randy, who was sitting on the hood of the car, cracking up.

Randy was now laughing so hard that he made Terrence start to chuckle at his own foolish antics. Terrence reached over, grabbed the blunt, and took a pull. It was something he rarely did, but he felt like he needed something to calm his anger.

"Oh, yeah, did you call homegirl?" Terrence asked, passing Randy back the Kush.

"Yeah, we on for tonight. She wanna meet at Reedy Creek Park around seven thirty or eight thirty," Randy informed.

Terrence nodded. He had been messing with his connect for a few months now, and the prices he was getting made the dope game worth swimming in. Hell, it even had him thinking about expanding deeper into the city where the real money was at, but whether he actually did so remained to be seen. He was well aware of the hardships he faced and the danger that lurked in the city. He was no stranger to danger, but at the same time, he wasn't stupid. His man, Dink, was a prime example that once you got into uncharted waters, the sharks came out to feast.

Stacey got up from the kitchen table to answer a knock at the front door. She looked out the small window and saw Cornell, Dink's brother, standing there with about three other men behind him wearing black hoodies. At first, she was a little hesitant to open the door because of the men Cornell had with him. Since she had known him for a while and he had always been real cool with her, she figured he wasn't a threat. Besides, Stacey was Dink's daughter's mother and everybody knew not to mess with her, even Dink's family. That was one reason why none of the other family members liked Stacey. They felt that Dink let her get away with too much shit.

"Wassup, Cornell?" Stacey said, opening the door.

"When was the last time you spoke to my brother?" he asked, brushing past her and entering the house.

Stacey copped an immediate attitude, oblivious to what the situation was with her daughter's father.

"Why? What's goin' on?" she asked, slamming the door in the rest of his boys' faces.

He walked in and looked around the living room. He remained quiet for a minute, grabbing a picture of Dink off the mantel and staring at it. Stacey still didn't know what was going on, but she wasn't going to let Cornell keep walking around her house looking around either.

"Cornell, what the fuck is up?" she asked, walking over to him.

"Sit down," he told her, nodding at the couch.

"No, I'm standing up. Now tell me what's going on."

Cornell didn't even know where to begin, or how to tell her that the father of her baby was dead. Seeing the look he had on his face and the tears that began to fill his eyes, Stacey started to put two and two together.

She looked toward the kitchen, where her daughter was, and covered her mouth. "Oh my God!" she said, taking a seat on the edge of the couch. "No, no, no, no, nooo!" she cried.

Cornell gritted, trying his best to hold back his tears. Now wasn't the time for crying. He already had it in his mind that he was going to find and bury anyone who had something to do with his little brother's death. It didn't matter who it was or where they were from. Looking over at his brother's seed only intensified his desire.

"Yo, Stace, I need you to call ya brother and find out what's goin' on out there in them streets. I know Dink was out there grinding wit' him . . . Yo, yo, yo," he said, snapping his fingers at Stacey, who was crying her eyes out. He needed her to focus on his instructions.

Cornell really couldn't care less about her tears or how she felt. In his eyes, she played a major part in why his little brother decided to go up north and get money. She was the one who introduced him to her brother, Terrence, who was originally from the A, otherwise known as Atlanta, but he had moved up north to dabble in the heroin game.

"Fuck all that. Call ya brotha and tell dat nigga he need to find out what happened to my brother. Tell dat nigga I want answers!" Cornell demanded through Stacey's cries.

"Mommy! Mommy!" her daughter yelled from the kitchen. "I done my food," she playfully said.

Stacey got up to go to her, but Cornell grabbed her by the arm before she could walk away.

"Yo, call ya brotha!" he snapped, squeezing her arm.

Stacey was still shell shocked about the whole situation, and she was a bit irritated by Cornell's demands. Her tears dried up quickly. She snatched her arm out of his hand and looked at him like he was crazy. She thought that he had to be that way because of his grip on her.

"I'll call my brotha later. Right now, I gotta go and attend to my daughter," she said in a stern voice and with an even more serious look.

She rolled her eyes and walked off toward the kitchen, leaving Cornell in the living room by himself. He eventually got up and walked out the front door. He was going to extend her some leeway because of the love his brother had for her. Cornell knew he would be back to see to it that his demands were met. The next time, he would do what was necessary, even if it had to be done by force.

"There she go right there," Randy told Terrence as they walked into the park.

Auntie was on the driving range, hitting a couple of golf balls. She had on the full golf getup and looked like she could be a pro, until she swung the clubs and her inexperience showed. Standing on the other side of the gate was one of her men, armed with a sub machine gun. She also had men in the parking lot and in the bleachers, so she felt totally safe and pretty much untouchable.

"Wassup, Auntie?" Terrence greeted, walking up and standing on the outside of the gate.

He took a good look around and noticed a couple of her men watching him closely.

"You know, I never really understood the whole golf thing," Auntie said, swinging at one of the balls and totally missing. "I'm more of a football girl." She smiled, tossed the club, and walked over to the gate where Terrence was standing.

Randy stood off to the side to give them a little space. He also kept his eyes on the men who kept their eyes on him.

"So, let's talk business," Auntie said as she pulled off her gloves.

"Yeah, well, I wanna go up a little bit with my numbers in hopes that you can come down on ya price," Terrence spoke through the gate.

Terrence's operation was small but did good numbers. Every month, he would buy between ten and fifteen kilos of heroin, most of which he would pump out of the trap houses he owned in the upper part of South Carolina. The rest of it would be moved in weight through a few people he knew in North Carolina, all but Charlotte. He had been warned, and his people had been warned, that the Queen City was off limits. The little dope houses he had in the outskirts of the city stayed under the radar, and that's the only reason he was eating anything out of the Charlotte area.

"So, what are you talkin' about? How much more do you want to buy?" she asked.

"I'm trying to get like twenty-five kilos at a good price," he told her.

She almost laughed at him after hearing the number. She thought that he was going to say a much larger number. She was already giving it to him for a cheap price. Him buying ten more kilos wasn't going to change her prices that much.

"Listen, Terrence, I usually don't answer my phone for anything less than fifty kilos. I been entertaining ya numbers because I thought that you would step ya game up. Now please, don't take this the wrong way. . . ." she said, shaking her head.

"Nah, I understand where you're coming from." He nodded. "Just let me know what you can do for me."

Auntie looked at him and smiled. She kind of liked Terrence and wanted to see him win. "Look, I'ma put you on to somebody,"

"Aww, come on, Auntie," he said in frustration. "Don't do me like that. I like doin' business wit' you."

"No, no, no. The person I'ma hook you up with will help you get ya weight up fast, and the product is the same as mine. I'll even put in a good word so the prices could come down for you."

Terrence scratched his head. He really didn't want a new connect, but it didn't seem like he had any other choice. He definitely wasn't trying to go back to his old supplier. His prices were high, and the dope wasn't as good as Auntie's dope.

"In good faith, I got ten kilos on hand right now for you. I'll give them to you for sixty-five grand apiece."

Sixty-five grand was a nice gesture, considering he usually paid seventy-five grand a kilo. He really didn't want to, but he accepted her offer, hoping that there wouldn't be any major differences with the new connect. The talk about the prices going down sounded even better. Exactly what Terrence needed to step his game up to another level.

Chapter 4

Gwen and Diamond walked into the Hearst Tower downtown, looking like they owned the place. Gwen had on a belted wrap dress by Roberto Cavalli, her long, curly mane draped down to her shoulders, and on her feet were a pair of Alejandro Ingelmo lace-up pumps. She was stunning.

Diamond looked like a bag of money also. She had on a silver studded Rebecca Taylor sheath dress, a pair of black Giuseppe Zanotti shoes, and her gold-and-black hair was pulled back into a ponytail. She turned a few heads with her Coke-bottle shape as she walked over to the elevator.

When they got to the seventeenth floor to meet with the building manager, the two girls looked around the empty floor in amazement. It was spacious, and although there wasn't a lick of furniture present, it still looked nice. At least twenty cubicles filled the space, and several small rooms lined the walls.

"Hello! You must be Gwen," a short, white man greeted them. "I'm Tom."

Gwen and Diamond returned the greeting and shook his hand before being led into a makeshift conference room. This was probably the only room that had a table in it. The girls could tell by the size that in the future, this room could be used as a conference room.

"As you can see, we just renovated this floor. It's fresh, so you can furnish it however you would like," Tom told them. "Did you bring your proof of business and the completed application?"

"Oh, yeah, I'm sorry." Gwen apologized and opened her Louis Vuitton briefcase.

Gwen had come fully prepared and wasted no time breaking down the nature of her business to Tom. All of her paperwork was correct, her credit score was over 700, and her bank was backing her 100 percent. That was key when dealing with white America. It wasn't like the hood, where she could toss money around and get what she wanted. This was a whole other ball game for Gwen, but it helped tremendously to have an MHB member as one of the bank's loan officers. Not only was she approved for the loan that she needed, but her credit score was hiked up to the max.

It took almost an hour to go over and sign the proper paperwork, but by the end of the meeting, Gwen and MHB had secured a seven-year lease for the seventeenth floor of the Hearst Tower. This was no doubt a huge step up from the hood. Both ladies looked out the floor-to-ceiling glass windows and observed the city they had called home all of their lives. Never in their wildest dreams did they imagine one day having an office in one of the downtown buildings they only got to see when riding the city bus through uptown on their way to school. They smiled at each other, knowing there was no stopping them now.

Tiffany and Alexus pulled into the Southside Tire Shop off Clanton Road in a black-on-black Chevy Tahoe. April and Portia pulled in behind them in a black-on-black Cadillac Escalade. Tiffany and Alexus were the only two who got out of the car, both clutching a handgun.

"You girls don't play no games," Noemi said, coming from the garage to meet the women.

"You know it ain't you, Noemi. It's a lot of nuts out here," Tiffany said, tucking her gun back into her waist.

Noemi didn't take the guns being drawn personally. Noemi hadn't expected anything less than how they came, plus she'd taken a liking to Tiffany over the past few months.

Tiffany kind of liked Noemi too. She had never seen a Mexican chick move as hard as Noemi; not to mention the fact that Niya used to tell her stories about Noemi's murder game back in the day.

"So, it's gonna take a little while for my guys to load up ya trucks. You girls wanna eat something in the meantime?" Noemi offered, leading them into the garage.

Tiffany declined the offer, only wanting to get straight to the business. Money still needed to be counted. With a wave of her hand, Tiffany had April get out of the second truck with a duffle bag full of money.

Noemi snapped her fingers several times at two of her men. They jumped out of their seats and headed to the back to grab the cocaine. Tiffany took the money from April and gave it to Noemi.

Tiffany couldn't lie; the food was smelling good. She could almost taste the Spanish chicken and brown rice that simmered in the air. It was irresistible.

"You know what, Noemi? On second thought, I think I can use a bite to eat," Tiffany said, looking over at Alexus and April to see if they were hungry too.

April followed them to the back, but Alexus stayed out front with Portia and watched as the men stuffed bricks of cocaine inside the specially made stash spots in the trucks.

Gwen and Diamond walked off the elevator on the ground level. They were heading toward the front door when a tall, muscular man bumped Gwen, damn near knocking the wind out of her. It felt like she had walked into a brick wall. When the man noticed what happened, he reached out to catch her before she fell.

"Damn!" Gwen yelled, yanking away from his hands.

She glared up at the man, frowning fiercely. He was a gentleman, and he was very apologetic for bumping her so hard. Gwen couldn't even stay mad at him. In fact, the longer she stood there looking at him, the more handsome he became. He had to be at least six foot six, 270 pounds. with a muscular build. He looked like a professional football player in a suit, but only cuter.

"My name is Terrence," he said, extending his hand.

Instead of walking off as she planned, she stood there with her had extended back to him. "Gwen," she greeted with a smile then turned around to walk away.

"Wait, wait. . . ." Terrence said, grabbing her arm lightly. "I know me bumping into you probably was enough, but you think I can get, like, two minutes out of your time?" he asked, looking in Gwen's eyes. "Just two minutes?" he asked again, holding two fingers up.

Gwen was interested in hearing what he had to say. She wanted to see if his brains matched how handsome he looked. She looked down at her watch then back up to him.

"You're on the clock," Gwen said, listening with all ears.

"I'm not gonna lie to you. I been in this building for a little more than a year, and this is the first time I've seen someone as beautiful as you," he said in a soft tone. "Do you got business here, or will this be the last time I see you?"

Gwen blushed for a second but got herself together quickly. She could tell that Terrence was a charmer. "You might be seeing more of me around here, and if you're interested in buying or selling your home, then stop by my office any time after next week and we can discuss it," Gwen replied, reaching into her bag and pulling out a card.

"Your office?" he asked, looking down at the card.

"Yeah, I'll be on the seventeenth floor."

"MHB Realty Company," Terrence said, looking down at the card. "You said you're on the seventeenth floor?" he asked, reaching into his pocket and pulling out a card of his own. "Jackson and Johnson Realty Company." He passed Gwen his card. "I'm on the sixteenth floor, right below you," he said with a grin.

Gwen took his card. She was shocked to see that this handsome man was going to be her competition. Too bad, because she was starting to think he was cute. Gwen went right back into her street mentality, dealing with competition the best way she knew how.

"I'm sorry, but ya two minutes is up," Gwen said, zipping up her bag. "I guess I'll be seeing you around." She nodded at Diamond and turned around to leave.

Terrence let her go this time. He didn't mind a little friendly competition on the block, especially since he was already established in the game. He just didn't want to rub Gwen the wrong way and possibly mess up his chances of getting with her later. Until she could realize that Terrence meant no harm, he was going to take the back seat and give her some space. Besides, she was new to the building, so Terrence had a little time to spare before he made his next move.

Tiffany, Alexus, April, and Portia drove back to the city in trucks loaded to the max with bricks of cocaine. On each return trip from scoring coke, Tiffany would be nervous as hell. Both trucks had approximately 150 kilos in them, more than enough to get the feds' attention if they were to be arrested for drug trafficking. That was something Tiffany wanted to avoid by any means necessary.

"Slow down, Lex," Tiffany told Alexus as they drove down the highway. "Make sure you use ya turn signals if you changing lanes."

"Tiffany, chill. I got this. Every time we come back from Noemi's you get paranoid. I made this run, like, a hundred times now," Alexus responded.

Alexus had a point. The very first time she and Tiffany made that run, Tiffany was so nervous driving back; she pulled over on the highway and told Alexus to drive. Since then, Alexus was the appointed driver. She was always on point with the speed limit, turn signals, and the State Troopers posted along the highway. She even made sure her seat belt was on at all times to avoid being pulled over for the smallest thing.

These were the precautionary steps they had to take in order to ensure that the cocaine would successfully make it back to the city and everyone would stay out of jail. April, the driver of the other truck, took the same precautions, and within an hour, both trucks and all four women were back in the city, safe and sound. Now, the only thing left to do was divide and package up the cocaine for the streets.

"It's gonna take about a week to furnish the place, but I don't wanna waste any time," Gwen said to Diamond as they drove.

"Did you talk to Auntie yet?" Diamond asked.

"Yeah, I'm supposed to be meeting up with her sometime in the next few days. We got enough dope to last us until then, plus Tiffany went to see Noemi today, so we should be straight."

Gwen handled so many drugs that she had to share the responsibility throughout the crew. Tiffany and Alexus were in charge of the cocaine aspect, while Gwen and

Diamond took care of the more profitable drug, heroin. Heroin was the reason MHB had to find a way to rinse the money in order to spend it the way they wanted.

In the middle of their conversation, Gwen's phone began to ring. She reached in her bag to grab it, and then looked at the screen to see that the number was UNAVAILABLE. Gwen sent it right to voice mail, not wanting to answer a blocked number.

That didn't stop the caller from trying again, this time with an unfamiliar number popping up on the screen.

"Yo!" Gwen answered.

"Hi, dis Larry down at Larry's Bar and Grill."

"Oh, hey, Larry," Gwen said, surprised to get a call from him.

Larry's was the local bar that just about everybody went to, even Gwen. She just never knew the phone number to the establishment.

"Yeah, I got Chad down here. He passed out in the middle of my floor. It was a wonder he could give me this number to call," Larry said, looking over at Chad, who was still lying on the floor.

"All right, Larry. I'll be there in, like, twenty minutes." Gwen assured him before hanging up.

"Is everything cool?" Diamond asked, hearing Gwen exhale in frustration.

"Yeah, everything's good. Take me to Larry's," she said, shaking her head while looking out the window.

Gwen explained the situation to Diamond on their way to Larry's. Gwen was getting fed up with Chad doing dumb shit. It had been over a year since Zion's death, and he was still in his grieving stage, like it happened yesterday. The way he was acting and keeping Zion's death fresh was making it hard for Gwen to let go. Every time she turned around, Chad was into something, and every time she tried to help, he would snap.

When they finally pulled up to Larry's, Chad had made it to his feet and was stumbling out of the bar. Diamond started to get out of the car, but Gwen stuck her hand out and stopped her. She had seen something that Diamond didn't see, which was a gun sagging in Chad's front pocket. She didn't want Chad to start acting stupid and mess around and start shooting.

"Just wait here. Let me take care of this," Gwen said, stepping out of the car.

Chad was wasted. He couldn't even walk, but he did manage to find his gun. He rested his hand on the butt of it while he struggled to lean against the wall. Gwen advanced toward him with caution, not certain if she could end up being a target herself.

"Chad!" she yelled as she walked up on him.

He pulled his head up, which seemed to weigh a ton, and tried to adjust his eyes to see who was calling his name. Gwen had to get within a couple feet of him for Chad to recognize who it was. He took his hand off his gun and reached out for Gwen like a child to his mother.

"My . . . My son," he struggled to get out through his slurred speech. "I want my . . . my boy."

The whole way to the car, Chad cried, thinking about his son, calling out Zion's name in the process. Gwen hated this exact thing. Hearing Zion's name called out like that brought tears to her eyes as well. How could she not think about Zion at times like this? Her mind traveled back to earlier that year, when she had done the hardest thing any parent could ever do, and that was to pick out the casket and clothes for her child.

"We have here the deluxe edition. This is considered the Cadillac of caskets. It includes everything one can have—"

"I'll take it," Gwen answered, cutting the funeral director off from his sales pitch.

She had been crying so much throughout the day, starting with picking out a three-piece, navy blue Polo suit for Zion to be buried in, that she had no more tears left to shed. She had put off the arrangements for as long as possible, but Zion's funeral was set for the next day. It was to be a closed ceremony, strictly with her and Chad. Because everyone had suffered and grieved so much during his hospital stay, she and Chad had agreed that it would be better to spare themselves and their family and friends more heartache with a long ceremony. Gwen had asked the funeral home to take care of all the arrangements, which was why she was unsure why the director was still trying to sell her something. She had only come by today to drop off the suit.

Before she was about to leave, the mortician came out and stopped her at the door. "The suit fits him perfectly. Would you like to see?" she asked, while holding her hand out in the direction of the small room.

Gwen's first instinct was to decline, but she knew she was going to have to prepare herself for tomorrow, so she figured it best to get it over with.

When Gwen stepped in the room and saw Zion lying on the metal tabletop, she wished she had followed her first instinct. Even the beautiful way the suit hung on Zion's body couldn't mask the death and paleness of his frame. It looked like he had white makeup all over his face and hands. Gwen's thought that maybe she had cried out all of her tears was incorrect, because they were now flowing freely down her face. Her legs became weak as her head began to spin.

The next sight that she had was the bright lights on the ceiling. It was shining directly in her face, because she was now lying on the floor. She was unsure how she had gotten there, but the mortician and funeral director were trying to help her up. At that moment, Gwen knew she had done the right thing to have a closed ceremony, because there was no way she and Chad would make it through a funeral.

"Everything's gonna be all right, Chad." Gwen tried to comfort him as she laid Chad down in the back seat.

The moment his body hit the leather seats, Chad went out like a light. He was out of it.

Diamond didn't try to say anything. She just watched as Gwen walked around to the passenger's side and got in the car. Diamond did the same and then pulled off while bystanders looked on.

Chapter 5

"Dis shit better not hurt, Niya," Melissa said, taking a seat in the chair.

Big Trina stood by the cell door to make sure the C.O. didn't walk in and catch them. Margret, the jailhouse tattoo artist, prepared her homemade gun and checked her ink level. Today was Melissa's big day. She was officially becoming MHB, only the third to do so in the entire jail over the past year and a half.

"So, where do you want it?" Margret asked, with the tattoo gun in her hand.

This was Melissa's first tattoo, so she really didn't know what the best and worst spots were. The letters had to be at least three and a half to four inches long in bold. Melissa's choice, surprisingly.

"I want it running down my side," Melissa said, lifting her T-shirt over her head.

Big Trina and Margret both looked at Niya, knowing that the side was one of the tenderest places to get a tattoo. They all remembered how much pain Niya went through when she got a picture of a tiger growling on her right side. It took over eight hours to do it, and Niya cried almost half of the time.

"You might wanna rethink that," Niya said, leaning back on her bunk. "Those side tattoos hurt like hell, girl."

Melissa thought about it for a minute, and then she made a decision that surprised everyone. "The pain from this tattoo is only gonna hurt for a little while, but the love

I'ma receive from being MHB will last forever," she said, looking over at Niya.

The whole room was quiet. Comments like that were the reason Niya felt Melissa was ready to be a part of the family. What Melissa said was accurate to the tee. The love that she would get from MHB was unlimited, unconditional, and everlasting.

"Damn, girl, I fucks wit' you," Niya said, getting off her bunk to give Melissa a hug. "I swear the girls are gonna love you," she said as she took a seat on the little gray table in front of Melissa.

For the next few hours, Melissa sat quietly as Margaret branded her body. It hurt like hell, but she took it like a trooper, not shedding a single tear, nor did she ask for a break. Niya looked on the whole time, and when it was finished, Melissa was officially MHB.

Chad woke up with a splitting headache. Khoula, his son, was jumping up and down on the bed watching the Cartoon Network, making Chad's headache even worse. He sat up in the bed and looked around the room. He hadn't been in Gwen's bedroom in so long that he had forgotten how it looked.

"Do you want something to eat?" Gwen asked, walking into the room with Kayla by her side.

"Nah, I'm good," Chad answered, getting up from the bed and heading to the bathroom.

Gwen could see that he had an attitude, but at this point, she couldn't care less about what he was going through. She had something she wanted to get off her chest, but at the same time, she knew she had to be mindful of the twins.

"What's ya problem, Chad?" Gwen asked, pushing open the bathroom door.

Chad whipped out his dick and started to urinate without even answering her. Gwen wanted to just walk up behind him and kick him right in his ass.

"You gonna answer me, Chad?" she asked in a low tone as she looked out at the kids playing on the bed.

"Who da fuck is you? I don't have to answer to you. . . . And where da fuck is my gun?" he shot back with his face twisted.

"You lost ya gun yesterday when ya simple ass got too damn drunk to walk. I had to come down to Larry's to pick you up."

"I didn't ask you to come get me. I was cool," he said as he brushed by Gwen to leave the bathroom.

"Chad, I'm tryin' to help you, but you're not letting—"

"Well, stop tryin' to fucking help me. You've made things bad as it is," he replied, walking over and grabbing his shirt off the floor.

That was the lowest blow Chad had shot at her thus far. She knew exactly what he meant by his comment. He was referring to Gwen being the reason Zion was kidnapped and killed. His comment hit Gwen like a ton of bricks. She was at a stage in her life where she was just starting to get over the guilt of being the sole reason for their son's death.

"Daddy! Daddy!" Kayla yelled, jumping up and down on the bed with her arms in the air.

"Hey, Princess," he said in a not too enthusiastic voice.

Gwen was still in a trance, thinking about what Chad had just said. She didn't even notice him checking the drawers and finding his gun.

"Yo, where my car keys?" Chad asked. "Yoooo!" he yelled, snapping his fingers in front of Gwen's face.

When she came out of her trance, she was hot. Words couldn't even describe the anger she felt, only physical contact. She slapped the shit out of Chad's face then followed it up swiftly with a flurry of punches. Chad took a couple of the punches to his face before he got himself together and gripped Gwen up.

"Fuck you, nigga. I hate you. I hate you!" Gwen yelled. "I didn't mean it. I didn't mean it," she cried as she continued to try to get loose from his grip so that she could keep swinging on him.

The cries from the twins didn't seem to make a difference at all, because Gwen and Chad kept fighting. Chad grabbed Gwen by her throat and slammed her against the bathroom door. He had his hands wrapped so tightly around her neck that it cut off her air supply. Gwen was struggling to get him off her.

"You killed my son!" he yelled, squeezing her neck as tightly as he could for a few seconds then letting her go.

Gwen slid down the bathroom door, holding her neck, wheezing and trying to get the air flowing through her lungs. Chad stood over her, looking down with built-up hatred in his eyes.

"It should have been you instead of him," he said before turning around and leaving the room.

"Where you goin', D?" Dollaz asked, sitting up in bed.

"Babe, every time I leave the room you don't have to ask me where I'm goin'," Diamond said, walking back over and taking a seat on the edge of the bed.

The injuries Dollaz had sustained from the shooting a while back had him feeling very insecure about where he stood with Diamond. He was temporarily paralyzed from the waist down. He had been undergoing intense therapy, trying to learn how to walk again. No matter how much she tried to convince him that she wasn't going anywhere, he just couldn't seem to get the idea out of his mind that Diamond was going to eventually leave him due to his difficulty performing sexually. He hardly ever became erect, and when he did, either it wouldn't last long or he could barely feel the warmth of the woman he loved so much.

"Aye, D, can I be honest wit' you about something?" Dollaz asked.

"Babe, you can talk to me about anything," Diamond responded. She could see the stress written all over his face.

"Ever since I got hit up, it's put a strain on our relationship. Sometimes I can see the frustration in ya face when my dick don't get hard at times. Then when I gotta take this bag off my stomach, you be looking disgusted, like you just wanna tell me you can't do it anymore," Dollaz explained.

Diamond felt bad, hearing the way Dollaz felt. She had to admit that at times, it was hard for her to maintain a relationship under these conditions, but at the end of the day, Dollaz was still her man.

"Baby, I'm sorry for the way you feel. I swear, I never meant to make you feel like I was tired. To be honest wit' you, babe, it do get rough sometimes, and I do get a little frustrated, but Dollaz, I need you to understand that I love you. I am in love with you just as much as I was before you got shot. I'm never going to leave you, boy. I don't care how rough it get. I'm riding wit' you until the wheels fall off," Diamond said, climbing further onto the bed and lying under Dollaz's arm.

Real love was hard to come by these days, so to have a female like Diamond, who was willing to love her man unconditionally and stand by his side when he was at his worst, made Dollaz appreciate what he had. Diamond was one of the rare women who were loyal to their men. They didn't make them like her anymore, and Dollaz was proud to say that she belonged to him.

"I love you, D," he said, kissing her forehead.

"I love you too, boo."

Gwen stood in the bathroom looking at her neck in the mirror. The twins had fallen asleep, and she was waiting on Niya's mom to pick them up so she could hit the streets. She still couldn't believe Chad had choked her out. This was the first time he'd ever put his hands on her to this magnitude, and the only reason he wasn't shot or stabbed behind it was because Gwen understood his pain to a certain extent. She finally felt the full weight of the guilt concerning the events that led up to Zion's death. The only difference between Gwen and Chad was that Chad would drink his problems away, while Gwen would busy herself with making money. So, as soon as Niya's mom picked up the kids, that's exactly what she was going to do.

Chapter 6

Diamond cruised through the parking lot of the Woodland shopping center until she pulled into an empty parking space in front of K's Hair & Beauty Supply store. The small strip mall had only a few stores in it.

Diamond reached in her bag and pulled out some papers, scanning through them to make sure she had the right ones. She also reached in and grabbed her gun to see if she had a bullet in the chamber. Instead of putting it back in her bag, she stuffed it into her back waist once she got out of the car.

"Please don't make this hard," Diamond mumbled to herself as she walked toward K's hair store.

There were still a few customers in the store when she entered, so she browsed around until they left and the store was empty except for the female cashier, who was well aware of what was going on. In fact, she gave Diamond the nod to let her know where Mr. Kwan, the owner of the store, was.

Diamond walked to the back of the store to the manager's office, looked around the store once more, then walked through the door. Mr. Kwan and the manager were sitting at Kwan's desk, counting money. The old, gray-haired Chinese man and the female manager both looked up to see Diamond watching them.

"Can you excuse us?" Diamond said to the manager.

The young female was well aware of who Diamond was and the reason she was there, so she attempted to get up and leave, but was stopped by Mr. Kwan.

"No, stay," he said, pointing to the manager.

Diamond smiled, walked over, and took the leather Bulgari satchel from her shoulder then placed it on the table where the manager and Kwan were sitting. They both looked up at Diamond like she was crazy. Mr. Kwan was more concerned about how she got back there.

"Can I help you?" Mr. Kwan asked, raising one eyebrow.

Diamond casually moved some of the money to the side then took a seat on the desk. She looked at the manager, and then looked at the door, indicating she wanted her to leave. Already knowing where this was going and anticipating her arrival, the manager looked over at Mr. Kwan then got up and left the room.

"I see business is good, Mr. Kwan," Diamond said, grabbing a stack of twenties and looking at it then throwing it back into the pile of money.

Mr. Kwan started to say something, but Diamond cut him off. "You had this store for a little more than twenty years. Hell, I even used to come here when I was a young girl." Diamond spoke calmly.

"I don't know what you want, young lady, but I think you better leave!" Mr. Kwan demanded.

Diamond wasn't about to be dismissed that easily. She reached into her bag and pulled out a large manila envelope.

"A'ight, let's get straight to the point," she said, pulling papers out of the envelope and tossing them onto the table in front of him.

"My proposition is simple. This store, equipment, products, along with popularity in this community, is worth an estimated 1.2 million, wholesale value. You been here for a very long time, so I'll even throw in a little extra for ya longevity," Diamond told him.

"What in da hell are you talking about?" Mr. Kwan snapped, looking at the sales agreement paperwork she gave him.

Diamond took off her glasses, put them in her bag, then shifted her hair over her right shoulder. "Look, Mr. Kwan, one or two things is going to happen today."

"Yeah, and what's that?" he asked in an irritated way.

"Today, I'ma buy this store from you. I'm going to cut you a check for 1.3 million dollars, and then you're going to sign over the deed. You can continue to run this place however you'd like, and all of your employees can keep their jobs. But at the end of the day, you all will work for me," she explained with a serious face.

Mr. Kwan sat there and laughed at Diamond like she was doing a stand-up comedy show. He wasn't taking her seriously at all. This wasn't the first time somebody had tried to buy his business. Just months ago, a realtor offered him 1.5 million to sell, but Mr. Kwan declined the offer. Now, here was Diamond, offering less money than the last, and she was demanding for it to be done as if he didn't have an option.

"And tell me, little girl, what happens when I get up out of my seat, grab you by that expensive weave you got in ya head, and throw you out of my store?" Mr. Kwan threatened.

Diamond went to reach for her bag, but Mr. Kwan leaned over and grabbed it first. He didn't know if she had brought a weapon with her, and he wasn't going to take any chances. He turned the bag upside down and emptied all of the contents out of it. As he scattered the items on the table, he was oblivious to the fact that Diamond had reached into her waist and pulled out a compact .45 automatic.

"Now, the flip side to that coin is a little bit different," she said, resting the gun on her lap.

After hearing that, Mr. Kwan lifted his head up from the table to see Diamond sitting there with the gun in her hand, looking down on him as if he were her prey. His eyes shifted slightly to the right, where he could see his large chrome .357 Magnum resting under his desk. Diamond was well aware of the gun, courtesy of her MHB sister sitting outside the room at the register.

"Don't be stupid!" Diamond said, taking the safety off her gun. "I'll empty my whole clip in you before you could get ya hands on it." She got up and walked around to the back of his desk.

Mr. Kwan snapped. He started yelling and screaming in Chinese, slamming one hand on the table and pointing at Diamond with the other. His whole face was red, and his blood pressure shot straight through the roof. The one thing he didn't do was reach for his gun, not even when she reached under the table to retrieve it. Diamond kept him at gunpoint the whole time. She wouldn't have hesitated to squeeze the trigger had Mr. Kwan tried to do anything crazy.

"If you choose not to sell, I can guarantee you won't make another dollar in this store. I'll make it so hard for you to sell anything, you'll need to borrow money from the bank just to keep the lights on," Diamond said.

Mr. Kwan wasn't fazed at all with Diamond's threats. He wasn't about to let a woman walk into his store and tell him what he was going to do with his business.

"You hear me clear, little girl. You do whatever you want. I'm not selling you shit. You haven't got the slightest idea who you messing wit'," Mr. Kwan said, shaking his head. "Now get da hell out of my store before I make you use that gun."

They stared at each other for a minute before Diamond tucked her gun back in her waist. She reached over and grabbed her bag off the table, along with her belongings that Mr. Kwan had dumped out. She tossed Mr. Kwan's .357 in her bag as well, then she casually walked out of the room without saying another word. She felt like nothing else needed to be said, and everything else would be communicated by actions.

Chad looked around the cemetery before tilting the bottle of Crown Royal up to his lips. Zion, his son, had been dead for almost two years, but the pain he felt made it seem like it all happened yesterday. Visions of how Zion's lifeless body felt in his arms haunted him day in and day out.

"Damn, li'l man . . ." Chad mumbled, squatting down in front of the tombstone. "I failed you, son," he whined, taking another swig of the firewater.

He missed the hell out of his boy. Zion was his first child, and it wasn't that he loved him more than he loved the twins, but it was something about the first child that made it hurt just a little more.

While Chad was kneeling down, he could feel and hear somebody walking up from behind. His instincts made him reach for the gun that was jammed in his waist. He pulled it out and was about to get up and turn around, but then he heard her voice.

"I miss him too," Gwen said, easing her way forward.

He didn't have to turn around to know who it was. He didn't say anything. Instead, he took another swig from the bottle and took his hand off the gun. She walked up and kneeled down next to Chad in front of the tombstone.

"Are you okay?" she asked, looking over at him.

Chad didn't say anything. He just took another swig. Since they had broken up shortly after Zion's kidnapping and the whole hospital ordeal, he and Gwen hadn't really spoken much. As much as he tried, he couldn't seem to stop blaming Gwen for their son's death. Instead of trying to stay and work things out, Chad felt that the best thing to do for both of them was to split.

"You don't have to say anything. I just need you to listen to me for a second," Gwen said as she turned to look at the grave. "I want you to know that I'm sorry. The reason that we're sitting here in front of our son's grave is me. I take full responsibility for that, and this is something I have to live with for the rest of my life. I think that's punishment in itself," she said, wiping the tears that fell down her cheek.

"I truly understand how you feel, and you have every right to be mad at me. But at the same time, I need you to let me deal with Mayo. You have two other kids who need their father right now. If you end up in jail or even dead, you're no good to them. I don't think that's fair to the twins or to yourself," Gwen explained.

Gwen didn't want to admit it, but she still loved and needed Chad. She loved her son, but at the same time, she loved the man who helped create him. To lose Chad would be just as devastating to her as losing Zion.

Right before she was about to say something else, her cell phone rang. She didn't answer it the first time, but then it started ringing again. She stood up, reached into her pocket, and grabbed it. A picture of Diamond popped up on the screen. If it was anybody else, she wouldn't have answered it, but seeing who it was made her feel compelled to take the call. She still had a business to run; plus, she wasn't really sure what else she could possibly say to get through to Chad.

"Did he sign?" Gwen asked when she answered the phone.

"Nah, he didn't sign, but I think he's gonna see things my way," Diamond said as she sat in her car right outside of Mr. Kwan's store.

Gwen stood up, leaned over, and kissed Chad on the top of his head. "I love you, boy," she said before walking off.

"I'm taking care of that situation as we speak," Diamond said, watching as her little hit squad walked across the parking lot toward the store.

"Yeah, but no blood," Gwen said. That meant that she didn't want Diamond to kill Mr. Kwan. That was the main thing she wanted to avoid.

His death would defeat the intended purpose of getting him to sell his business. If he died, it would be even harder to purchase the property from whoever was in line to get it next. Right now, the takeover had to run as smoothly and as quietly as possible. Unnecessary attention was the last thing Gwen wanted.

"Yo, my nigga, come look at all these new mafuckas," Mayo's celly said, calling him over to the window.

New guards came into the jail often. It was like a revolving door for them also. County was one of the worst jails in the system, mainly because everybody that was beefing in the streets came through there and continued beefing on the inside. The more violent the inmates were, the less safe the staff was. There were some who quit, and then there were others who transferred to the penitentiary where it was less violent.

"Damn, shawty got a fat ass," Mayo said, watching the only female guard walking through the yard with the male officers.

"I'ma kick it wit' shawty as soon as I get the chance. She look like she'll move out for a nigga," he said, watching her disappear back into the building.

Mayo knew that it was on a first come, first serve basis. Half the inmates in the jail was gonna be trying to get at the new guards. That's how most of the drugs and cell phones got into the jail. All one had to do was manipulate the guard and finesse his way into making them become mules. It all boiled down to whoever had the best mouthpiece. Whoever was lucky enough to have a guard was considered to be the man in the jail. Mayo definitely was trying to be that man, and he had more potential than 90 percent of the jail population to make it happen.

Diamond's crew went straight to work when they entered the hair store. One person held Mr. Kwan and the workers at gunpoint, while three other females ransacked the place. They spray painted all the hair that was lined up on the wall, knocked over racks, and poured premium gas from a five gallon can over everything. They busted out the counter glass, damaged hair care products, and stained the carpet with red paint.

Mr. Kwan watched as they ruined his store and damaged thousands of dollars in product. It was killing him to see his store be destroyed. When he attempted to stop the girls, he was smacked in his mouth with the butt of a gun, knocking out two of his front teeth.

It took the crew less than fifteen minutes to destroy just about everything in the store. One of the girls walked up to Mr. Kwan, who was standing behind the counter spitting out the blood that kept flowing into his mouth. He looked at her with a more submissive stare.

"If you call the cops, we'll kill you," she said, reaching into her pocket and pulling out a lighter. "And if you don't sell, we'll burn dis bitch to the ground and then kill you," she threatened, flicking the lighter and waving the fire in his face.

The heavy aroma of gas, plus the knowledge of it being all over the store, had Mr. Kwan too scared to do anything other than nod his head. He wished he could have sold the store right then, but he actually wasn't in the position to do so. He had investors who had financially helped him a while back when his business was about to go belly up. He was in deep with a prominent realty company and wasn't going to be able to do anything until his debt was paid off with the interest the company had him locked into.

Whatever the case was, he was going to try to make something happen. He loved his business, and he didn't want to lose it like this, so he was going to do everything in his power to save it.

"Tell ya boss we can work something out," Mr. Kwan said, lowering his head in humility.

Desks, chairs, fax machines, printers, tables, computers, and all kinds of office furniture were delivered to the seventeenth floor where MHB Realty was located. Gwen and Niya had agreed to use MHB as the name, but instead of flaunting its true meaning, they made the name sound a little more professional. Mortgages, Homes, and Businesses is what MHB stood for now.

Gwen stood in her office, looking out of the large floor-to-ceiling window, taking in the sight of the city. Everything was coming together nicely. Tiffany, Portia, Alexus, and April were all out and about, trying to buy up every property available in Charlotte. Diamond, on the other hand, was taking a more mobster approach with trying to get already established businesses to sell. She gave two options: either sell or lose the business altogether. Ironically, it was working, because within a couple of days she had muscled in and bought several storefronts.

"Gwen, Auntie is here to see you," Deja, Gwen's personal secretary said as she entered her office.

"Send her in," Gwen responded.

Moments later, Auntie walked into the office. She had a huge smile on her face when she walked over and gave Gwen a hug.

"You moving up in the world," Auntie said, looking out the window at the city.

"Yeah, well, I think it's time to take dis shit to another level. What's the point of making money when the government won't let you spend it unless they know where it's coming from?" Gwen said, walking over and standing next to Auntie by the window. "What about you? How are things looking in the gulf?" Gwen asked, referring to recently beefed-up security on the coast.

"Everything looks good right now. You know all the Coast Guard want is more money. That's something else I need to talk to you about," Auntie said, turning to face Gwen.

"I have to go up to fifty-K per kilo," Auntie said. "My hope is that everything goes back to normal by the end of next month. And just so you know, everybody else has to pay sixty-K a kilo."

"Come on, Auntie. You don't have to explain all that. I know you'll take care of me when you can. You always do." Gwen smiled.

The ten thousand–dollar hike in the prices wasn't bad, especially since Gwen was making well over one hundred grand from each kilo. The profit was still crazy, and Gwen was still going to benefit from it. She was a genius who knew how to capitalize on situations like this. If everybody else in North Carolina had to pay between sixty and seventy grand for a kilo of heroin, a lot of business was about to come Gwen's way, and she was ready for it.

***

Mayo pulled up on the new correctional officer in the hallway on his way to the laundry station. He couldn't help himself once he saw her. Even though she had on the standard correctional officer uniform, her ass still sat right in her pants. Her long, curly hair dropped down past her shoulders, and her size five feet looked cute in her work boots.

"Damn, Ms. Nealy," Mayo said, looking at the name that was on her shirt. "How you like the job so far?"

"It's cool. I'm not really feeling where they got me at right now," Ms. Nealy responded.

She wasn't the stuck-up type like some of the female guards that worked there. She actually was a little friendly, something Mayo picked up on from the very first words that came out of her mouth.

"Now, look, make sure you stay out of trouble in here," he joked. "You already know niggas is gonna be tryin' to talk to you. Just tell them you're my girl and nobody will say nothing else to you," he said with a smile.

Ms. Nealy smiled back. "Oh, you the charmer, huh? What block are you on?" she asked, looking up and down the hallway at the few inmates who were either going or coming from their units.

"I'm on D-block cell 122." He checked out her body while she continued looking down the hallway.

Three guys huddled up by the kitchen area caught Ms. Nealy's eye. She put a stop to the conversation her and Mayo were having and walked off to confront the men and send them back to their unit.

As Mayo watched her walk off, he grabbed a handful of his dick through his pants, imagining what it would be like if he could fuck her from the back. Her ass bounced with every step she took, bringing back the sad reality of what Mayo was missing out on in the streets. There were thousands of women just like her, and some even badder, on the other side waiting for men like Mayo to come home. The fact was that Mayo had to do at least the next ten years in prison. That was a long time, and once he was shipped out to his prison, everything was going to change.

If Mayo wanted to make a move on Ms. Nealy and try to get her in pocket before he left, he needed to get on his job. Once he went to court and pled guilty, it was only another thirty days before he was sentenced, and then another eight weeks before he was packed up and shipped out. That meant he only had twelve weeks to do his thing, which was more than enough time, as long as he could get to her when she was alone.

"How can I help you today, Mr. Kwan?" Terrence said, closing his office door and walking back over to take a seat at his desk. "Is everything all right?"

Mr. Kwan reached into his bag, pulled out a couple of wads of money, and placed them on the desk. It was the exact amount of money he owed Jackson & Johnson for the loan he took out back when his business was struggling. Terrence looked at it and raised an eyebrow. He was curious to know what was about to follow.

"I–I . . . just wanted to pay off the rest of the loan so we can p–part ways now," Mr. Kwan said as his eyes darted around the room.

Paying off the loan was cool. It was the parting ways part that got to Terrence. He wasn't sure if Mr. Kwan had forgotten the agreement they had at the outset of the loan, but he sure as hell was going to remind him about it.

"Did you forget our arrangement?" Terrence asked, pushing Mr. Kwan's money back to his side of the table.

"I remember what we agreed on, but I will not be able to sell you my business," Mr. Kwan told him.

Terrence chuckled without humor. It took everything in him not to reach across the table and punch Mr. Kwan in his mouth. Terrence didn't even get the chance to say what he was about to say, because his office phone started ringing. He gave Mr. Kwan the evil eye as he answered it.

A brief conversation ensued, and Mr. Kwan could tell by Terrence's facial expressions that whoever was on the other end wasn't giving him any good news. Mr. Kwan even thought about getting up and leaving the office, and for a second he even attempted to do so.

"Have a seat, Mr. Kwan," Terrence said, hanging up the phone. "Now, explain to me why you won't be selling me the business?" He sat back in his chair and interlocked his fingers over his stomach.

"Because I already sold it," Mr. Kwan said, putting his head down like he was ashamed for doing it.

"What did you just say?" He had heard him the first time, but he just wanted to hear it again to be sure.

"I sold the business already. I didn't have any other choice," Mr. Kwan started to explain.

Terrence wasn't trying to hear any excuses. The only reason he loaned Mr. Kwan the money was so that he could eventually buy the property from him. That's how his company was built, and that was how he sustained it to keep the public eye off his other business.

If Terrence didn't have other important matters to attend to, he would have dealt with Mr. Kwan in another way. The phone call had saved him.

"Get da fuck out of my office!" Terrence said, grabbing the two wads of money and throwing them at Mr. Kwan.

Mr. Kwan looked at him in confusion, wondering why Terrence wasn't taking the money.

"I'm not done wit' you yet. Whoever you sold the store to, you better give the money back," Terrence snapped, pointing to the door.

Mr. Kwan got up and left, passing Randy, Terrence's right hand man, on his way out the door.

Randy came in and took a seat, unenthusiastic about the bad news he had to tell Terrence.

"What happened?" Terrence asked, still a little irritated by what Mr. Kwan was trying to pull.

"Some motorcross kids found Dink's body by the dirt bike trails early this morning. He was shot in his head twice," Randy said, shaking his head.

Terrence's blood began to boil instantly. Dink was his sister's baby father and a major part of his organization. He trafficked dope all around the outskirts of Charlotte, mainly in Gastonia, Rockhill, and Belmont, but often flirted with the idea of cutting in on some of the money coming out of Charlotte. That's what had cost him his life.

"I told that nigga not to be messing around with those niggas out in Charlotte. Do anybody know who did it?"

"Nah, but some kid who was out there riding his bike told the cops he saw a couple of chicks jump into a truck right before he came across the body," Randy explained.

Terrence sat back in his chair, resting his chin between his thumb and his index finger. He went into deep thought, wondering if the females had something to do with the murder, and if so, for what reasons they would want to kill Dink. All kinds of scenarios ran through his brain, but none of them could wrap around anything that was remotely close to the truth. It was one of the disadvantages Terrence had, being from Atlanta. He didn't know too much about anything that was going on up top, and he definitely didn't know anything about MHB, or how they ran the streets of Charlotte. It had gotten ugly, and if he didn't let it go, it could get even uglier for him or whoever else interfered with what was going on in the city that belonged to a group of females who weren't taking any shorts.

Gwen stood by her office door, waving at Auntie, who was getting onto the elevator. Immediately after watching the elevator doors close, Gwen closed her door, locked it, and closed the blinds on all of her windows so that nobody would be able to see inside.

The day after Gwen was approved to move into the new office suite, she had a walk-in safe built inside her office. It took two days to complete, and once it was done, Gwen began to move most of MHB's money into the safe. She didn't do it because she didn't trust her crew. It was done because she wanted to have easier access to the money instead of having to travel an hour and a half outside the city, where their major stash house was located. Not just that, but the money was more secure right there in her office than it was stashed previously. The building was like a fortress in itself. The security was tight, and no one could just walk in the building without having a reason for being there. It was like having a safe within a safe.

Gwen punched in her eight-digit code then placed her thumb on the key pad for fingerprint recognition. After a series of beeps, the door slowly swung open. She could never get tired of stepping into that room and seeing shelves of money right before her eyes. The scent of the money alone gave her a natural high. It wasn't everything, but Gwen had a little more than fifteen million dollars sitting in her office, at her disposal.

She slowly walked into the six by nine safe, letting her fingers glide across the piles of money on the shelves. She shook her head, amazed at how far she'd come in the game, and all the things that were sacrificed for her to make it to this point. Gwen stood there for a moment, reminiscing to herself, but came back to earth once she realized she had a job to do. Five million dollars was the cost of the shipment of dope scheduled for delivery by tomorrow morning. Gwen had to have the money counted out and in Auntie's hand before the day was out. Right now, that was the only thing she really had time to do, and frankly, that was the only thing she wanted to do.

Chapter 7

Mayo looked down at his watch as he continued to jog around the track in the yard. Ms. Nealy walking across the compound was unexpected, but he saw her, Mayo sped up, hoping to catch her eyes before she disappeared into the building. Mayo was constantly working out, so his body was ridiculously cut. He wasn't huge and bulky, nor was he thin and ripped like Bruce Lee. His size was close to perfect, standing six foot one, weighing 215 pounds.

"Hey, Ms. Nealy," Mayo said, slowing his pace once he caught up with her by the front gate.

She couldn't help but to notice how sexy his body looked, seeing that all he had on was a pair of sweat pants and some running sneakers. The sweat dripping off his body made him look even sexier, but Ms. Nealy couldn't draw too much attention to herself by looking at him so hard. Although it appeared that no one was watching, they were. The guards in the towers were watching, along with the guards who were in the rec yard. More importantly, the inmates were watching, trying to see how much of a connection Mayo and the new guard had. If it looked like Mayo had her locked in, nobody was going to shoot their shot at her, but if the vibe between the two wasn't where it was supposed to be, the wolves would come out.

"I'll be working ya block today, so I'll talk to you later," Ms. Nealy said before turning off the walk and heading for the units.

Mayo didn't have to say anything and didn't want to at that point. He didn't want to draw any unnecessary attention either. Since she was working his block this shift, he had all night to holler at her, and having her in a more isolated area was better anyway.

"Feliciano! Come to the office!" the guard yelled over the speaker. "Feliciano! Come to the office!" the guard yelled again out into the common area.

Melissa took one ear bud out of her ear when Niya gestured to her. "The C.O. want you," Niya told her, looking up at the TV to see what she was watching.

She passed Niya the Walkman and walked over to the correctional officer's office.

"Yo, what's up?" Melissa asked, standing at the door.

"I need you to pack ya shit and head down to R and D," the officer told her.

"For what?"

"Look, the lieutenant called up here and told me to tell you to pack ya shit."

Melissa just walked away and headed back over to where Niya was. She didn't know why she was packing up so early. Her release date wasn't until next month, and as far as she knew, she didn't have any open cases pending in Philly.

Niya noticed the distraught look on her face. "What happened?" she asked Melissa, taking the ear bud out of her.

"The C.O. just told me to pack my stuff up and go down to R and D," Melissa explained. "I need you to walk me up to the lieutenant's office so I can see what's going on."

"Girl, nine times out of ten, if they told you to pack up, then ya ass is going home," Niya said with a huge smile on her face. "I'll walk you up there, though."

When they got to the lieutenant's office, Niya was right. Melissa was being released to a halfway house early. Sometimes when the system got overcrowded and female prisons needed the bed space, those who had months to go tended to get released early, as long as their case didn't have anything to do with violence. Melissa had 365 days for bank fraud, a white-collar crime that wasn't violent at all. She fit the criteria perfectly.

Melissa looked at Niya, almost not wanting to leave her new best friend behind. Her eyes began to fill up with tears. Niya, seeing the hurt on her girl's face, quickly made a joke to ease the pain. "Shit, if it was me, girl, I would be crying and packing at the same time." Melissa laughed, and they embraced one more time before Niya turned and headed back to her cell.

Right before the institution's four o'clock count, Melissa was taken to the bus station and released. It was on such short notice that she didn't have time for her family to send her money so that she could get a plane ticket. The bus ride all the way back to Philly was going to take a couple of days, but Melissa didn't mind. She was so happy to be free. She couldn't care less about how long it was going to take her to get home. As long as she got there, it made no difference.

"Rachel, I told you I was on top of it," Terrence said into the receiver. "No . . . No, I don't know yet!" he yelled.

Terrence pulled his head back from the phone, not wanting to hear his little sister yelling at him about something he had no knowledge of. It wasn't just her that was snapping out about Dink's death. Damn near the whole city of Atlanta, Georgia, was in an uproar about the situation. Bottom line, people wanted answers, especially his family, who was far from the streets.

"Rachel, just give me a couple of days," Terrence said. "I'll let you know something as soon as I hear anything."

He sat back in his chair and put both of his hands on top of his head. He looked out his office window into the cubicle area and made eye contact with Randy, who was flirting with one of the female workers. A simple nod of the head from Terrence got Randy to stop doing what he was doing and make his way to the office.

"What up, T?" Randy asked, coming into the office.

"Yo, you didn't hear anything yet about that situation with Dink?" Terrence asked, leaning up in his chair.

"Nah, not really. Everybody I know keep talking about some bitches that supposed to be running this city. They call themselves MOB . . . MHB, or some shit like that," Randy answered. "They got a bar in the city somewhere. Me and Mike supposed to be goin' through there to see what it look like."

"Nah, nah, don't take Mike. Take Tianna wit' you. If it's a chick bar, she can find out more information than you could," Terrence directed.

Tianna was from the hood for real, and she didn't mind putting in work if necessary. She was born and raised in North Philadelphia but migrated to South Carolina with her mom and step pop after her stepfather shot a man in his head in broad daylight in front of the whole neighborhood. Tianna was one of the many people who witnessed it. Since then, South Carolina was her home, but North Carolina was where she worked with her uncle, Terrence.

"Oh, yeah, and I need you to take a look at something too when you come in tomorrow. I'm losing a couple of businesses, and I'm tryin' to figure out why," Terrence said, shuffling around some papers that were on his desk.

"No problem, T. I'll check it out first thing," Randy responded. "I'ma go jump on this shit wit' Dink tonight, and I'll call you later and let you know what happened."

He gave Terrence dap then left his office.

"Yo, homie, let me holla at her for a minute," Mayo said, tapping the arm of the guy who was standing in the doorway of the C.O.'s office.

For a second, the guy acted like he wasn't going anywhere, but that only lasted for a second, because when he turned to see that it was Mayo, he did what he was told. Over the past year, Mayo had really made a name for himself. After he got stabbed and was almost killed, he turned around and had several brutal fist fights that ended in his victims being sent to the infirmary. Not too many people wanted drama with him or the li'l crew he had riding with him.

"You ignorant," Ms. Nealy said with a smirk on her face.

"He wasn't talking about shit anyway," Mayo responded, looking over his shoulder at the guy sitting down at the TV. "So where you from out there?" he asked, changing his tone to a calmer one.

His ruggedness was attractive, along with everything else about him, but Ms. Nealy was there for other reasons.

"Boy, you know you ain't supposed to be asking me where I'm from. I like my job." She smiled.

"I like ya job too. Whatever we talk about stays between us. Scout's honor," Mayo said, raising two fingers in the air.

Ms. Nealy thought Mayo was cute, and he didn't seem like the type who would go running his mouth to other inmates. She felt comfortable for some reason, and it showed, because all the way up until lockdown time, she entertained Mayo's conversation. They talked about many things they weren't supposed to talk about, and Mayo even managed to get her to flirt with him a little.

This was how it all started, and it looked as if Mayo was going to get all the time he needed, because Ms. Nealy would be working his unit for the next quarter. If he got that far in one night, there wasn't no telling what he could accomplish over the next eight weeks.

Gwen took her glasses off and rubbed the corners of her eyes. She'd been looking at paperwork all day and still couldn't understand the legalities of running the realty company. It was too much work, and it was taking up a nice amount of her time trying to figure stuff out.

Within a few weeks, Diamond had tackled five major stores in Charlotte, including one supermarket, two check-cashing places, and a steakhouse. She wasn't even done yet. She had her eyes on a few other businesses that generated large quarterly profits.

Tiffany and her boyfriend, Toast, tore down the auction, buying just about every property that went up. In a week's time, they bought more than fifteen houses for very cheap prices. Most of the houses were fixer uppers, but Toast didn't mind doing the work so that the houses looked good enough to sell.

Alexus's job probably was the hardest. She had to buy land. It was different than buying a house. Location was everything, and Alexus had to strategically purchase acres of land that had the potential to generate a lot of money, whether it be by developing something on that land or by selling it to someone who wanted it more than she did. So far, Alexus had purchased over a hundred acres of land, mainly in the city because she found that it was easier to buy vacant lots nobody ever used. She'd already pitched the idea of building houses in some, and turning vacant lots downtown into parking lots.

Everything from Diamond's businesses to Alexus's parking lots were sitting on Gwen's' desk, giving her nothing but a vicious headache. A knock at her office door snapped Gwen out of it.

"Gwen, there's a Mr. Johnson out here to see you," Deja said, peeking her head into the office.

"You can send him in." Gwen let out a deep sigh. "Oh, and Deja, can you bring me some coffee?"

Gwen turned around in her chair to look at the mirror she had hanging up on the wall behind her desk. She felt beat, and she was sure that she looked the same way. She quickly stroked and fluffed her hair then put her glasses back on before he got to the office.

"Damn, ya office is bigger than mine," Terrence said, looking around when he entered.

"You bought gifts?" Gwen asked, looking at the box he had in his hand.

"Yeah." He smiled, passing her the box. "It's like a housewarming gift, except you're in an office."

Gwen took the box and set it on her desk without opening it. She knew that if a man was bringing a woman gifts, he was going to want something in return. Before Gwen opened it, she wanted to find out what that something was.

"What do you want, Terrence?" Gwen chuckled, leaning back in her chair.

"Why do I have to want something?" He sat down in the chair in front of her desk.

Gwen had to set aside the fact that he was as handsome as they come. She couldn't let his dark, thick, wavy hair, his thick eyebrows, and smooth dark chocolate complexion fool her. She could tell by his devious grin that he was there for something more than welcoming her to the building.

"All men want something. Now go ahead and spit it out," Gwen said.

"A'ight, you got me," Terrence confessed. "I see you been running around this city buying up everything you can get ya hands on. All that's fine and dandy. I just need you to stop buying up my shit," he said in a more assertive manner.

Terrence had done his homework and found out that MHB had bought the store from Mr. Kwan, and two other stores he had his money invested in. Several other properties he had his eyes on were also purchased by MHB through some kind of a back door deal.

"I hope you're not scared of a little competition," Gwen said, leaning up in her chair with a smile on her face.

"Competition? You can't possibly compete with me. I own more houses in Charlotte than any other realty company out here. I got businesses that are in debt to me more than they are with the banks. I own Charlotte!" He sat back and crossed his legs.

"You own Charlotte?" Gwen smiled, looking at how serious Terrence looked when he said it.

He had no idea who he was talking to. Gwen was about to fully inform him but decided against it. She wanted to stay as low key in corporate America as possible, but on the other hand, she did want to have a little fun with Terrence. He seemed too cocky and confident that he had the city on lockdown. It was somewhat cute, but Gwen wanted to put him back in his place.

"Look, Terrence. We both got a business to run—"

"Have dinner with me?" Terrence asked out of nowhere, cutting Gwen off in the middle of her sentence.

"Excuse me?" Gwen asked, pulling her head back and raising one eyebrow.

His question threw her for a loop. It wasn't just the question in itself. It was the way he asked and how he looked asking it. His stern, aggressive demeanor turned humble, and the look on his face was sincere. She really didn't know how to take him.

"No." She smiled at how cute he looked sitting there.

"Well, what about lunch?" he shot back.

"Nooo!" She giggled and grabbed two handfuls of her hair and pulled it into a ponytail.

The more he looked at her, the more beautiful she became to him. He didn't want her to know right now, but he had been feeling Gwen ever since he bumped into her. He wasn't really into chocolate women, but Gwen was an exception. Even through the suit she was wearing, he could see that she had a body out of this world.

"So how about I pick you up in the morning for breakfast?" Terrence smiled, licking his lips like he was LL Cool J in the flesh.

Gwen continued to smile as she shook her head. She couldn't believe how determined he was to take her out. She did find Terrence to be handsome, plus it had been a while since somebody showed interest in her this much. A date wasn't going to come cheap though. She would make Terrence pay like he weigh or keep it movin'.

"I'll go out with you under one condition," Gwen said, looking over at her computer screen and typing a few letters on the keyboard.

"You name it . . . you got it," Terrence said, sitting up in his chair to be more attentive.

"You got a house on the north side. Its estimated value is only around fifty thousand. Sell it to me for seventy-five thousand and we can go wherever you want," Gwen said, looking at the list of properties Jackson & Johnson owned.

"Done!" Terrence said without hesitation.

He didn't have to think twice about it. Two things made it easy for him to entertain the offer. One, it was the fact that he was selling a house in a known drug area and making a twenty-five thousand dollar profit in the process. Two, he couldn't help but to visualize in his head all the freaky shit he wanted to do to Gwen. If he could make his fantasies come true and make some money at the same time, it was a win/win for him.

Gwen, on the other hand, was playing chess. The house on Oaklawn Avenue was a power move, because that was all she needed to set up shop in that neighborhood. There were only a few areas in Charlotte that MHB didn't corner during their rise, and Oaklawn was one of them. If Gwen could get a house there, it would be a lot easier for her to ease her way in and take over their set from the inside out. The only problem she had and wasn't aware of, was that Oaklawn actually belonged to Terrence.

Chapter 8

Diamond climbed over Dollaz and straddled his face while he palmed both of her ass cheeks and pulled her throbbing wet pussy down to his mouth. He stuffed his tongue inside of her, swaying his head from side to side, causing Diamond to moan in pleasure as she looked at her bare breasts through the mirror on the wall behind the headboard.

She began moving her hips back and forth, getting both penetration from his tongue and stimulation to her clit from his nose. It didn't take long at all for her to feel a tingling sensation in the pit of her stomach. She grabbed the headboard with one hand, then reached down and held onto the top of Dollaz's head with the other. She began fucking his face as though she was riding the dick, and the more Dollaz sucked on her box, the wetter it got

"Oh my God!" she moaned, looking down at Dollaz.

He looked back up at her, squeezing her ass harder and pushing his tongue farther inside her. Diamond was at her tipping point and was ready to explode. Dollaz could tell that she was about to cum because of the way her face twisted and how her rhythm slowed down. He took his tongue out of her center then started sucking on her clit while at the same time licking on it. It drove Diamond into shock.

"Ohhhh, shit, boy!" she whined as her whole body went into convulsions. "Ohhh my God!" she cried out.

Dollaz kept licking and sucking, swallowing every drop of her cum as it poured out of her nectar box and into his mouth. Diamond tried to dismount his face, but Dollaz wouldn't let her. He held onto her ass and continued sucking and French kissing her clit.

Within seconds, another orgasm erupted from Diamond's love tunnel, causing her body to spaz. She tried to get up again, but Dollaz still wouldn't let her. He wanted to make sure that he satisfied her completely, since he lacked in other areas. He kept eating her pussy until Diamond caught a cramp in her leg.

"What is you doing, boy?" Diamond asked, collapsing onto the bed.

Dollaz reached over and grabbed the towel from off the nightstand. His whole face was wet and white, like he had just bathed his face in milk.

"Dollaz . . . What's goin' on, babe?" She turned to face him.

This was the first time Dollaz had ever ate her pussy in that way. She knew that it wasn't just a coincidence, and that he had to have his reasons for going so hard. She knew Dollaz well enough to know something was going on.

"Are you satisfied?" he asked, patting his face with the towel. "Be honest," he said, looking down at his limp dick.

The truth of the matter was that Dollaz's insecurities were only getting worse. He felt like it was only going to be a matter of time before Diamond would want a long, stiff dick inside of her guts as opposed to just getting some head all the time.

"Dollaz, look at me." She tapped his arm. "You really don't know who you got layin' in this bed wit' you? After all this time, you still have your doubts about me? I don't know what else I have to say to you for you to understand, but boy, I love you, and I'm not going anywhere, so you really don't have to try that hard," she said, flopping back onto the pillow. "Oh, and I was satisfied the first time you made me cum."

Dollaz rolled over, wrapped his arm around her waist, and pulled her closer to him. He gently kissed her on her shoulder and then spoke softly. "I'm sorry, babe. I'm trippin'. I love da shit out of you, and I swear I don't wanna lose you," he said, rubbing the small of her back.

"That's the thing, babe. You're not gonna lose me. You have to get that through ya head. You say that you love me, so you gotta trust me."

Hearing her say those words for the hundredth time finally made Dollaz realize that he had something special lying next to him. If Diamond wanted to leave him, she would have done so already, and Dollaz knew it. She stayed by his side through this whole ordeal. Dollaz didn't want to be the one who messed that up, because ultimately, he was the only one who could drive their relationship to total destruction, something he and Diamond would like to avoid.

"You sure this the house?" Terrence asked, looking out the passenger's side window.

"Yeah, Davis said this was the address the witness gave when he was giving the statement. Look, he got two dirt bikes sitting in the garage," Randy said, pointing over at the house.

Officer Davis was one of the few cops Terrence had on his payroll down at the station, so his information was pretty much reliable. At that point, Terrence didn't have any other choice but to rely on him, since the people down in South Carolina were putting even more pressure on Terrence to find out what happened to Dink. It got so bad, Dink's uncles threatened to come up North and shut the whole Charlotte down. Terrence knew they weren't playing, and the last thing he wanted them to do was make the streets hot where he ate.

Terrence and Randy jumped out of the 745 BMW and walked up to the door. After knocking a few times, a teenage white kid answered. He was nervous as hell, seeing two large black men standing at his front door. He almost slammed the door in their faces.

"We're not here to cause any trouble," Terrence said, seeing the fear in the young man's eyes. "I'm just tryin' to find out what happened to my friend. I know you talked to the cops already, but I really need to hear it from you."

Any initial signs of a threat had dissipated once the young kid heard why they were there. He stepped to the side and let Terrence and Randy in.

Terrence sat there for about an hour questioning and getting as much information as he could pertaining to the night Dink was murdered. The young kid didn't see much. When he pulled up to Dink's body, the assailants had left. It wasn't until he climbed the dirt hill on his bike that he saw a black SUV and two women jumping inside. It was too dark, so he was unable to see the female faces nor the license plate number to the truck, but he did recognize something else.

"Is that all you can remember?" Terrence asked.

"Oh, there is one other thing I didn't tell the cops. There was another car out there too. It was either white or silver, and it looked like a sports car or something. That car I could see parts of the license plate because it was closer to the track. I couldn't really see the numbers, but I know it started with MH. That, I'm sure of," the young kid explained.

The description of the cars weren't enough to go on alone. A thousand cars in Charlotte fit that description. Terrence just took the mental note of it, then he and Randy got up and left without further questions.

***

Chad pulled back up to the Super 8 motel off Sugarcreek Road. where he had been staying for the past few days. The motel room was shabby and run down, but none of that mattered to him anymore. As long as he had a place to rest after a long night of drinking and smoking, he was cool. Lately, all Chad did was smoke weed, pop pills, and drink brown liquor until he passed out. This had become his daily routine. It was the only thing that seemed to help with the hurt, and he was cool with it. Chad walked over to the CD player and placed in the disc that had become his sole refuge. Tupac's "Shed so Many Tears" blasted through the speakers. The lyrics were like sweet words from God playing through his mind.

Chad stood up and started waving his hands and rapping along, like he was on stage with the legendary rapper. Chad had nearly lost himself completely into the rhythmic melody. The death of his son, mixed with the alcohol and drugs had really taken a toll on him, and all he wished was that he could trade places with Zion. It made him feel like less of a man to know that he wasn't able to protect his child from the streets. That was part of the reason why he really didn't want to be around his twins. He felt that if he was unable to protect Zion, how could he be there to protect the twins?

"Man, who da fuck is dis?" he mumbled to himself, as the ringing of his cell phone interrupted his rap performance. Looking over at his phone sitting on the other side of the bed, he really didn't feel like being bothered with anyone, so he didn't even answer it. Instead, he sat back on the bed and took in another deep pull of the Backwood filled with Grand Daddy Kush. He then followed it up with two more oxycodones and a swig of Crown Royal.

"Damn, God, why not me? Why take my son? Now tell me how a nigga supposed to get through the shit? Tell me!" he screamed, looking up at the ceiling. Chad was about to lay back on the bed when the second Tupac song begin to play and he felt like maybe the Lord was giving him an answer to all his pain.

I smoke a blunt to take the pain out, and if I wasn't high probably try to blow my brains out. . . .

Chad looked down at the gun on the bed, the nickel-plated .40-caliber sparkled in the dimly lit room. The drugs had his body totally numb.

He couldn't even feel the tears that were rolling down his face. He took a seat on the bed, exhaled deeply, and grabbed the pistol. The song was now like an instruction manual.

Ms. Nealy walked down the range doing her routine count of the inmates and stopped at Mayo's cell. He was in there with his shirt off, doing pushups before they called block out for the showers. Mayo didn't even know she was standing at his door until he got off the ground after finishing his set.

"What, you just came in?" he asked, looking down at his watch.

She smiled then nodded in the affirmative. Her eyes couldn't help but to wander, scanning his sweaty body and locking onto the print from his dick bulging through his gray sweat pants. He looked sexy as hell.

"You see something you like?" he asked, grabbing a handful of his dick. "Don't be shy." He smiled.

Ms. Nealy looked over Mayo's shoulder to see where his celly was.

"He's at work," Mayo said before she could even ask.

She still couldn't say what she wanted to say, because other inmates were sure enough ear hustling. Instead, she just nodded her head in the direction of his dick. Mayo didn't hesitate to whip out his semi hard stick, letting it swing in the air while Ms. Nealy looked on. She licked and bit down on her bottom lip seductively before shaking her head.

"It's yours whenever you want it," Mayo said, tucking his member back into his sweats.

Ms. Nealy gave him a wink before walking off. The two had been at it over the past week, talking and flirting with each other all day. Mayo had her locked in too, because she wasn't giving any other inmate the time of day. She was focused on him, and the way things were going now, it wouldn't be much longer until she stepped her game up.

"Gwen, he's here," her secretary announced, tapping on the office door.

Gwen got up from her desk and looked at herself in the mirror. She wanted to make sure she was dressed properly, even though she hadn't the slightest idea where Terrence was taking her. Just in case, she kept another outfit in her car that was a little more relaxed than the clothes she had on.

Gwen shut down her computer. She closed the blinds to her office windows and turned off the lights before heading out to the front, where Terrence was standing and looking urban. He had on a pair of blue 7 jeans, a white Polo V-neck T-shirt with some white, black, and gold chains, and on his wrist was a rose gold Rolex. His New York Yankees hat cocked slightly to the side gave him that hood look. He looked like he came straight out of Brooklyn.

"Now I feel overdressed," Gwen said, walking up to him. "Just give me like thirty minutes so I can—"

"Nah, you don't gotta change. You look good." He smiled, checking her out from head to toe.

She had on a black leather skirt, a yellow blouse with a hip white tuxedo-style overcoat and a pair of Charlotte Olympia platform pumps. She opted for a simple ponytail, but even then, she still looked good.

"So where are you taking me this evening?" Gwen playfully asked.

"You wanna know something crazy? I still haven't decided yet," he said, getting onto the elevator behind her. "I know they have a carnival going on downtown," Terrence suggested.

"A carnival?" Gwen asked, surprised he would pick that to be the destination for the night.

"Yeah, a carnival. Don't tell me you're too good to go to a carnival," Terrence shot back.

Gwen smiled and shook her head. She actually loved the carnival and had been to the very one he was about to take her to just a couple of days ago with the twins. Gwen probably looked like it, but she was far from bourgie. In fact, she enjoyed the basic things in life over the more luxurious. It had always been like that, and though Terrence wasn't aware of what he was doing, in Gwen's eyes, he was starting out good this evening.

Tianna sat in front of the bar watching female after female enter the establishment. Wednesday night was ladies night at MHB's Bar and Grill. Free food, open bar, and male bartenders who stripped drew women there in droves every week.

A tap on the passenger's side window made Tianna jump. She leaned over to see Tiffany motioning for her to roll down the window. Tianna didn't at first, but then two other females walked across the street and surrounded the car. She could see that at least one of the females was strapped. She rolled the passenger's side window down to see what the females wanted.

"If you're a cop, we have boys in blue night on Sundays," Tiffany said, looking around the inside of the car.

"Do I look like a fuckin' cop?" Tianna shot back with an attitude.

The female who was strapped placed her hand on the butt of the gun resting on her hip. Tiffany gave her a quick glance to let her know to cool out.

"Well, if you're not a cop, then who are you, and why are you sitting out here instead of in there?" Tiffany asked, nodding at the bar.

"I heard about this place, but I see I'm not welcome here," Tianna said and stuck her key in the ignition.

"Wait, wait . . . It's ladies night. You are welcome here," Tiffany told her.

MHB was still growing, and new recruits came through daily. Tiffany could see from her response to the cop comment that Tianna had some fire in her. Females like her learned to love being a part of MHB.

After a few minutes, Tiffany convinced Tianna to join her inside the bar. Right before she got through the front door, a silver 2011 Chevy Camaro pulled up to the front of the bar and caught everyone's attention. Tianna and Tiffany watched as Diamond hopped out of the car. Tianna knew that it had to be somebody of importance because Diamond just left the car running with the door wide open. It only took a couple of seconds for another female to run over, jump inside the car, and pull off, only to park the vehicle down the street. It was at that moment Tianna realized that there was something more to this all girls club than what she thought.

***

Gwen and Terrence strolled side by side as they exited the carnival. Gwen had one giant stuffed animal in her arms and Terrence had another in his, both of which, he won by shooting a basketball.

"It's definitely better when you come at night," Gwen said, holding her giant bear in the air.

Terrence had been the perfect gentleman, totally different from the man Gwen thought he was. Conversation was everything on this date. Terrence talked about being from South Carolina and gave a brief history on how rough it was coming from the streets to making it to where he was now. He talked about his business and some of the goals he had planned for his future. He even had the courage to talk about relationships.

"So, what time do I gotta have you home by?" Terrence asked, opening the passenger's side door for her. "And don't tell me that you're grown either." He smiled and grabbed the bear from her to put in the back seat.

Gwen stood outside of the car, watching as other carnival attendees left. She didn't know why, but she was really feeling Terrence. She was digging his whole persona, and that was confusing, because she hadn't looked at another man in that manner in a long time. At times, she even felt a sexual connection, picturing her naked body wrapped up in his strong arms. It was crazy.

"Well, I did tell my babysitter I would be home by one, which gives you approximately one and a half hours before I need to be back at my car," Gwen told him.

Terrence closed the back door then walked up to Gwen, who was leaning against the car. He confidently placed his hands on her waist and gazed into her eyes.

Gwen looked up at him, and for some odd reason, she felt submissive to him. She didn't know if it was his size or the way he looked down on her, but Gwen felt like she wasn't in control of her body at that moment.

"I'ma make you mine," Terrence said, pulling her body closer to him then leaning in to kiss her. His full, thick, soft lips pressed against Gwen's ever so gently.

Oh my God! I'm kissing this boy! Gwen thought to herself.

She couldn't believe it, and neither could Terrence, who swore he was going to be rejected.

"I just wanted to get that out of the way, so by the end of this date, it won't be awkward for either of us when I kiss you good night."

Gwen just shook her head with a smile on her face before turning around and getting into the passenger's seat. Not only was Terrence handsome, successful, and a gentleman, but he was also spontaneous, another good quality Gwen looked for in a man. Terrence was catching all green lights riding with Gwen down this road.

Chapter 9

"Housekeeping!" the Spanish maid yelled as she knocked on Chad's door in the early morning hours.

Chad didn't answer, so the maid took it upon herself to enter the room despite the DO NOT DISTURB sign on the door.

"Housekeeping!" she yelled once more as she walked through the door. The smell of urine and feces smacked her clean across the face almost immediately. "Oh God!" she said, covering her nose with a towel.

The TV was on, and there were bags of food on the bed, but no sign of Chad. That was until the maid walked up to the bathroom door, which was slightly open. A pair of legs were the only thing she could see through the small crack.

"Sir! Sir, are you okay?" the maid asked, pushing the door open.

She jumped back in fear at the sight of Chad lying face down on the floor. His blood and brain matter was everywhere, along with urine and his own shit. She didn't even check to see if he was alive or not. Like a professional sprinter, she bolted out the door. It was the first time she'd ever seen anything like this.

The motel manager darted up to the room after the maid informed him of what she saw.

"Hey, guy!" the manager said, kicking Chad's lifeless leg.

The manager, covering his nose with a towel, leaned in and checked Chad's wrist for a pulse. There was none.

Judging from how cold and stiff Chad's arm was, the manager determined that he was long gone. The only thing he could do at this point was reach in his pocket, pull out his cell phone, and call the cops.

Bringing drugs and cell phones into the jail wasn't all that Mayo wanted from Ms. Nealy. He also needed somebody out in the streets making moves for him and getting messages to the people he needed to send messages to. Not only that, but Mayo wanted some pussy, bad. Hell, everybody in jail wanted some pussy, but some were more fortunate than others when it came down to having a female guard in pocket. Mayo was close to that point.

"Yo, you make my day every time you walk through that door," Mayo told Ms. Nealy while standing at her office door. "It's crazy, 'cause you know what you do to me too."

"Is that right?" she responded with a smile.

"Yeah, you sexy as hell too. You can't imagine the shit I'll do to you," Mayo said in a seductive way.

"Boy, you better stop playin'. You couldn't handle half of what I got," she shot back.

Mayo grabbed a handful of his dick through his sweat pants and looked at her with lustful eyes. At this point, he was tryin' to fuck now. The heavy flirting had reached its peak. It was time for Mayo to go all the way in.

"How about we just fuck and get it over with?" Mayo bluntly said. "After you do the count for the night, let me out with the other two unit orderlies," he suggested.

"But what about them?" she said, referring to the other two orderlies. "Where are they gonna be?"

"Don't worry about them. I'll take care of all that. You know I run this block," he assured her.

Ms. Nealy sat there and thought about it for a minute. She was trying to see if she was going to be able to get away with what she had in store for Mayo. Everything had to be planned perfectly or she could end up losing her job.

"Look, I got the next two days off. When I come back, we'll find a way to make it happen," Ms. Nealy told Mayo.

Mayo was a little disappointed that it couldn't go down that night, but waiting a couple more days wasn't going to kill him. He had Ms. Nealy right where he wanted her, and once he finally got a chance to put his dick inside her, he was going have her moving out hard for him, both inside the jail and out on the streets. She was going to really be his bitch.

Terrence and Randy sat in Terrence's office, waiting for Tianna to come through. She had called Randy early that morning and told him that she needed to talk to him and Terrence about what went down at the MHB bar the night before. It had to be important, because she sounded somewhat excited over the phone.

"Yo, my nigga, we gotta do something fast about this Dink situation," Terrence told Randy. "My li'l sis and his people keep callin' up here wanting some answers. I know it won't be long before they send somebody up here to make dis muthafuckin' city hot, and you know I can't afford for that to happen," Terrence said.

"Yeah, I spoke to this connect, and she supposed to be right by the end of the week. She told me to call her today for the time and location where we supposed to meet," Randy explained.

"Plus, we gotta get this money to the bank too. The first of the month is in a couple of days, so we gotta push as much money through the wash as possible this month," Terrence added.

Their conversation was interrupted by Tianna, who walked into the office, slung her bag on Terrence's desk, and took a seat on the leather couch next to it.

"Tee-Tee, tell me something good," Terrence said, focusing his attention on her.

"I was at that bar last night, and one thing about those bitches, they sure know how to party." She laughed and lay back on the couch.

"A'ight, get to the point," Terrence urged.

"Well, I was sitting outside when one of the chicks from MHB approached my car. . . . To make a long story short, I was on my way into the bar when a nice, silver Chevy Camaro pulled up in front of the door. I don't know why I remembered Randy telling me about the truck and the car that the witness saw pulling off from the track the night Dink was killed."

"That could have been a coincidence," Randy said.

"Yeah, I thought the same thing, until I saw the license plate number." She pulled out her phone.

Tianna was so smooth with her work that after she left the bar, she took a couple pictures of the Camaro.

Terrence took the phone and started looking through the photos. There were about five or six pictures from every angle of the car.

"A sports car," Terrence mumbled to himself, thinking about what the witness had told him.

When he got to the license plate pictures and saw MH-443 across the tags, his heart started to race. Tianna was right. This wasn't a coincidence, and from the way she had described the female that got out of the Camaro, it sounded like these were the chicks Terrence was looking for.

"I know her from somewhere."

"Oh, and that's Diamond," Tianna said, pointing to the screen. "That's the one who got out of the car. I think she might be the boss, because the whole night she acted like she ran the place, and everybody seemed to know her," Tianna informed.

Terrence wracked his brain trying to figure out where he had seen Diamond before. One thing about him, he never forgot a face, but in this case, he couldn't remember for the love of God where he'd seen her. He stopped thinking so hard, knowing that it would eventually come back to him.

Terrence sat back in his chair and stared at the pictures. He was finally getting somewhere, and thanks to Tianna, he now had a name and a face to work with. If Diamond didn't do it, Terrence felt that she more than likely knew who did.

"If you want me to, I can take care of it," Tianna offered, reaching over and grabbing her cell phone from him. "It'll be fast and quiet," she said, tucking her phone in her bag.

"Nah, nah, nah. We gon' be smart wit' dis shit. The witness said he saw three bitches dat night. If Diamond's one of them, that means it's two more out there. I'm trying to touch all three of them," Terrence responded.

Until now, Terrence had been on chill mode, not really getting into any beef. It'd been a while since he had to put in some street work, but to him, it was like riding a bike. He just had to be smart about it, because Charlotte really wasn't his hometown. Maneuvering around the city the wrong way could definitely get him killed ASAP.

"You starting to become a permanent fixture in this office," Kea joked.

Gwen was knee deep in paperwork; sales agreements, deeds, financial reports, bank statements, rent receipts, and all other kinds of paperwork cluttered her desk. She looked up at Kea and shook her head, smiling at how true her statement was.

"Yeah, well, as soon as you finish taking care of that situation, I got a nice, cute corner office for you, so you can take care of all this." Gwen tossed some of the papers in front of her in the air. "So how's everything coming along? Is he comfortable yet?" she asked.

"Yeah, he's real comfortable. I'm just waiting for the green light from you," Kea said, taking a seat in the chair in front of the desk.

Mayo thought that he had gotten away with murder and wasn't going to have to stand trial for what he'd done. He was living as if everything were peaches and cream, but Gwen was plotting and planning his death. At first, she didn't know how she was going to be able to get to Mayo because he was locked up, but then she concluded that he had to be touched on the inside. The only way that was going to happen was if Gwen got somebody on the inside to touch him. A regular inmate wasn't good enough. About a year and a half ago, Mayo was stabbed up by Prada's folks, but he lived through it. In fact, the stabbing just made him stronger. His status in the jail skyrocketed because he got stabbed, fought back, and didn't tell at the end. Killing him was going to have to be strategically planned.

"Just keep ya eyes on the situation and I'll let you know when it's a go. It shouldn't be that much longer," Gwen told Kea. "But on another note, what's going on wit' you and ya sister? Are y'all cool again?"

"Whoooo, girl. That's another story," Kea responded, shaking her head in frustration.

Gwen knew that the situation with Kea and her older sister was a sensitive issue, so she didn't ask any further questions. She didn't want Kea to become unfocused on the mission at hand. Out of all the females Gwen had access to in her crew, she felt that Kea was the only one capable of pulling off the unthinkable. Gwen only wished that she could be the one who looked Mayo in his eyes right before he died, but she understood that it couldn't be her. It had to be somebody else, and as long as it was somebody from MHB, Gwen was cool with it.

"He doesn't have any identification on him at all?" the young African American detective asked, looking down at his partner, who was checking through Chad's pockets.

"No, but he got some oxycodones," he said, passing him a small Ziploc bag with a few pills left in it. "Do you think it was a robbery or a possible suicide?" The detective was familiar with the drug, which could produce both.

"There are eighty milligrams too. Shit, one pill is like shooting up two or three dime bags of heroin," he told his partner. "Hell, that's enough to make anybody crazy enough to eat a bullet," he continued.

"Yeah, but just to be careful, let's wait for the crime scene crew to come and see if he has gunpowder residue on his hands. I'm pretty sure this was the weapon used," the detective responded while holding the nickel-plated handgun.

To the detectives, Chad was just another addict who looked like he had decided to do himself and society a favor; but they still had to find out who he was, so the process had to be followed, and that would start with his body being taken to the coroner's office. They had to find out the official cause of death and run his fingerprints. For now, Chad was going to be labeled simply as John Doe.

Chapter 10

The sun shone through Diamond's living-room window as she walked over to the money machine and pushed the start button. She'd been counting money all morning, trying to get ready for the bank run scheduled for one o'clock that afternoon. So far, she'd counted a little more than two hundred grand, and the only reason it took so long was because drug money came in all types of bills, mainly tens and twenties.

"D!" Dollaz yelled out from upstairs.

Diamond walked over to the bottom of the steps with her cup of coffee in her hand.

"Yeah, babe?" she answered.

"Dr. Reed just called. He wants me to come in this afternoon for therapy. I'm not gonna be able to make the bank run wit' you, but I'ma call Ski and tell him to go wit' you."

"Nah, babe, it's cool. I can take myself. Plus, I was going to stop by the office and talk to Gwen after the run," she said, looking up the steps.

"You must be crazy if you think I'ma let you walk out this door with all that money. As a matter of fact, fuck the doctor. I'm coming out."

"No, babe. Go to ya appointment," Diamond insisted.

She knew how much it meant to Dollaz to get his legs back, and the only way he was going to do that was by going through the intense therapy regimen Dr. Reed had him on. He really couldn't afford to miss one day.

Diamond wanted him to start walking again just as bad as he wanted to.

"A'ight, babe. Call Ski and tell him to be here by twelve thirty. I'll have one of the girls take you to the doctor's office," Diamond said, bending to Dollaz's demands.

She really did love Dollaz. Despite his physical disability, Diamond still listened to him and took his advice whenever he voiced his opinion about something. Most of the time, he was right. Even in this instance, Diamond could understand his concern, since she was traveling with a large amount of money. The bank wasn't that far away, but the wolves were still out there, and they were always on the hunt.

Gwen walked from her office to the copy machines, which were in a room on the far end of the floor. Her head was buried in the paperwork she was about to copy, so she didn't even notice Terrence getting off the elevator. He noticed her right away and followed behind her, enjoying the view of her ass switching side to side in her linen khakis.

When she got to the room and up to the copy machine, she was startled by Terrence, who walked up behind her and grabbed her waist. She looked over her shoulder to see that it was him, and then gave him a stiff elbow to his gut.

"Boy, don't be walking up on me like that," she said, turning back around to look at the copier.

After the carnival date a few days before, Gwen and Terrence had become closer, connecting more on a mental level than anything. The physical connection was crazy too, but Gwen had yet to give him a shot of pussy. It'd just been a lot of heavy kissing and touching for now, but all of that was about to change.

"Can I take you somewhere tonight?" Terrence asked, moving her hair to the side so that he exposed the side of her neck.

"You always wanna take me somewhere. You better cool out before you get yaself into something you can't handle," she shot back as she placed the paper on the glass.

"Yeah, and what's that supposed to mean?" He gripped her waist a little tighter and pulled her ass against him. "Don't talk shit you can't back up."

"I'm tryin' to save you. I ain't tryin' to be responsible for corrupting you. It's more to me than you think."

Gwen did have a crazy life. She had more responsibilities than any other female in Charlotte. Terrence wasn't ready at all, but it wasn't going to stop him from trying his hand. He was feeling Gwen, so much so that he wasn't sure whether it was lust or just a genuine liking that made him want to dive deeper into her personal life.

"If you scared of me, just say you scared," Terrence said as he kissed her on the side of her neck.

His warm lips sent chills down Gwen's spine. She closed her eyes and imagined what his lips would feel like down below. It made her wet just thinking about it. She turned around to face him. "You sure you wanna go down this road?" Gwen asked, staring up at him with sex in her eyes. "Shit can get real dark for you once you cross these borders."

Terrence couldn't care less about how dark it could get, and the way Gwen was talking made it seem like he couldn't handle what she had. It only turned him on even more. "I'ma pick you up tonight at nine o'clock. Make sure you bring ya overnight kit wit' you."

He pulled Gwen's body closer to his then leaned in and pressed his lips against hers. Gwen practically melted in his arms. When he released his hold on her, she was almost tempted to grab him, lock the door, and let him blow her back out right there on the spot.

Gwen let him leave, but not before getting one more kiss from him, hoping it would keep her satisfied until later.

Diamond sat in front of the house, waiting for Ski to show up. He was supposed to be there by twelve thirty, but he was running a little late, due to the traffic. He did get a chance to call Diamond and let her know, but it was already one o'clock, and Diamond was getting impatient. She jumped on the phone and called Dollaz, who was already on his way to therapy. The call went straight to voice mail.

"Come da hell on," she mumbled to herself.

She was frustrated, and she wasn't trying to waste any more time. She walked back into the house and grabbed the small duffle bag. After locking the house up, she tossed the bag into the trunk of the Camaro.

Just in case Ski was close, she waited for a few minutes to see if he would pop up. He didn't, so Diamond said, "Fuck it." She got into the car and pulled off.

The drive to the bank was nerve-racking. Although she was doing the speed limit, using her turn signals and wearing her seat belt, she still felt nervous for some reason. This wasn't even the first time that she had traveled with large amounts of money on her, so she really didn't know why she was shook the way she was. The realty company afforded her with a valid excuse to have that much money on her, so it wasn't that.

After about forty-five minutes of driving into the city, Diamond finally made it to the bank safely. The bank manager, Rebecca, who was also MHB, made sure that the money was deposited directly into the realty company's account. The whole money laundering situation was set up to perfection. It was damn near impossible for them to be popped by the feds, especially since they had somebody in the bank to make sure the IRS stayed in their lane.

"A'ight, Becca, I'll talk to you later," Diamond said before leaving the bank.

Next stop was the office. Diamond didn't really spend that much time at MHB Realty because she put in a lot of work hours on the streets. When she did stop by, it was to have lunch with Gwen or just BS around.

When Diamond walked up to the driver's side of her car, she instantly felt something was wrong. It was as if the black Ford Explorer 4x4 appeared from out of nowhere and came to a screeching halt right in front of Diamond. It was only about a couple feet away from hitting her. When she turned around, both the front and rear passenger's doors swung open. The only thing Diamond really saw were the guns pointed right in her face.

"Get in the car," the masked man sitting in the back seat said, motioning to her with his guns.

"I'm not getting in ya car. If you gon' shoot me, then go ahead and shoot!" Diamond shot back.

She turned back around as though she was going to attempt to get into her car. Once the door was open, her gun would be in arm's reach, and if she was lucky enough to get her hands on it, she was going to open fire without hesitation.

The chances of her getting that off were slim to none, because as soon as Diamond got her key in the door, she was knocked over the back of her head with a lead pipe. The guy who hit her caught her body before it hit the ground, then tossed Diamond into the back seat of the jeep like a rag doll. It happened so fast that none of the few pedestrians who were out there noticed anything going on. The Ford simply pulled off calmly, blending in with the rest of the traffic.

***

"Where you taking me?" Gwen playfully asked, reaching over and smacking Terrence on the arm.

Gwen didn't know exactly where she was, but she did know it was right outside the city limits. It was nighttime, so she really couldn't see that well. What she did notice was that it was a lot of land and not too many houses in the area. It looked country.

After driving a few more minutes, Terrence pulled off onto a rocky dirt road that led up to a large piece of open land. Motion sensor lights lit up around the house when the car pulled into the driveway. Gwen looked in awe at the huge, beautiful house.

"This better not be ya house." Gwen smiled.

"This is just one of them," he said, gathering his things in the car. "I hardly ever come out here."

"Dis shit don't make no sense." Gwen got out of the car and looked up at the house.

It looked even bigger from outside the car. The night-lights lined the walkway along the driveway up to the front of the house. Gwen didn't say anything right away, but she swore she could smell water in the near distance.

"If I would have known you was bringing me to your home, I wouldn't have wasted a perfectly good outfit," Gwen said, stopping at the bottom of the stairs and looking down at her clothes.

Terrence had to admit Gwen looked sexy as hell. She had on a pink pencil skirt, a white blouse with a yellow leather biker jacket over it, and on her feet were a pair of Louboutin heels. In her hand was a cute clutch by Alexander McQueen. Her overnight bag was still in the car.

"So you gon' come in or stay out here?" Terrence smiled, opening the front door.

Gwen shook her head as she climbed the steps. She bumped Terrence on her way inside for not helping her up the stairs in her heels.

When she got inside, she was impressed with the way he'd decorated the house; hardwood floors throughout, cedar wood stairs and banisters, plush leather furniture with glass tables and a red brick fireplace in the center of the living room.

"You swear you gon' get some tonight." Gwen chuckled, looking around the house.

Terrence smiled at her comment. "Come on, silly. Let me show you around the rest of the house," he said, grabbing her hand and walking backward toward the staircase.

Diamond woke up, only to be drowning in a bathtub full of water. She inhaled water through her nose and mouth as she tried to breathe. Randy pulled her head from the water, allowing her to get a second's worth of air before he shoved her head back into the water. He repeated this act several times, bringing Diamond to the edge of death then pulling back just in the nick of time.

The last time he pulled her head up from the water, he let her almost lifeless body drop to the floor. Tianna stood at the entrance to the bathroom looking on. It took her a minute, but eventually Diamond came to, coughing and throwing up water and the meal she ate for breakfast.

"Now look, shawty. I can do dis shit all day . . . or until I end up killing you. I just wanna know who made the call for Dink to be killed," Randy said, taking a seat on the toilet.

Diamond didn't say anything. Snot, water, and vomit ran down her face. She was still a little discombobulated, so she was unable to answer the question.

“Let’s just shoot dis bitch!” Tianna said, pulling a 9 mm from her front pocket.

Diamond already had it in her mind that they were going to kill her, so she definitely didn’t have anything to say. That only made Randy more upset. He leaned over and punched Diamond clean across her chin.

Tianna pointed the gun at Diamond’s head.

Randy quickly reacted, pushing the gun away from Diamond. The gun went off in the process, but the bullet missed Diamond and went into the floor.

“What da fuck is you doin’, Tianna?” Randy snapped. “We need dis bitch alive. If she do know something, I know one sick muthafucka who can get it out of her,” Randy said, looking down at Diamond.

The person Randy was talking about was well experienced in making people talk. Randy had seen firsthand what Terrence could do, and he knew that Diamond wouldn’t last five minutes being in the room with him alone. There was no question that Diamond went hard in the paint, but the fact still remained that she was a woman, and it was only so much pain a woman could take before she cracked. Terrence knew that, Randy knew that, and deep down inside, Diamond knew it too, but she was going to hold on for as long as she could to preserve the lives of her friends.

Gwen and Terrence sat on the balcony outside his bedroom, looking out at the large pond in his backyard. It had to be the size of an Olympic swimming pool, and what made it look so beautiful were the underwater lights Terrence had installed a while back. You could actually see fish swimming around the pond, unharmed by the lights.

“You know, when my brain becomes cluttered with all the bullshit goin’ on in my life, I come out here and get peace of mind,” Terrence said, looking out at the water.

Gwen could feel the sense of peace he was talking about. It seemed like the view overlapped all the bad, and for the first time in months, Gwen didn't think about Zion, Chad, or Mayo, nor did she worry herself with the piles of paperwork sitting on her office desk.

"Hold up for a second," Terrence said, getting up and walking into his bedroom. He came back out with a few pillows and a couple of thick comforters. He tossed them on the edge of the roof that slightly lapped over the balcony, and then jumped on the rail and climbed onto the roof.

"What are you doin'?" Gwen chuckled, watching him as he brushed off his clothes.

"Come on," he said, leaning over and sticking his hand out over the ledge.

"Boy, I'm not coming up there on that roof," Gwen replied. "I think I'm scared of heights." She smiled.

"Trust me," he told her, wiggling his fingers for her to grab his hand.

Gwen looked up at him and let out a sigh. He just stood there with his hand out, waiting for her to grab it. Gwen looked back at the pond then back up at Terrence. She got up from the chair and reached for his hand. "You better not drop me," she said as she took off her heels and allowed him to pull her up to where he was.

The rooftop was slanted in certain places, but smack dab in the middle of the roof was an evenly flat surface about thirty square feet. Terrence led her to it with the comforters and pillows in hand. The view of the pond was even better from the roof.

Gwen stopped and did a full 360 degree turn, looking into the open field and the bright city lights in the far distance. "Now how many of your bitches did you bring up here?" Gwen playfully asked, turning back around to face him.

Terrence wrapped his arms around her waist, resting his hands on the lower part of her back. He pulled her closer to him then leaned in and kissed her. Gwen held onto his arms, returning the kisses and allowing his tongue to roam freely inside her mouth.

"I swear on my mother that I never even brought another female to this house," he said, looking into her eyes.

From the sincere look that he gave her, Gwen believed him and didn't second guess it.

"I'm not gonna lie, Gwen. I want you bad," he confessed.

His hands traveled from her lower back, around her ass, and then down the back of her thighs. His touch was driving Gwen crazy, especially when his hands began to go underneath her skirt. Her body became more submissive the higher his hands traveled.

"Don't be scared," he whispered, palming both of her ass cheeks.

In one swift motion, he lifted Gwen off the rooftop. She wrapped her legs around his waist and locked them. Terrence held her up with one arm while squatting down to spread the comforter out with his free hand. Gwen kept her arms wrapped around his neck, watching as he laid out the makeshift bed.

It was a little chilly out, so when he laid her down, he took another blanket and put it over them. Gwen was nervous. She hadn't had sex for almost a year, and she hoped to God that she could handle Terrence.

"I got you now," Terrence said, leaning in to kiss her.

He peeled off his shirt and didn't even give Gwen the chance to unbutton her blouse. He popped it open then stuffed his tongue in her mouth before she could complain. He shimmied his pants down, and at the same time, pulled off her pink lace panties.

The aroma from her box was sweet, like she bathed in fruit. Terrence had to taste it. He started by kissing and licking around her stomach, biting down on her side as he made his way farther down. Gwen couldn't believe what she was allowing him to do to her.

Her skirt remained on, but it was hiked up over her waist, making it easier for him to point his face inside her garden. Gwen moaned, feeling his lips softly kiss around her labia. Her jaw dropped and she looked down at Terrence like he was doing something strange to her. The way he wiggled his tongue around inside of her almost felt like a small, warm, wet dick.

"Sssss!" she hissed, throwing her head back in pleasure.

An orgasm was right around the corner, and Gwen could feel it down in her gut. She spread her legs wider, reached down, and grabbed her vulva. Gwen felt a little embarrassed to cum in his mouth, but at this point she really couldn't help it. Her body went into shock, and the fluids flowing from her pussy poured into Terrence's mouth. He cleaned up good, too, swallowing every drop of her.

"Oh my fuckin' God!" Gwen yelled.

She brought his head up to hers and threw her tongue into his mouth. His dick was rock hard and didn't need guidance in finding her entrance point. His thick member tunneled down into her warm, pulsating canal until the full length of it was inside her. Gwen bit down on the top of his shoulder in pleasure, her nipples rock hard from the light breeze that passed through the blanket. As Terrence took his time stroking Gwen slowly and passionately, she looked up at the stars in the sky and felt like she was sampling a piece of heaven.

"Yo, my nigga, hold on," Ski told Dollaz when he looked over and saw Diamond's car on Front Street. "Yo, I found her car!" he said, jumping out of his car and walking over to the Camaro.

"It's no sign of her," he said, looking in the car then up and down the street.

When Diamond didn't pick Dollaz up from therapy as they had planned, he called five times and began to get worried when he couldn't reach her. He called around to everyone, asking if they had seen her, but nobody had. Ski informed him that by the time he got to the house, she was gone.

Dollaz sat in his wheelchair and scratched his head. He didn't know what to think, but it seemed like all the negative things found their way into his thoughts.

"Where da fuck are you?" Dollaz mumbled to himself.

If he only knew how much Diamond needed him. She was tied up, gagged, and beat up pretty badly, hoping and praying that her nightmare would end soon. Little did she know that it had only just begun, and she was going to need a little more than a prayer to get her out of the vicious situation she was in.

Chapter 11

After sleeping on the roof and waking up together to watch the sunrise, Terrence and Gwen finally took it back into the house. There was no rush for either one of them to get to work, because they both were bosses.

“You know you gon’ buy me another shirt,” Gwen joked, buttoning up one of Terrence’s long-sleeved Polo shirts she had found in his closet.

She smiled as she walked over to him and threw her arms over his shoulder while he sat at the desk, looking at the computer screen.

Terrence stopped what he was doing once he felt her touch. He grabbed her hand and kissed it. “How about me and you just chill out for today? We can get something to eat, do a little bit of shopping, and just kick it,” Terrence suggested.

“What?” Gwen shot back. “Let me find out you getting all soft,” she joked, kissing the side of his neck.

Terrence jumped out of the chair and spun around the bedroom with her, pecking her lips with his like a bird. She couldn’t get enough of how easily he manhandled her and picked her up at will.

When he laid Gwen down on the bed, she felt a vibrating sensation.

“That better not be what I think it is.” She chuckled as she reached under the covers and felt around. It was her cell phone under the sheets. When she grabbed it, Terrence looked at her with the puppy dog face, not wanting her to answer it.

"Don't look at me like that, boy." She smiled, looking at the UNAVAILABLE on her screen.

It could only be one person calling from an unavailable number, and that was Niya. This was a call Gwen couldn't ignore. "Yo," she answered, reaching up and caressing Terrence's chest as he sat on top of her.

After the operator came through, Gwen pushed five to accept the call. "Hey, sis!" she said in a chipper voice.

"G, when was the last time you spoke to Chad?"

"A couple of days ago. I snapped on him about him not spending much time with the twins and—"

"Chad is dead!" Niya said, cutting her off.

"What?" Gwen yelled into the phone, pushing Terrence off her and jumping up off the bed.

"The chaplain called me down to his office this morning and told me. He put me on the phone with a detective who told me that Chad committed suicide a few days ago," Niya explained.

The phone went completely silent. Gwen walked out onto the balcony, rubbing her head. The news wasn't sinking in right away; it was as if she were waiting to wake up from a bad dream.

Niya gave her a moment to get herself together, knowing exactly the way she was feeling. She had been crying half the morning after receiving the news herself. Even with everything that had happened between them, Niya still had tremendous love for Chad, and that would never change. She only wished she was home to help him through his time of need.

"You still there, G?" Niya asked, trying her best to hold back the tears that continued to form in her eyes.

Gwen nodded her head, forgetting that Niya couldn't see her. Truth be told, Gwen was sick. She felt somewhat responsible for his death, thinking that she should have kept a better eye out on Chad, knowing that he was out there riding reckless. Niya finding out about his death before her only further proved the fact that she had been neglecting Chad.

"Take your time and get yaself together, sis. Then call around and make sure that what the cops said happened is what happened to him," Niya said. "I'll call you back later on tonight, okay?" she said.

Gwen nodded first, but then verbally said yes before hanging up the phone. She looked out at the pond and shook her head, hoping the view would help her gather her thoughts, but it didn't. It wasn't working in the least, nor was Gwen going to stick around and wait for its tranquility to kick in.

Terrence dropped Gwen off to her car then headed for the office to catch up on some paperwork and find out what happened yesterday when Randy and Tianna set out to find Diamond. Until now, he had been pretty much in the dark about the situation. His cell phone was turned off the moment he had picked Gwen up for their date. He didn't want any interruptions, and he knew that if he kept his phone on, he'd never enjoy the night.

As Terrence drove down the highway, he looked up at his rearview and saw a black SUV dipping in and out of traffic. The truck got closer and closer, until it pulled up on the driver's side. Terrence didn't panic, because at this point, he knew what it was. The passenger's side window of the truck came down, and Randy sat up in the seat. Terrence rolled his window down as well.

"Yo, we got da bitch!" Randy yelled through the whipping winds. "She's not talking, though. I think you might wanna holla at her!" he yelled.

Terrence nodded then pointed with his two fingers for Randy to lead the way. They darted in front of Terrence's car and got off at the next exit. It took another thirty minutes for them to get to a trap house they had off Patrick Street. That's where they had Diamond under heavy watch.

Terrence walked up the stairs and to the bathroom door, where one of the armed workers was standing. Diamond looked dead. Blood covered her face and body, and she wasn't moving at all. He looked over at Randy with a confused look on his face.

"Watch out. She ain't dead," Randy said, entering the bathroom and kicking Diamond's leg. "Wake up, bitch!" Randy yelled, kicking her leg again.

When she didn't respond, he grabbed a handful of her hair and lifted her head. He smacked her cheeks a few times, which did the trick in waking her.

She was groggy from the dope Randy shot her up with before he left, so it took her a minute to adjust her eyes. When she did, she couldn't believe she was looking at Terrence. She blinked her eyes several times to make sure her eyes weren't deceiving her, but the image didn't change. Sure enough, it was Terrence.

"Damn, shawty. Look like you had a rough night," Terrence said, walking over and taking a seat on the edge of the tub. "My people tellin' me you don't wanna talk." He reached over and lifted her chin.

After looking at her for a minute, Terrence began to recognize her blood-soaked face from somewhere. He felt the same way he did when he saw her picture on Tianna's phone. He didn't remember her, but Diamond sure knew who he was.

"Where do I know you from?" he asked, leaning in to get a better look at her.

Diamond didn't say anything, and that wasn't because she didn't want to, but rather because her jaw felt like it was broke, and the slightest movement of her mouth gave her excruciating pain. Her silence only made Terrence upset. He drew the Glock he had tucked in his waist and pointed it at her face. Diamond looked up at him with emptiness in her eyes. She welcomed the bullet, as opposed to giving up her friends.

Terrence was about to pull the trigger but stopped when he saw the MHB tattoo on her.

"Y'all MHB bitches swear y'all run this city," he said, looking back up into her eyes.

Diamond dug deep down and found enough strength to respond to what he said. Through the pain from her jaw, and knowing that more than likely she was about to be killed, Diamond spoke. "We do run this city," she said, spitting a glob of blood onto Terrence's shoes.

Before Terrence was about to pull the trigger, it clicked. He finally remembered where he recognized Diamond from. He took the gun and moved her hair from the side of her face to be sure. Clear as day, the female that was walking with Gwen the day he bumped into her in the Hearst Tower was lying there in front of him. He lowered the gun from her head then scratched his own head as he went into deep thought.

"Yo, what's goin' on, bruh?" Randy asked, seeing Terrence's confused look.

"Get da fuck outta here," Terrence mumbled.

He was putting everything together now. If Diamond was MHB, then more than likely Gwen was too. Thinking even harder, he realized that Mortgages, Homes, Businesses actually stood for MHB, and the boss of that company was also Gwen, who probably was the boss of MHB. Shit was getting deep, and the more Terrence thought about it, the more it made sense.

"Yo, we can't kill dis bitch right now," Terrence said.

"Why not? Dis bitch killed Dink," Randy responded.

Terrence looked at Randy like he was crazy. "Do I answer to you now?" Terrence shot back, getting up and walking to Randy. "I said don't touch her," he said through clenched teeth. "Do I make myself clear?"

Randy knew to stay in his place before it got dark for him. He lowered his head in humility.

"Clear," Randy answered in a low tone.

Terrence stuffed his gun back in his waist and walked off. Randy looked over at Diamond, who looked back up at him with a smirk on her face. Randy thought that she was going to die, but it wasn't going to happen, not now anyway. He looked at her and shook his head then walked off, trying to catch up with Terrence to find out what was going on.

Gwen couldn't stop crying as she looked down at Chad's body lying on the metal drawer. She couldn't believe it. It was like her heart sank into her stomach, and she found it hard to breathe, looking at his pale face. The bullet had traveled quickly through his upper skull, so all that could be seen was a small entry and exit wound right above each ear. The doctor stood far off to the side, giving her time and space to grieve.

The detective in the room wasn't so respectful. He had a few questions to ask so that he could wrap up his investigation.

"Ma'am, where was he currently residing?" the detective asked with his pen and pad out, ready to take notes.

Gwen looked up and wiped the tears from her cheeks. She explained to the detective that Chad was living with her and not at the address they had in the criminal system, which was Niya's house.

"Well, if he lived on the east side with you, what was he doin' in a motel way on the other side of town?" the detective asked.

That was one thing Gwen couldn't understand about the whole situation. Not just that, but it was hard for her to believe that Chad would kill himself. This was something most black men would never consider. She did know that lately he was using a lot of drugs and alcohol to mask his pain. That pain was so hard that she had even considered it once herself, and had it not been for Chad, it would be her lying on that metal bed being identified.

Damn, why wasn't I there for him, like he was for me? Gwen thought. The two most important men in her life were now gone, and it was only one person she could think of to blame outside of herself.

The detective tried to ask a few more questions, but Gwen wasn't up for it. She snapped on the detective and then stormed out of the coroner's office. Her hurt turned into anger, and the only thing that was on her mind when she left of the coroner's office was putting an end to that other person's life. Mayo's number was up, and Gwen wasn't going to wait another minute. She whipped out her cell phone as she walked through the parking lot.

Kea picked up on the second ring. "Yo, wassup?" she answered.

"It's a green light on that. And make sure that shit hurt," Gwen said before hanging up the phone.

Terrence stepped off the elevator and walked onto the floor of MHB Realty. He stood by the elevators and looked at all the females walking around, answering telephones, and sitting with potential clients. He slowly walked toward Gwen's office, all the while looking around. Shockingly, he noticed that most of the women had MHB tattoos on their necks, arms, hands, and feet, and they weren't ashamed to flaunt them.

"Can I help you, Mr. Johnson?" one of the secretaries asked from her cubicle.

"Yeah, is Gwen in?" he asked, noticing that she, too, had an MHB tattoo on her wrist.

"She didn't come in yet. Do you want to leave a message for her?" the secretary asked politely.

"Nah, that's okay. I'll come back a little later," he told her before heading back to the elevator.

Terrence went downstairs to his own office. When he stepped onto the floor, it was quiet and his employees sat at their cubicles with nervous looks in their eyes.

"Molinda, what's goin' on?" Terrence asked his receptionist.

"They been here since nine this morning," she said, nodding in the direction of Terrence's office.

He looked back and saw about a half dozen people sitting around his office. They looked hood, too, dressed in black hoodies and tan Timberland boots. Seeing his little sister Stacey sitting in the middle of everybody, he knew exactly who they were.

"Here we go," Cornell said when Terrence entered the room.

Cornell was Dink's older brother. He was the one who kept pressing the issue about getting some answers concerning Dink's death. Terrence knew him, but not that well, especially not well enough to continue to allow Cornell to be sitting in his chair with his feet up on his desk.

"Yo, you wanna get up out my chair, homeboy?" Terrence asked, not even taking the time to acknowledge his sister.

Cornell didn't even look at him.

Terrence wasn't going for it though. "I'm not gonna ask you again, my man," Terrence said, walking around to the back of his desk.

Cornell jumped up and stood toe-to-toe with Terrence when he walked up on him. There was obvious tension in the room, and most of it was coming from Cornell and his crew, who were in murder mode behind Dink's death. They felt that Terrence wasn't making enough progress in taking care of the situation, so they came up North to make shit hot.

"Everybody just cool out. We ain't come up here for all that," Stacey said, breaking the silence in the room.

Cornell stood to the side and let Terrence sit in his chair. He took a seat on the other side of the desk.

"Yo, what you know about my brother's death?" Cornell asked with an attitude.

"Just like I told my incompetent sister," he said, looking up at Stacey. "I'm working on that situation."

"That's not good enough," Cornell said, shaking his head. "My li'l bro was up here fuckin' wit' you, which makes you partly responsible for his death. Now you either tell me what you know, or I'ma take it out on you!" Cornell threatened.

"Take it out on me? You got me fucked up," Terrence said, pulling the gun from his hip.

Terrence started a chain reaction, because the other three males that were in the room all pulled out guns and pointed them right at Terrence. Terrence had his gun pointed at Cornell, who was unarmed. A couple of the employees who watched as guns were drawn, were tempted to go for the elevator but stopped when they noticed a man with a black hoodie on, standing by the elevator doors with his hand under his shirt.

"If you gon' shoot, nigga, then shoot. If not, tell me what you know so we can get da fuck up outta here," Cornell said aggressively.

It wasn't that Terrence was bitching or anything. He just figured if he told them what he knew, they could deal with it from there on out. He could save some time and money, plus a lot of unnecessary bloodshed.

"It was some bitches from a crew out here called MHB," Terrence said, lowering his gun slowly. "I don't know how many of them there are, but I do know they run this city and they're not hard to find. The problem is, you gotta find out which ones did it," Terrence said.

"Yeah, well, we do things a little different down South, homeboy," Cornell said, getting up from his seat. "We gon' kill as many of them as we can. Then, after we feel like we caused enough grief in this city, we'll leave. So from here on out, just stay out of the way," Cornell said and walked out of the office.

Terrence gave his sister the evil eye as she followed behind Cornell and his crew. She stopped at the door and turned around to say something to him, but Terrence gave her a dismissive stare to let her know he wasn't tryin' to hear nothing she had to say. As far as he was concerned, Stacey wasn't his sister right now, and whatever happened to her at this point was on her.

Chapter 12

"Lockdown!" Ms. Nealy yelled from her office.

Mayo was already in his room, preparing to give Ms. Nealy some of the best dick she ever had. A couple hundred push-ups, a few hundred sit-ups and about five hundred back-arms had his body nice and tight. He took a quick bird bath in his sink to freshen up, then dabbed on some oils from the commissary.

"A'ight, my nigga. As soon as she open this door after count, I need you to go out there and start cleaning up," Mayo told his celly so that he would have the cell to himself.

"Damn, my nigga, you da man," his celly shot back, extending his hand for a pound.

Mayo walked over to the door and looked out the narrow window, watching as Ms. Nealy and another guard walked around counting inmates. He was more so looking at Ms. Nealy's ass swaying from side to side as she walked up to every door. Just the thought of sticking his dick between her cakes made his dick hard.

When she passed by his door, she smiled and gave him a wink of the eye to let him know that it was on. Mayo just fell back, sat on his bunk, and waited for the count to be cleared by the center control. The whole time he sat there, he thought about all the things he was going to do to her in that cell. Visions of him fucking her from behind ran through his mind, causing his dick to become rock hard.

"Yo, my nigga, as soon as she pop this door open, you gotta get da fuck out," Mayo reiterated.

He was hyped up and ready to go at this point. His dick was so hard, pre-cum seeped out into his boxers. He was going to fuck Ms. Nealy like no other. He didn't know it yet, but Ms. Nealy was going to fuck the shit out of him as well.

"Bitch, you better stop playin," Tiffany joked, playfully punching April in her arm while they sat at the bar.

There weren't many people at MHB Bar & Grill on a Wednesday night, so Tiffany and April took that time to plan the surprise party they were going to give Alexus for her birthday.

"Y'all better hurry up. You know that girl gon' be walking through that door any minute," Tanya, the bartender, said as she wiped off the bar with her rag.

Moments later, the front door swung open and in walked Cornell, pulling the hood off his head. April looked over and saw him but didn't think anything of it, so she turned back around to finish looking at the party themes with Tiffany.

"Can I get you something?" Tanya asked, walking over to him.

The visible MHB tattoo on her neck made Cornell waste not another second in doing what he came there to do. He pulled the .38 snub nose from his jacket pocket, pointed it at Tanya's chest, and squeezed. The first bullet hit her center mass, while the other entered her top right shoulder, sending her backward.

April fell out of her chair when she heard the shots. Tiffany looked over and saw Tanya's body crashing into the shelves, knocking down dozens of bottles of liquor. She jumped up, and by that time, Cornell had turned the gun on her.

One of the bullets just missed Tiffany's head, while the other two knocked chips of wood from the bar into the air. April managed to retrieve her gun from her bag while she was on the floor, and began shooting wildly in Cornell's direction. He didn't even duck behind anything to avoid the gun spray. He didn't have to, because April's aim was off, shooting from the ground.

"Tell Dink I'ma ride for him," Cornell said, firing his last shot and hitting April in her neck.

Tiffany finally retrieved her gun from her bag, spinning around to the .38 being thrown at her. It hit her on the top of her head, stunning her for a second. By the time she readjusted her eyes, Cornell had taken off out of the bar.

"Oh my God! April!" Tiffany yelled, dropping down to the ground next to her. "Come on, girl, hold on!" she yelled, wrapping her hands around her neck.

The bullet had hit a major artery, sending blood straight down her throat and into her lungs. Tiffany couldn't stop the bleeding no matter how much pressure she put on the wound. She looked down at April, whose eyes were rolling to the back of her head.

"Call the ambulance!" she yelled to the only two patrons in the bar.

They came from behind the tables with their phones in their hands, dialing numbers. Their efforts were to no avail, because April was dead and Tiffany knew it. She closed April's eyes with her blood-soaked hand then fell back against the bar. She was still in shock and couldn't believe what had just happened, or why it had happened. She heard Cornell loud and clear when he said Dink's name. She never thought that his death was going to come back on her, and even to someone who was as innocent as April, who didn't have a clue about what was going on and who Dink was. All Tiffany knew now was that the beef was officially on.

Alexus, Gwen, and two other MHB members climbed into the truck and headed off to meet up with some new clientele. Gwen really didn't feel like doing too much of anything, considering she had to prepare Chad's funeral, but the only way she could take her mind off his death was by staying busy.

"Gwen, are you okay?" Alexus asked, looking over at her staring hard out of the passenger's side window.

Gwen snapped out of her daze and looked over at Alexus. "You ever feel like you wanna put this life behind you and start over?"

Alexus didn't want to answer the question in front of the two newly pledged MHB members. This wasn't the kind of conversation they needed to hear, and they definitely were a little too fresh in the game to hear the boss questioning herself about being MHB. They just wouldn't understand.

"Well, we all need a break sometimes," Alexus responded, trying to clean up the conversation. "We'll talk about that later, though, 'cause we about to get off on the next exit," she told her, pointing to the sign.

Gwen couldn't lie; being the boss of MHB was starting to take its toll. So many good things in her life were sacrificed behind being MHB. In a sense, it felt like MHB was the one who took her son's life, and now she felt the same way about Chad. The regular life she used to have was far over, and the simple things she took for granted were replaced by mountains of responsibilities that took up her life.

The more she thought about it, the more she started to hate her position. The only reason she hadn't quit by now was because so many young females depended on her for guidance. So many young females became MHB because of Gwen, and she didn't want to just turn her back on them. She felt obligated to stay in charge.

"We, like, ten minutes away," Alexus announced in the car so everybody could get ready.

One of the girls in the back got up, reached into the third row seat, and grabbed a large duffle bag. In the middle of Gwen cocking a bullet into the chamber of her Glock .40, her cell phone went off. She grabbed it from the center console and saw that it was Tiffany.

"Yeah," Gwen answered, resting the gun on her lap.

She could hear sirens and people yelling loudly in the background before Tiffany even said a word. At this point, Gwen became very attentive and sat up in her seat.

"Tiff, what's goin' on?" Gwen asked.

"Tanya and April is gone," Tiffany spoke, watching as the coroner rolled April's body over to the van.

"What do you mean gone?" Gwen shot back looking over at Alexus to see if she had heard what Tiffany said.

Tiffany broke down all the events that took place in the bar, and how the gunman gave reference to Dink's name before killing April. She also reminded Gwen that Diamond still hadn't popped up, which made her think that she might be dead somewhere. Gwen leaned up and put her head on the dashboard.

"Meet me at the spot in one hour!" Gwen told Tiffany then hung up the phone.

"I don't even wanna know right now," Alexus said, shaking her head. "Let's finish taking care of this." She pointed at the meeting place.

Mayo heard the sound of keys outside his door, so he jumped up from the bed and walked over. Ms. Nealy was walking through the pod, going to the selected doors and opening them so the orderlies could go out and clean. Per Mayo's instructions, only three out of the normal five cells were going out.

When she got to Mayo's door, his celly was already on point, waiting at the door.

"Boy, you gon' get me in trouble," Ms. Nealy said, stepping to the side to let Mayo's celly out.

"Come on," Mayo said, backing up and taking off his shit. "Time is precious." He licked his lips.

Ms. Nealy stood at the door, hesitating to enter his cell. She knew that once she was in, she'd be committing herself to see it through. Her heart was racing, but she couldn't back down now. It was a lot more than sex on the line, and Kea wanted to make sure she did it right.

"You ain't really tryin' to do anything, boy," Kea teased, looking like she was about to walk away.

Mayo wasn't trying to let her go. He was ready and horny as a pit bull. No way was he was going to let her leave.

"Hold up, hold up, where you goin'?" he asked, walking over to the door.

She backed up a little, gave him a seductive grin while biting her bottom lip. It drove Mayo crazy. He reached out and grabbed her before she could walk off and pulled her into the cell. She didn't resist much, and stumbled into the cell giggling.

"Girl, stop playin' wit' me!" Mayo said, kissing Kea while at the same time unfastening her belt.

She returned his kisses, stuffing her tongue down his throat. He walked her over to the bottom bunk and sat her down. Clumsily, he push her backward and pulled off one of her pants legs. He left her panties on, but just pulled them to the side.

Kea tightened her walls and braced for impact.

Mayo almost had to pry her legs open in order to get inside her. When his dick finally reached the pussy, he wasted no time pushing the whole head of his member deep into her canal. Kea moaned from the deep penetration. She opened her legs up a little wider, allowing him to go in deeper.

"Smack me," she moaned, looking up at him. "I like it rough." She dug her nails into his chest. "Fuck dis pussy, nigga."

Mayo didn't do it at first, but when Kea reached up and smacked him clean across the face, he joined in the rough sex. He smacked her lightly and she giggled. She reached back up and smacked him again, this time harder than the last time.

"You can't handle this pussy!" she taunted, reaching up and grabbing his neck.

He drew his arm and backhanded the shit out of Kea's face. It damn near knocked her out, but she managed to look back up at him with a smile.

"That's what I'm talkin' about!" she smiled, biting her lower lip.

Mayo was pounding away. Tight, warm, wet pussy never felt better, especially coming from a guard.

"You better not pull out either," she told him.

She could tell by the way Mayo looked that he was about to cum. She pulled him down to kiss her so that it would take his eyes off what Kea was about to do. The harder he pounded, the easier it was for Kea to reach down into her back pocket and pull out the jailhouse shank. She kept it down by her side while she continued to kiss him. Mayo still didn't notice what she had in her hand. He was so focused on sucking Kea's tongue that nothing else mattered.

"I'm about to bust!" Mayo said, picking up his pace.

Kea could feel his cum oozing inside her, and as soon as she saw that he was at his weakest moment, she struck. She grabbed him by his neck and lifted him up from her face.

He looked at her and smiled.

Kea did too.

"Gwen said she'll see you in hell!" Kea said before shoving the flat, sharp, metal shank into his neck.

She quickly pulled it out and hit him two more times in the neck with it, causing blood to squirt out onto her face.

Mayo was in shock. He tried to punch her, but grabbing his neck was more important. She pushed him off her, rolled out of the bed, and grabbed her radio dangling from her belt. She yelled into the radio for help then pushed the panic button. Mayo struggled to keep his eyes open as the blood poured out from his neck.

Within seconds, a team of guards rushed the block, searching cell by cell for Kea. She could hear the keys jingling, but they weren't coming to the cell.

"I'm in here!" Kea yelled, getting the attention of one of the guards.

When the guards walked into the cell, it was a bloody mess. Mayo had pretty much bled to death, and Kea was lying between the lockers, covered in blood, with her pants halfway off. Everything so far was going according to plan, but the assassination of Mayo wasn't quite over yet.

Terrence and Randy sat in the truck, waiting for the new connect to pull into the parking lot. Drama was in the hood, but Terrence couldn't let it stop his business. Money still needed to be made, and dopefiends needed their product. Terrence was trying to cop as much dope as he could, since Auntie had told him that a drought was coming soon. That was the last thing any dope boy wanted to be caught up in. A drought could really set a nigga back, and Terrence couldn't afford any setbacks.

"So wassup wit' da bitch?" Randy said, referring to Diamond, who was still being held hostage.

Terrence couldn't decide whether to kill her or let her go. He couldn't stop thinking about Gwen and how much he was feeling her. At the same time, he had a lot of questions that needed answers. How Gwen answered them would determine if she lived as well.

The only problem Terrence had was getting in touch with Gwen to find out what was going on. The last time he saw her was when he dropped her off at her car the morning after they had sex. She wasn't answering her phone, nor was she coming into the office, as far as Terrence knew. It was like she went M.I.A.

"Yo, I think that's her," Terrence said, nodding at the black Cadillac Escalade that pulled into the lot.

All four doors to the Escalade opened up and out jumped four women. Two were heavily armed with AR-15s. They all walked up to Terrence's truck, surrounding it like a pack of curious lions.

"Get da fuck outta here," Terrence said, seeing Gwen amongst the pack of women.

Terrence exited the truck with his 10 mm in his hand. Randy did the same, clutching an AK-47 in both hands. For now, everyone kept their guns lowered to the ground.

"Are you serious?" Terrence asked, walking up to Gwen.

She was shocked to see that it was him. Auntie said she had some new clientele lined up, but the last person she thought would be standing there was Terrence.

"I see we both have our own little secrets," Gwen said, leaning against his truck.

"So, it is true. You really are MHB?" Terrence spoke, looking at her and then over at the females holding the assault rifles.

Gwen could only nod her head. There was no use in lying now, plus at that point, she really couldn't care less about what somebody thought about her. She had so much going on in her life right now it was making her sick.

"So you mean to tell me that all this time—"

"Stop! Look, I'm here on business. If you wanna score, you gotta do it now, 'cause shit lookin' real crazy," Gwen said, cutting him off.

Terrence turned his face up at her, surprised that she was talking to him in that manner.

"What, did you forget?" Terrence shot back, referring to the night of passion they had shared.

Gwen grabbed him by the arm and pulled him to the side, away from everyone else. She definitely didn't want everybody involved in her personal life.

"It's not like that, Terrence. I just got a lot goin' on right now," she said in a much softer voice.

"Did you have something to do with killing Dink?" Terrence asked. "I know you run MHB, so don't act like—"

"Dink? What you know about Dink?" Gwen took a step back with a curious look on her face.

She had just hung up the phone with Tiffany, and now he was sitting there asking about Dink. Automatically, she thought that he may have had something to do with the shooting at the bar. If he did, the situation was about to turn ugly, especially with all the assault rifles on deck.

"Look, Gwen, I fucks wit' you. And if you did have something to do with it, it's some people in the city from down South that's out to kill you and whoever else they can find from MHB," Terrence warned.

He really couldn't believe that he had told Gwen about Dink's people. When he saw her face-to-face, everything changed. He went from thinking about killing her, to wanting to save her life.

Gwen, on the other hand, had murder on her mind and all she wanted to know was where Dink's people were so she could do to them what she had done to Dink.

"Take me to where they at!" Gwen demanded.

"I can't," he responded, looking away from her.

"What you mean? These bastards just killed two of my friends and another one is missing. If you know something, Terrence, let me know," Gwen pleaded.

Terrence wanted to tell her, but he really didn't know where they were. He hadn't talked to his sister since she left his office, and because of the way she came, he didn't have any plans on calling her either. There was one thing he could help with but was reluctant to do so, because of the possible repercussions behind it.

"Look, I might know where ya missing friend is," Terrence said.

Alexus and one of the armed females overheard him, and it immediately sparked some hostility.

"You know where Diamond at?" Alexus butted in, walking over to where they were standing.

The other female walked beside Alexus, pointing the AR-15 at Terrence. Randy lifted the AK-47 and pointed it at Gwen, Alexus, and the armed female, while the second armed female pointed her gun at Randy.

"Whoa! Whoa! Whoa!" Terrence yelled. "Lower dat fuckin' gun!" he screamed, pointing at Randy. "Tell ya people to lower da shit," he told Gwen.

"I can't do that, Terrence!" Gwen shot back.

Her girls were trained to go, and they weren't going to hesitate setting it off. Randy could see that in their eyes too. That's why he didn't lower the AK like he was told.

"Gwen, look at me. Do you think for one second that I wanna hurt you?" Terrence said, looking Gwen in her eyes.

She didn't think that he was out to hurt her, but none of that mattered. All Gwen wanted was Diamond, and if she didn't get what she wanted, bullets would start flying. As Gwen and Terrence locked eyes, it was like the earth stopped spinning. The tension in the air could be cut with a butter knife. Terrence had a choice to make, and it was totally up to him to make the right one, because in the event he chose wrong, Gwen already had her mind made up to put him and Randy down.

Chapter 13

"Can you please state your first and last name for the record?" the homicide detective said, pressing the record button on the tape player.

Several other prison officials were in the room as well, sitting attentively with their note pads and ink pens in front of them. The events that took place in Mayo's cell had to be explained in detail, and there was only one person alive who could tell that story. Mayo's celly thought he knew what was going on, until he saw all the guards rushing the block. The prison staff asked him for a statement, but he declined, sticking to the G code of never talking to the cops.

"My name is Kea Nealy," she said in a low tone.

Kea's acting skills were excellent. She sat there in front of the group of men like she was intimidated by their presence. The warden had to stop the interview to bring another female guard, because he could tell that she was uncomfortable.

"Can you tell us what happened last night?" the detective asked softly as if he cared.

The obvious bruises on Kea's face and neck told most of the story, but it was the bruises between her legs that told the rest. Immediately after the encounter took place, Kea was taken to a local hospital, where nurses used a rape kit to determine that the small tears in her vagina were consistent with a female who was resisting penetration. That came from when Kea tightened up her canal as much as she could while Mayo shoved his large member in her. Making Mayo pretty much pry her legs open to get to the pussy also helped the ruse.

What sealed the deal was Mayo's cum, which was found inside Kea. She had taken a morning after pill to kill any chances of getting pregnant. As far as the possibility of catching an STD, Kea had made sure Mayo had a clean bill of health before anything. Several trips to the jail's hospital afforded her the opportunity to check Mayo's health record. That was courtesy of a fellow MHB member who worked as a nurse at the jail.

"So, Ms. Nealy, is there anything else you wanna tell us about the incident?" the detective asked.

He looked around the room to see if anybody from the prison staff had any questions, but they didn't. Kea had this whole hit on Mayo mapped out to perfection. She left little to no room for doubt, and when she left the office, she took with her any suspicions that might have been lingering around the room.

It was broad daylight when Gwen pulled up to Patrick Street and hopped out of the car with her gun in her hand. Two other cars pulled up right behind her, and MHBs locked, loaded, and ready for whatever jumped out of them.

Niggas standing on the corner of the block were staring at the women hard, but Terrence had already given them the heads up to let them do what they had to do and leave. That was all negotiated in the deal Terrence made with Gwen the night before. For Diamond's life, Gwen or nobody else from MHB could retaliate for his people snatching her up.

"Come wit' me," she told Alexus. "Everybody else wait out here," Gwen directed, walking up to the house she had recently bought from Terrence.

When she got up to the door, it was already partially open. Gwen and Alexus proceeded through the door, guns in their hands, cocked, and ready to shoot. According to Terrence, nobody else was supposed to be in the house but Diamond, so if anyone other than her jumped out of the woodwork, they were getting shot.

"Keep ya eyes open," Gwen spoke, leading Alexus up the steps.

The whole house was silent, and for a minute, Gwen didn't think Diamond was going to be there. It kind of felt like a setup. Gwen was relieved when she got to the back room and saw Diamond lying on the ground. She was half-naked and still knocked out cold from a concoction given to her less than twenty minutes ago. It was codeine and Xanax mixed together, something Terrence knew for sure would put her to sleep.

"Oh, shit, D!" Gwen said, running over and kneeling down next to her.

She cradled her in her arms, checking her wrist to see if Diamond had a pulse. It was a little weak, but Diamond was alive. The blood had been wiped from her face and her body, but Gwen could still see the traces of it on her bra and panties.

"Hold this," Gwen said, passing Alexus her gun.

She took off her jacket and wrapped it around Diamond before lifting her up. She carried her out of the house and to the car. With tears streaming down her cheeks, she laid her down in the back seat. Just as Gwen got into the driver's seat, her phone went off. She wasn't going to answer it, but when she saw that it was Terrence, she just had to give him a piece of her mind.

"What da fuck is wrong with her?" Gwen snapped into the phone, looking back at Diamond.

"Nothing. It's just a little cough syrup. She'll be awake in about an hour," Terrence responded. "Aye yo, I need to talk to you about something important."

Gwen couldn't entertain anything he had to say right then. If she wasn't a woman of her word, she would have blown his head off for this stunt he pulled. She'd put niggas in the ground for less, so it kind of ate her up not to ride on this one. Making matters worse, when Diamond finally did wake up, Gwen had to give her the news of the "no retaliation" deal she had made with Terrence.

"By now, dese bitches know we here," Cornell told his boy. "I know I bodied at least one of those bitches at the bar," he said, toting his sour diesel stick.

Cornell and his crew had been riding around the city all day, finding more spots owned by MHB. For his little brother, Dink, Cornell was ready to literally burn the city down. He didn't care who was in his way.

"Yo, pull over right here so we can get some gloves and shit," Cornell said, pointing to the small shopping center.

They pulled into the shopping center and parked right in front of a hair store. "Damn, Niki, run in here with me," Stacey said, seizing the opportunity to buy a wig while they were in the city.

The wig wasn't to look good in, but rather to disguise herself while riding around with Cornell. He was crazy as hell and didn't care anything about cameras when he went to put in work. Niki was a little harder than Stacey when it came to gunplay, but she also felt the need to change her look.

"Yo, don't be in there all day. I'ma go over here and grab this shit and come right back," Cornell told them.

The group of four dispersed. Cornell and his man went in one direction, while Stacey and Niki went into the hair store. Cornell didn't take long at all, because he knew exactly what he was going into the department store to grab. Duct tape, latex gloves, gas cans, and some rope were all he needed, which he got and was out of the store within ten minutes. When he got back to the car, the girls were still in the hair store.

"I just told these bitches to make it fast," Cornell said with an attitude, looking into the window of the store.

Stacey looked out the window to see him standing there with an attitude, so she and Niki sped up.

"Yo, my nigga, we gon' turn dis shit up and get da hell out of here," Cornell said, leaning against his car.

"Man, fuck it," his boy responded. "Dese bitches killed my folks."

Cornell relit his weed, looking at the store's window. A sign on the window caught his attention as he inhaled the weed smoke. He tilted his head sideways like a curious dog, then got up from the car and walked over to the window. He stood there looking at the small six by nine-inch MHB sticker in the righthand corner of the window.

"Yo, you see dis shit, homie?" Cornell said, waving his boy over to the window.

He thought he was tripping for a second when he saw the realty sticker, but just to squash all curiosity, he stepped into the store to ask a few questions.

"Yo, who own this store?" Cornell asked the female cashier who was ringing up Stacey and Niki's items.

She didn't know what to say, so Cornell clarified his question to get a better answer. "Do MHB own this store?" Cornell asked, pointing to the sticker on the window.

The cashier simply nodded her head with a half grin on her face. Cornell looked at the woman a little harder, noticing the MHB tattoo on the back of her hand. Cornell threw his head back in frustration, fed up with how much shit MHB had their hands in. He looked around the store and noticed the camera in the corner pointing at the cash register.

"Y'all bitches gotta go!" Cornell said, reaching into his waist and pulling out the .38 he loved so much.

The cashier looked at him, but all she saw was the flash before the bullet crashed through her forehead. Her body fell backward and onto the floor.

"What the fuck, Nell?" Niki said, covering her ears.

Mr. Kwan came from the back of the store but was met by gunfire from Cornell once he saw him. Mr. Kwan dipped back into the room as Cornell sent three more shots at the door.

"No! No!" Stacey yelled, grabbing Cornell before he could walk to the back of the store.

As she pulled him out of the store, Niki went behind the counter to retrieve the surveillance tapes. She stepped over the female's lifeless body and began pushing buttons on the monitor, but nothing happened. She wasn't leaving without the tape. Without wasting any more time, Niki grabbed the whole nineteen-inch monitor and yanked it off the shelf. She exited the store with both the monitor and the wig she was buying and jumped into the back seat of the awaiting car.

"Go get her some more water," Gwen told Porsha.

Diamond finally woke up, thankfully in the comfort of the condo. She was thirsty as hell for some reason, having already drunk two bottles of water within the last seven or eight minutes. Luckily, the bruises that she sustained weren't serious enough to make a hospital run, but her jaw still hurt a little, along with her arms and ankles from being tied up for so long.

"So, how do you feel?" Gwen asked as she sat on the couch with Diamond.

"I'm all right, but I'll feel much better when I put a bullet in Terrence's head for kidnapping me," Diamond responded.

Gwen had forgotten that she didn't tell Diamond about the deal. She turned and looked at Diamond with a sad face. "I made a deal with Terrence," Gwen spoke. "In order for you to be returned alive, MHB made a pact not to retaliate in any way," she explained.

"Tell me that you're joking," Diamond said, sitting up on the couch. "They kidnapped me, beat da shit out of me, and was two seconds away from killing me, and you're sitting here telling me that we're gonna honor that shit?" Diamond asked.

"I'm sorry, D. We have honor it," Gwen said.

It was a tough pill to swallow, but Diamond had to. She couldn't go against one of the most important pillars MHB was built on. Honor was one of the things that made MHB so strong. In time, Diamond would get over it, and it might be sooner than expected, because she already had jokes.

"Dat nigga must got a golden dick for you to be making deals like that." She chuckled, taking another swig of the water.

Gwen and Alexus chuckled too, but only Gwen knew that there was a little truth to what Diamond said. Before Gwen could continue to talk, the locks to the condo's door started to unlock. Seconds later, Kea walked in looking joyful, even with a black eye. Until then, Gwen had forgotten that she was supposed to put the work in on Mayo. Kea was so busy with the detectives, prison officials, and the hospital, she hadn't had time to call, but she definitely brought good news.

"Is it done?" Gwen asked as Kea walked toward her.

"Girl, you're not gonna believe what I had to go through in order to get these pictures." Kea smiled as she rambled through her bag.

She pulled out a small yellow envelope, which contained about ten pictures of the crime scene in Mayo's cell. Gwen reached in and pulled out the pictures, and tears came to her eyes when she saw the first flick. It was a picture of Mayo lying on top of the steel table, pale-faced, with the word *deceased* next to his head. The rest of the pictures were horrific to the average eye. It showed Mayo's lifeless body lying in a pool of blood in his cell. It showed the three fatal stab wounds up close, and it also showed the shank that was used. Last, but not least, Gwen saw a picture of Kea standing outside the cell with blood all over her face and clothes like she was Carrie.

"Sweet!" Diamond said, bending her head to see the pictures. "You pulled dat shit off."

Gwen jumped up with tears running down her face. "Thank you so much!" she said, giving Kea a huge hug.

She'd been waiting for this moment for what seemed like a lifetime, and now it was finally here. It was a feeling that couldn't be described with words. It was like a huge burden was lifted off of Gwen's shoulders, and she only wished Chad was still alive to see what she had done. She knew that he would have loved to share the moment with her.

Gwen looked up to the sky and spoke. "Babe, it's done. Give Zion a hug and kiss for me."

"What you up in here thinkin' about, homie?" Randy said, walking into the office.

Terrence was at work, but he wasn't actually working. On his desk was a bottle of Scotch and a glass of ice. He had been drinking all morning, thinking about the events that had taken place over the past few days. One particular person he couldn't get off his mind was Gwen.

Randy had a feeling it was more to Gwen than what Terrence was telling him. He just never questioned him about it, and wasn't going to. Whatever was going on, Terrence was going to have to fight those demons alone.

"Well, I'ma let you chill out in here. Whenever you ready to leave for the day, just call me. I'll be waiting out here," Randy said and tapped on the door before leaving.

Some alone time was exactly what Terrence needed in order to get his affairs together. Between Gwen, Cornell, and his crew, and finding another drug connect, Terrence definitely had to draw up a new game plan if he wanted to stay relevant in Gwen's eyes, the dope game, and corporate America.

Chapter 14

Chad's funeral was low key, and only immediate family members were invited, aside from the few MHB members who were there to support Gwen. In total, about fifty people were there. The location was undisclosed, so the many friends that Chad had would have to wait until his public viewing, which was scheduled for the next day.

"They're together now," Ms. Evette, Chad's mother said, scooting over and putting her arm around Gwen.

She was talking about Chad and Zion being together in heaven. Gwen was being strong, not wanting to cry, but when Ms. Evette said that, it brought tears to her eyes. For a moment, she wished that she could be in heaven with them, so that they would be a family again. The two men she loved most were gone, never to walk the face of this earth again. The more Gwen thought about it, the more hurtful it was.

"Ms. Evette, if you don't mind, I have to leave," Gwen said, looking over at her with tears falling from her eyes.

Ms. Evette understood. It was hard for her to sit there and look at her only child in a casket.

"I'll keep the twins for as long as you need me to," Ms. Evette told her, leaning over and kissing Gwen on her forehead.

Gwen wiped the tears from her face, got up, and walked over to the casket. She reached into her bag and pulled out the pictures of Mayo's dead body.

Tucking the pictures on the side of his body, Gwen leaned down and kissed him on his cheek. "Rest in peace, my love," she whispered in his ear before she stood up straight and walked away.

As she walked down the aisle, the MHB members in attendance got up from the pews and followed behind her. They almost ran into her back when Gwen stopped suddenly right before they got to the front door of the church. She looked over and saw Terrence standing next to a statue of Mary.

When Tiffany saw him, she immediately reached for her gun. She didn't know what type of shit he was there on. All she knew was that Terrence had become an enemy of MHB.

Gwen stuck her arm out, telling her crew to stand down. The look in Terrence's eyes told her he wasn't there to start any trouble. Tiffany stayed on point anyway, holding the P-80 Ruger down by her side.

"Just because I told you we weren't gonna retaliate doesn't give you the right to show up here," Gwen said, walking up to him.

Terrence was lucky Diamond wasn't there, because she probably would have taken this as a breach of the verbal contract.

"I didn't come here to provoke a war," Terrence said.

"Yeah? Well, why are you here? I know you don't know the man lying in that casket," Gwen shot back.

The other attendees weren't aware of what was going on in the back of the church.

"I'm here for you, Gwen," he said with a sincere look in his eyes. "I know you might think I'm the—"

"Not right now," Gwen said, cutting him off. "Now ain't the time or the place for this. My son's father is laying up there in that casket right now," Gwen told him.

Gwen did want to talk to him, but she was right; now wasn't a good time for that. Aside from Chad's funeral, Gwen had a host of problems going on, one being Dink's people running around the city causing havoc with anything and anybody claiming MHB. After the murder at the hair store, someone came back later on that night and burned it to a crisp. The MHB Bar & Grill was also burned to the ground, and several cars that had the MHB logo were shot at. One MHB member was stabbed and left for dead in an alleyway off Nixon Street. Cornell and his crew were going extra hard, and Gwen didn't have any way of finding out who was responsible for it all. It was like chasing ghosts around the city.

"Look, I'll call you later on. We'll talk then," Gwen said in a low tone so only Terrence could hear her. She didn't want to just blow him off, but at the same time, she didn't want everybody in her business.

Terrence read between the lines well and humbly dismissed himself.

Gwen and her girls waited a few minutes, and then they left too.

Niya got off the bus in Durham, North Carolina, and took in a deep breath. She smiled, thinking of how surprised all the girls were going to be to see her. She had decided to keep her early release a secret, so she could get some time in with Eagle before she assumed her post again. Being free felt amazing, and she was enjoying every second of it. Even the long-ass bus ride from Arizona to North Carolina didn't feel too bad. The most important thing was the fact that Niya was a free woman after serving a little under two years in prison. The early release was due to the new federal Good Time bill, which had recently passed.

The sun was beaming, and Niya couldn't believe how hot it was in the middle of October. As she was walking through the bus station, she noticed a bunch of flyers on the ground. She stopped and picked one up when she saw the letters *MHB* on one of them.

"MHB Realty," Niya mumbled to herself.

She smiled at the flyer, happy to see her crew moving the way they were. They had come a long way without her around, but now they didn't have to go any further without her, because she was back on the streets. The whole MHB was going to be ecstatic to see her, and Niya was ecstatic to be reunited with them.

Terrence pulled his phone out as he, Randy, and Tianna walked through the lobby of the Hearst Towers. Stacey was calling him, and he wanted to know why, because he thought he had made himself clear that he was through with her.

"What?" he answered, pushing the elevator button.

"Hey, bro. I was wondering if we could talk," she said in a low voice, as if she didn't want anybody around her to hear her conversation.

"It's nothing for us to talk about. I told you not to bring those stupid-ass niggas up here and you did anyway. Y'all got da whole fuckin' city hot right now!" he snapped as he waited.

"But we family. I need ya help!" she responded.

"We only got the same Dad, so that just makes us—" Terrence stopped. Even he didn't like the words that were coming out of his mouth. It was a little too late, because Stacey had heard enough. She was hurt to hear him say that.

"Stacey, I'm sorry," Terrence said, missing his elevator and walking back out into the lobby.

"No, I guess I deserve that for everything I've done."

"Nah, you don't deserve that. I'm being a fuckin' idiot right now. It's just . . . ya people makin' it hard for me to eat right now," Terrence told her.

"Yeah, I know. I didn't know they were going to do all of this. These muthafuckas are crazy. I don't wanna be here. I wanna go home!" she pled, still at a whisper.

Dink was her son's father, and she wanted nothing more than to see the people responsible for his death to be held accountable, but the stuff Cornell was doing was a little too much for her. Stacey had never killed anybody, and the first person she ever saw murdered was when Cornell shot the cashier at the hair store. It was at that moment she knew that shit was real. She wanted out, but getting out wasn't a simple option. She didn't know what Cornell would do to her if she tried to go back home now.

"Stacey, just tell me where you at and I'll come get you," Terrence said, walking toward the exit.

"I'm at the Madison Inn right off of Pinegrove." Stacey said, walking over to the window. "I'm in room 108, but I'll be standing outside waiting for you. And please, bro, don't come by yourself. I don't know what dese crazy niggas is gonna do."

Terrence assured her that he would be there, and that he wasn't going to come alone. She really didn't have to tell him that part, because he hardly ever traveled alone. If it wasn't Randy following him around all day, it was Tianna, but in this case, he had both.

"Wassup, cousin?" Tianna asked, seeing the look Terrence had in his eyes.

"Nothing. I just gotta go pick up my sister before she get herself into trouble," he responded as he walked toward the door.

As he was walking toward the door, Gwen, Tiffany, and Alexus were entering the building. Gwen was hoping that he could help her find the men responsible for the carnage happening to her people. If anybody would know, it would be him. Gwen just hoped that he would help her at this point.

"Damn, that's crazy that you're here. I need to talk to you," Gwen said, walking up to him.

When he saw Gwen, it was like his brain short-circuited, and all he could see was her. It happened just about every time he encountered her. It took Tianna to remind him about Stacey, but even then, he still put Gwen's concerns first. That's probably because he wanted to talk to her about some shit he had on his chest.

"Yeah, where do you wanna talk?" he asked.

"Can you come up to my office in about an hour?" Gwen needed a little bit of time to get some things situated. "I have something to take care of real quick."

Terrence looked at his watch. That's about how long it was going to take him to pick up Stacey, so an hour was good timing. He agreed to it before he, Tianna, and Randy walked out of the building, while Gwen, Tiffany, and Alexus proceeded to the elevators.

The cloud of weed smoke was thick inside the small motel room where Cornell, Stacey, Niki, and three other men were sitting. Everyone in the room except Stacey had latex gloves on, jamming bullet after bullet into clip after clip. Cornell noticed that she wasn't participating, but he didn't say anything. He had other plans for Stacey, ones that didn't include her seeing tomorrow. She was Dink's baby momma, but he really didn't like her from the jump. He even put some of the blame for his death on her, since she was the one who encouraged Dink to get some money with her brother Terrence.

"Yo, after today, we goin' back home, so make sure you go hard when the time comes," Cornell said, slapping a clip into his .40 cal.

Cornell pretty much felt that after this last massacre, his work in Charlotte would be done. Truth be told, he was ready to go back home anyway, but he wasn't going to leave without saying good-bye to a few people.

It took twenty more minutes for everybody to be locked and loaded, suited and booted, and ready to go out the front door. Stacey was scared as hell, hoping Cornell wouldn't say anything if she chose to stay back. He really didn't mind. In fact, right before he walked out the door, he told Stacey to fall back and wait for him there at the motel. She was somewhat relieved when he directed her to do that, but Niki and everybody else that was there knew that the outcome for Stacey wasn't going to be good. Cornell was vicious, and if he felt at any time that there was a weak link in his circle, he was going to terminate their contract.

"First thing we gotta do is get all of this money out of here," Gwen said, closing the blinds to her office windows.

"You don't think those fools are gonna be stupid enough to run up in here, do you?" Alexus asked.

"Yeah, Gwen, those niggas ain't that stupid," Tiffany chimed in, walking over to look out the window.

Gwen didn't think Dink's people were crazy enough to wander into the Hearst Tower, but she really wasn't going to take any chances. After all the damage they'd done in the city thus far, she wouldn't put it past them. They had already proven themselves to be treacherous.

"Oh, and send out an e-mail and let everybody know to be on point. Our bitches that's in the street got the green light to blast anything movin' wrong," Gwen said, walking over to the safe door.

Tiffany walked over to the computer and jumped on top of the e-mail situation immediately. Tiffany could write one e-mail and send it out to every member of MHB at the same time. The e-mail would go straight to their cell phones within seconds of pushing the SEND button.

"Lex, help me with this," Gwen said, punching the numbers into the keypad.

This was the first time that Tiffany or Alexus had seen the safe open, so when Alexus stepped inside, she felt the same way Gwen did every time she saw that money.

"Damn, girl!" Alexus said, looking around at all the stacks of money. "I didn't know you had all this."

"We!" Gwen corrected. "This is all of our money. Me, you, Tiffany, Diamond, and Niya. All I'm doing is stacking it up for us. As soon as Niya gets home, we gon' break dis shit down correctly," she said, grabbing a couple of duffle bags from the top shelf.

Alexus squatted down and opened one of the bags, while Gwen tossed money into it. This was the most money Alexus had ever seen at one time. It took about ten minutes to get all the money into two duffle bags and one Louis Vuitton suitcase. Once it was all packed up, Gwen jumped on the phone to call a few girls to escort her to the stash house outside of the city, where the money would be safe.

"Yo, I think Cornell gon' mess around and make me kill him, my nigga," Terrence said as he pulled into the motel's parking lot.

"Whatever you wanna do, I'm ridin' wit' you, bruh." Randy responded, reaching under his seat and grabbing his gun.

If Terrence decided to drive off a bridge at 100 miles an hour, Randy was going to put his seat belt on. The love he had for his boy was unquestionable, and if Terrence had to run down on Cornell, Randy was going to be gunning for his head too, along with Tianna, the silent killer.

Stacey was walking out the door when Terrence pulled into the parking space in front of the room. Everyone jumped out of the car, and they were all strapped. Stacey had a confused look on her face and only wanted to get the hell out of there. The look Terrence had in his eyes told her that wasn't about to happen.

"Is he in there?" Terrence said, walking toward the door, holding his gun in his hand down by his side.

Stacey stood in front of him with her arm out to stop him. "It ain't nobody in there. Let's just get da hell out of here," Stacey said, pushing Terrence backward toward the driver's side door.

Stacey just wanted to get as far away from Cornell as she could. The vibe that she got from him before he had left the motel made her a little more afraid of him.

"Yo!" Terrence called over to Randy. He simply nodded his head at the motel room door.

Randy walked over to the door and kicked it in, aiming his gun as he entered the room. It took seconds for him to clear the room. He walked back out and cut at his neck, indicating that nobody was in there.

"Where did they go?" Terrence asked.

Stacey knew that he was up to something. She could tell by the look in his eyes that Terrence had his mind made up, and his final conclusion came down to Cornell being wiped off the face of the earth.

"They should be goin' back home today. They got one more place they wanna hit, then Cornell said that they were done," Stacey said.

"And where is that?" Terrence asked.

"I don't know. Cornell said MHB had some type of realty company," Stacey told him.

Terrence's eyes shot wide open. His heart began to race uncontrollably as he rushed to get back in his car. He almost pulled off without letting anyone in the car. Randy knocking on the window snapped him out of his zone. He put the car back in park then unlocked the doors so everybody could get in.

Terrence couldn't believe Cornell would be so bold and stupid as to go downtown, late Friday afternoon, to put in some work. More importantly, he couldn't believe that he was going after Gwen. Just the thought of it had him amped up. Gwen didn't know it, but Terrence had developed strong feelings for her in the short period of time that he'd known her. He cared about her enough that he didn't want to see her go out like that. If it was within his power, he was going to make sure that it didn't happen.

Cornell, Niki, Cub, Killa, and Tec all walked into the Hearst Towers looking like they were supposed to be there. They weren't wearing the usual war time attire of black hoodies, jeans, and boots. Everybody had on a suit, except for Niki, who had on a black pencil skirt and a white blouse. Her black leather jacket concealed the two semi-automatic handguns tucked away in her back.

"Can I help you, sir?" the female receptionist asked when Cornell walked up to the front desk.

"Yes, I was looking for the MHB Realty Company. I was told that their offices are in this building." Cornell spoke in a professional tone.

The woman looked down at her listing then lifted her head. "Their offices are on the seventeenth floor. The elevator right over there will take you up," she said, pointing to the elevators.

Cornell and his crew walked back through the lobby past several guards with no problems. No one in his camp appeared to pose any threats.

Once on the elevator, Cornell, Killa, Cub, and Tec unbuttoned their blazers, reached in and pulled out their handguns. Niki reached behind her back and pulled out her two compact Chrome .45 automatics. They didn't care about the cameras on the elevator or the armed guards that would be waiting for them downstairs. Cornell was about his business, and as the elevator climbed up toward the seventeenth floor, everyone in that elevator was ready to go.

Terrence sped through the late-day rush hour traffic, almost having several accidents in the process. He swerved in and out of lanes like he was a race car driver, pushing the BMW 750 to its max. Tianna struggled to stay on one side of the car as Terrence maneuvered the V8 like it was a toy.

"Slow down, bruh!" Randy said, wanting to avoid being pulled over by the police before they got there.

Terrence really didn't have to slow down, because he was already off the downtown exit where traffic was bumper to bumper. The good thing about the Hearst building was that it was only three blocks away from the expressway exit.

"Tianna, when I get out of this car, I want you to pull up and double park right in front of the building," Terrence told her while digging into his center console and grabbing the gun.

He looked outside his window at the cars that slowly passed him. His lane was moving super slowly, frustrating the hell out of him. He cocked the .357 Sig slightly to make sure he had one in the chamber. Once he confirmed he was locked and loaded, he threw the car in park and jumped out without saying anything.

Randy jumped out right behind him, while Tianna climbed over into the driver's seat. By the time she looked up, Terrence and Randy were running up the street.

Cornell and his crew stepped off the elevator and onto the seventeenth floor. They walked across the small hallway and through the glass double doors of MHB Realty. A few females were sitting in their cubicles. All it took was a female walking past with an MHB tattoo on her calf muscle to set Cornell off.

"Can I help you, sir?" the secretary asked, looking over her computer.

Cornell looked over at her. She, too, had an MHB tattoo on her neck, clear as day.

"Yeah, you can help me," Cornell said, reaching for his waist and pulling out a large chrome .50-caliber Desert Eagle.

She didn't even have a chance to scream before Cornell squeezed the trigger. The large bullet exited the gun with fire on its tail. It hit the young secretary in her left eye, damn near knocking the whole side of her face off. The force of the bullet knocked her clean out of her chair.

The rest of his crew drew their weapons too, spreading out on the floor and gunning down everything that was moving.

"Oh, shit!" Tiffany yelled, jumping up from the desk.

Gwen rolled off the brown leather couch, barely getting out of the way of a bullet that came crashing through the office door glass. Alexus backed away from the glass windows and pulled out her seventeen-shot 9 mm. Gwen crawled over to the safe door, reached up, and punched numbers into the keypad blindly, desperately wanting to get inside. Tiffany dipped behind the desk, avoiding more bullets coming through the office door.

"Tiffany, here!" Gwen yelled, sliding her a black .45 automatic from out of the safe.

The gun didn't make it all the way across the room, coming short a few feet from the desk. She crawled out to get the gun, and when she got to it, she looked up and saw a man in a suit coming through the shattered glass door. He had his gun aimed at Tiffany, but something in his peripheral view caught his eye. He looked over and saw Alexus standing there with a gun pointed right at his head. She pulled the trigger without hesitation, sending a hot lead ball into his head.

"Cuuuuuuubb!" Cornell yelled, looking back toward the office and seeing his man's body fall to the floor.

Two MHB workers, who brought their guns to work every day, engaged in a shootout with Cornell's crew. They took refuge behind some cubicles at the far end of the floor. Niki and Tech occupied themselves with trying to get to them, but they were standing their ground.

Terrence and Randy darted through the lobby toward the elevators. Security was about to stop them, but calls started pouring in on their phone. People from the eighteenth floor called in with reports of gunshots sounding like they came from the seventeenth floor.

"You think they're here?" Randy asked, standing at the elevators with Terrence.

Just then, two of the six elevator doors opened. People rushed out of them and raced across the lobby.

"Yeah, they're here!" Terrence answered, walking over and getting onto one of the empty cars.

Bullets continued to crash through the office windows, forcing Gwen, Alexus, and Tiffany to stay low. Cornell stood about ten to fifteen yards across from the office, trying to pick Gwen and the girls off one by one. He couldn't really see into the office because the blinds were covering the windows.

"I'ma kill every last one of y'all bitches!" Cornell yelled, firing another shot into the office.

Gwen crawled over and sat with her back against the wall. She nodded at Alexus, who was sitting right up under the window. Alexus reached over, grabbed the string to the blinds, and yanked it as hard as she could. When the blinds went up, Gwen had a clear view and a clear shot at Cornell, which she took.

One bullet hit him in his chest, while a second one took a nice chunk out of his right shoulder. He let off two shots wildly before dipping behind a partition. The vest he had on under his suit saved him, but the bullet still knocked the wind out of him.

Gwen didn't stop there. She kept firing bullet after bullet into the cubicle where Cornell took refuge. Bullets hit the computer screen, the monitor, the chair, and knocked holes the size of golf balls in the thin, wooden partition.

Niki and Tec started to back up to the elevators when their ammo got low. In a flash, they were out the door and down the fire escape.

Terrence and Randy just missed them, because as soon as the emergency exit door closed, the elevator doors opened.

Terrence and Randy cautiously entered through the broken glass doors into a room of silence. The first thing Terrence saw was the dead secretary's body on the ground; then he looked to the back to see the two armed MHB workers aiming guns right in his direction. The only reason they didn't shoot was that they recognized Terrence.

Randy split off, trying to clear the rest of the floor. He slowly walked to the other side of the cubicles, looking up and down the aisle with his gun in front of him. He wasn't expecting Killa to jump out from behind one of the partitions with a knife, but he did, and it happened so fast, Randy only got one shot off before a Rambo knife was jammed into his gut.

Killa took it out and jammed it back into his gut a second time. Fortunately, Randy didn't let go of the gun. He raised it to the side of Killa's head while he was bear-hugging him, and pulled the trigger.

Terrence turned around for a hot second after he heard the second shot, but he didn't see anything because it was happening on the other side of the cubicles. His focus was on Gwen anyway, so he turned back around to continue heading for the office.

"Gwen!" Terrence yelled, walking down the aisle toward the office.

Gwen peeked her head from behind the wall and saw Terrence. She then looked over at the cubicle Cornell dipped behind and saw how close they were to each other.

"Terrence, watch out!" Gwen yelled.

Cornell peeked over and saw Terrence approaching. He dipped off, crawled around the back way, and ended up right behind him.

The two armed MHB workers wanted to shoot at Cornell, but he had Terrence right in front of him, and they both were standing in front of the office. They just couldn't take the risk, and Randy was nowhere in sight.

"Dick head!" Cornell said, raising the gun.

When Terrence turned around, Cornell shot him in his chest. Tiffany jumped up from behind the desk to capitalize on their situation, but she was met by gunfire. Cornell let off a quick two rounds, hitting Tiffany in her chest before she could get a shot off. She fell to her knees and then flat on her face.

"No, no, no, nooooo!" Gwen screamed, dropping her gun and crawling over to Tiffany.

She rolled Tiffany over and cradled her in her arms. Alexus was in shock. She just sat under the window with her back against the wall, staring at Gwen holding Tiffany.

Gwen didn't have her gun in her hand, so she posed no threat. Cornell walked over and stood over Terrence, who was still alive.

"You chose these bitches over my brother. Now you gon' die right along wit' 'em," Cornell said, aiming the gun directly at his head.

Cornell was so caught up in the moment that he didn't hear the soft footsteps walking up behind him. At the very moment he was about to pull the trigger, he felt something press against the back of his head. He hesitated pulling the trigger, but the person standing behind him didn't. The shot was muffled somewhat from the gun being so close to his head. The bullet crashed through his skull and ripped more than halfway through his brain. It was lights out, and he didn't even get a chance to get the shot off. His body dropped right next to Terrence's.

Terrence looked up and saw a female standing there with the smoking gun in her hand. He figured it was just another MHB member, but what he didn't know was that the woman standing over him was the boss, Niya.

Chapter 15

Three white hearses covered in flowers turned the corner and drove straight down Tryon Street. This was the last drive through the city before Tiffany and the other two MHB females were laid to rest in the Pinewood Cemetery in Charlotte.

There had to be at least 200 cars following behind the hearses, most of which carried MHB members. The city was pretty much shut down on this Sunday, and not a lick of traffic was moving if it wasn't going in the direction of the funeral. Just about every MHB member showed up in support, wearing their MHB hoodies and showing off their MHB tattoos.

"What you thinkin' about?" Niya asked Gwen as they sat in the back seat of a limousine that followed directly behind the third hearse.

Gwen didn't say anything at first. She just sat there thinking about all the things that had happened to her over the past couple of years. She lived a hectic life and had lost her family to the streets, along with a few close friends. It all had become too much for her to bear.

"I'm done, Niya," Gwen said in an exhausted manner. "I can't keep livin' life like this," she said, wiping the tears that fell from her eyes.

Niya scooted over and wrapped her arms around Gwen. She knew exactly how Gwen felt, because there were times when she felt the same way.

"Shit, girl, I thought you was gonna be done a long time ago!" Niya chuckled. "Hell, I'm just about done too. I'm all the twins got now. Plus, we gettin' too old for dis shit!"

They broke into laughter, thinking about how true that statement really was. Niya and Gwen had orchestrated one of the largest female movements in the history of Charlotte and paved the way for young females to come. It would be an understatement for anybody to say that they did their thing. They did more than that, and put in more work than most men. They did it all and made more heavy sacrifices. They were like queens in the hood, and once they departed from the game, they would become legends.

After the funeral, Gwen stopped by the hospital to check up on Terrence, who had been through a surgery and two blood transfusions. The bullet had done some serious damage, but the doctors said that he was going to make it.

When she got up to his floor, she noticed an increase in security around his room. It was not hospital security, but hood security, and even a few familiar faces Gwen knew. They were five deep outside his room, with two inside with him. When Gwen walked up, she didn't even have to say anything. The men just parted without question, letting her pass.

Randy was sitting in a wheelchair next to Terrence's side, with his head resting on the edge. When he looked up and saw Gwen, he smiled.

"How are you?" she asked, putting her bag on Terrence's bed by his feet.

"I lost one of my kidneys and one of my lungs collapsed, but other than that, I'm good," he answered. Sometimes being stabbed by a knife can be worse than being shot, especially if you are stabbed in the right place.

"So, how's he?" she asked, walking over to the other side of the bed.

"He woke up for about five seconds, and you're not gonna believe what he said," Randy said with a smile on his face.

"What?" she asked, looking down on Terrence.

"Dis black-ass nigga had da nerve to call out ya name, talkin' 'bout . . . Gwen, I love you," Randy said. "If he didn't have that big-ass hole in his chest, I would have woke him up just to kick his ass," he joked.

Gwen smiled then pulled up a chair to sit next to him. One of the nurses came to the door and chased Randy back to his room, so Gwen was left in the room with Terrence all alone.

She'd never really had a chance to thank him for being there for her, nor did she have the opportunity to let him know how she felt about him. She didn't go as deep and as far as Terrence did by saying that he loved her, but Gwen did like him a lot. Even though he ended up being shot before he could run in and save the day, Gwen felt like his intentions were just as good. He was willing and did take a bullet for her, and for that, Gwen was going to stay right by his side until he woke up. She wasn't sure if anything was going to come about from being there for him, but she damn sure was going to see it through, in hopes that maybe Terrence could be the one whom she shared her newfound life with—a life without MHB.

Chapter 16

South Carolina

Tec pulled up to Niki's house and honked the horn. Since the episode up north, they'd been spending a lot of time with each other. One could say that they were somewhat a couple now. Their relationship had gone from gun-clapping side by side to fucking just about every night since Cornell, Killa, and Cub were killed in the Hearst Tower shootout.

"I'm comin'!" Niki yelled as she walked down the steps.

She switched her fat ass down the walkway and straight into Tec's car. She was looking good in her Tru Religion jean set and Jordans.

"What you in a rush fo'?" Niki asked, closing the door behind her.

"You not gon' believe what I stumbled across," Tec said, looking over at Niki like he had found Noah's ark.

"What you talkin' about?"

"I know where dem bitches live!"

Tec had been plotting his revenge ever since the day Cornell, Killa, and Cub were murdered. He had driven back up to North Carolina to do some homework and had come up when he found and followed Gwen home.

"You tryin' to finish dis shit?" he asked Niki with a serious look on his face.

One thing about Niki, she was down for whatever. "Yeah, fuck it. Let's do it."

Tec looked at her and smiled. He loved having a bitch that would ride or die with her man. This was something he could really get used to.

He put the car in drive and was about to pull off when out of the blue, two big, black Suburbans pulled up in front of him and behind him, boxing in his Cadillac CTS.

"What da fuck?" he asked and reached for his gun under his seat.

He didn't know who it was until all eight doors to the trucks swung open and eight females with MHB hoodies jumped out with large assault rifles in their hands. Everybody had a chopper, and every one of them was pointed at the car.

"Ah, shit!" Tec yelled, ducking down in his seat.

Niki ducked down too, but it was to no avail. All eight choppers opened up at the same time, sending hundreds of bullets into the car. There was nowhere for them to hide, especially since the girls opened fire a mere ten to fifteen feet away from the car. Needless to say, both Tec and Niki were dead before the last bullet hit the car.

In an instant, all eight woman jumped back into the truck and pulled off, leaving behind what was left of the beef.

Apparently, Tec wasn't the only one doing his homework.

PART TWO

Chapter 17

Heavy rain fell down on the hood of Niya's silver 2014 Aston Martin as she and Eagle sat waiting for Contez to pull up. For a minute, she didn't think that he was going to show. Niya called his cell again, but this time, it went straight to voice mail.

"What do you think?" Niya asked, gazing over at Eagle, who was busy looking at some Hayabusa motorcycles on his iPhone.

"Just give him a few more minutes," Eagle answered, not taking his eyes off the screen. "One thing I know about these Africans is they never miss out on a chance to make money," he continued, now lifting his head up from the display of the phone.

For some reason, Niya just didn't feel right sitting on the dark, empty street. Maybe it was the hundred grand in cash sitting in the back seat. She and Eagle were strapped, but in her mind they were still like sitting ducks. She remembered the countless times she and her girls had set niggas up the same way, and Niya wasn't trying to get caught slipping.

"We can set dis shit up at a later date," Niya said as she started the car up.

"Nah, nah. Look!" Eagle said, pointing at a Mack truck that was turning onto Commercial Drive.

Niya turned the car off and watched as the truck began to back into the garage in the middle of the long, narrow street. She grabbed the Glock .40 from out of the center console and cocked it back slightly to make sure there was a bullet in the chamber. Eagle looked over and smiled at her. *Damn, this chick is sexy and dangerous*, he thought to himself.

"What? I don't know these mafuckas, and you know you don't one hundred percent trust Africans any fucking way," she added with one eyebrow up and a smirk on her face.

This was going to be the first time Niya had met Contez in person. Eagle was the one who had somewhat of a relationship with him, having done time with Contez's little brother in federal prison a while back. Upon connecting with him when he and Niya hit Philly, Eagle did a few small-time deals with Contez, just to feel him out. Once it was established that Contez did good business, Eagle decided to kick it up a notch, and so it was now time for Niya to get involved.

Niya opened the door and stepped out into the rain, throwing her hood over her head then making a dash for the garage. Eagle jogged right behind her, not really fazed by the rain drops pounding down on his bare head. The service door next to the garage was unlocked so Niya didn't have to wait to gain entry. She entered with her gun tucked into her back pocket and Eagle on her heels.

"Eagle, my friend!" a short, skinny, big-headed man greeted as he came from behind the Mack truck.

"This must be the lovely Niya," he said, extending his hand.

Niya shook it and gave him a little smile. The two other men that were with Contez began speaking in Mandingo, but Contez quickly stopped them and informed them to speak in English so Niya and Eagle wouldn't feel uncomfortable.

"Jedi will be home in less than sixty days. I know he can't wait," Eagle spoke, walking Contez around to the back of the truck.

"Yes, my little brother will join us soon." Contez smiled. "Now, let me show you what I have."

Contez jumped up onto the rear bumper of the truck and opened the back door. Eagle and Niya climbed into the back of the truck behind him and were somewhat startled by what they were looking at. There were more guns than they had expected.

"I got AK-47s, M-16s, .45s, and I even have a few of these," Contez said, reaching into one of the crates and pulling out a grenade.

Niya picked up one of the AK-47s from out of the crate, holding it with both hands. She looked around and had to admit that she had never seen this many guns in one place and at one time. When Eagle said that Contez was into the gun-running business, she didn't know that it was this deep.

"So what's the price on these puppies?" Niya asked, holding the AK-47 in the air.

"Like I told Eagle, if you buy in bulk, I can give you a good price. If you only want one or two, I'ma charge you a thousand dollars per firearm."

"How many do you have?" Niya asked.

"As many as you can stand," Contez answered back quickly.

Niya leaned up against the inside of the truck and looked at Eagle. She had no idea what to do with a bunch of AK-47s. Although MHB didn't have many assault rifles, they were all spades in the handgun department. The look on Niya's face told Contez that maybe she wasn't that interested in all the military weapons.

"Maybe I might have something else you like," Contez said, digging deep into one of the crates, "I already have a buyer for these, but I can get more" he said, pulling out the contents from deep inside of the crate.

Contez put the folded-up brown towel on top of the crates and began unraveling the contents.

"These come straight from Africa, Sierra Leone's most prized possession."

Niya and Eagle walked closer and stood looking over Contez's shoulder. Niya's nipples got rock hard at the sight of the diamonds. Never had she seen a diamond sparkle so hard, even with the little light that was present. The stones were so clear, and when they glimmered, it appeared as if they were water. Just as she was about to gain her composure, Contez stepped back and allowed Niya and Eagle to get an even closer, more personal look at the jewels.

"How much are these worth?" Niya said, holding one of the stones up to her face.

"These stones are worth a little more than a million dollars. I can get more, but it's going to take a while," Contez replied.

"Damn! A million dollars. Are you serious?" she asked, wanting to make sure she had heard correctly.

Contez began to explain how the rainy season lasted throughout the summer in Africa and how the best time for him to get more stones would be after that time elapsed. Niya wasn't trying to hear any more of what he was talking about. Looking at and holding those diamonds in her hands did something to her. She didn't want to let them go.

"Here, get these damn things away from me." Niya smiled, backing up and letting Contez walk back up to the crate.

"Yeah, I know how tempting they can be," he responded, looking down at the stones.

Niya looked out to see where the other two Africans were at then turned back around once she saw they weren't anywhere in sight. Eagle could see the look in

Niya's eyes, and he wasn't sure if he liked it. He knew something was wrong, but before he could say anything or try to stop her, Niya pulled the gun from her back pocket. At that point, it was too late for her to try to turn back. Besides, Eagle knew she didn't have any intentions on doing so anyways.

She aimed the gun right at the back of Contez's head and squeezed the trigger.

Pop!

The bullet went in through the back and came out the side. Blood splattered all over most of the diamonds, and Contez's body dropped and slumped over the crate that sat in front of him.

Yelling in their native language, the two Africans ran from the front of the truck to the back door, with guns drawn. One got a shot off, hitting the interior top of the truck before Niya fired back, striking and killing one of them instantly. The other African took off running out of the garage, dropping his gun in the process.

Eagle simply stood there looking at Niya with a confused look on his face. With the gun in one hand and a smirk on her face, she grabbed Contez by the back of his collar and pulled him off the crate.

"What?" she shot back, wrapping up the diamonds. "Don't act surprised. You know I don't like these funny talkin' muthafuckas no way."

"I told you he was a good dude," Eagle snapped.

Niya didn't seem to take him being upset seriously at all, jumping down off the truck and continuing on like nothing had happened.

"Are you going to drive this big-ass truck or what?" Niya said, tucking the gun back into her back pocket.

Eagle still continued looking at her like she was crazy.

"What makes you think I know how to drive this big-ass thang?" he asked

"Well, you so good at navigating this one, I thought you could handle it," Niya responded while grabbing Eagle's crotch, hoping that her joking would ease his anger with her.

"You got issues. You know that, right?" he asked before jumping down off the truck, brushing by her and walking out the garage door.

Not wanting to leave a truck full of guns behind, Niya decided that she would drive it herself. She pulled Contez's body out of the truck and tossed it to the side, then shut the door. Moments later, she was backing the Mack truck out of the garage and pulling off down the street. Eagle sat in the Aston Martin, shaking his head, watching as Niya drove away.

Chapter 18

"We have to send a crew out to the property on Johnson Road. There is water everywhere," Diamond said, entering the office where Gwen and Alexus sat.

Due to the shooting that took place at the Hearst Towers building eight months ago, MHB Realty was forced to relocate out of the downtown area. No high-rise in the city would let them rent out office space, so Gwen had to improvise in order to keep the business running smoothly.

At first, the four seventy-five-foot trailers were supposed to be temporary, but as time went on, Gwen and the rest of the girls had adapted and become used to the new work environment. The trailers sat on several acres of land off of the I-85 service road, which meant it was easily accessible to the highway. The view was also a plus, overlooking a lake surrounded by trees and wildlife.

"How in the hell do we have water damage? We just got the roof fixed on it two months ago," Gwen asked, lifting her head up from her desk.

Diamond shrugged her shoulders and took a seat on the edge of the desk. If it wasn't one thing, it was another, and the whole going legit thing was more difficult than either had expected. Without the constant flow of drug money coming in, there was a lot of work to be done in order to maintain a legal and profitable business. A lot of the work had recently fallen into Gwen's lap. It was a good thing Alexus had been around to help with the twins, allowing Gwen to focus in on the MHB business.

She let out a sigh, removed her reading glasses, and leaned back in her chair. Gwen was really just about at her breaking point. Her thoughts were interrupted by the sounds of her two pit bulls barking out front. When she leaned over and looked out of the small window, a Cadillac Escalade and Cadillac CTS pulled up in front of the trailers. Gwen looked over at Diamond, then Alexus, wondering if either was expecting anyone. The looks on their faces said no.

Diamond, who stayed strapped, led the way, stepping out onto the front steps. Gwen stood at the threshold, watching as several men got out of the vehicles. She and Diamond had told Alexus to stay inside. Lexus was like everyone's little sister, and although she would get it in when provoked, she wasn't the naturally violent type.

"Damn, Gwen. Long time no see," a familiar voice greeted from the group of men.

It had been a while, but Gwen knew all too well who the man was. Right before Niya went to prison, MHB and these same men were about to go to war. Rell was the head nigga in charge, but after he had been gunned down in CMC Hospital, his right-hand man, Nose, who was now standing before Gwen, had stepped up and took the reins.

"What's up with you, Nose?" Gwen asked, stepping out onto the porch.

"You know, same shit, different day." He smiled. "I see MHB still got the streets on lock."

"Ahhh, you been in jail for a while. Maybe you didn't get the word that we ain't in the streets anymore," she responded, leaning on the rail.

"Yeah, I heard something like that, but I find that hard to believe," he answered.

MHB really wasn't in the streets to the extent that they controlled the drug market anymore, but they were definitely taxing the dealers for selling drugs in the neighborhoods they once claimed. The streets called it taxing, but Gwen referred to it as "paying rent."

"So did you come here for a reason, or did you simply drive all the way out here to make small talk?" Gwen asked.

"Nah, shawty, I just wanted y'all to know that I was home, and to let you know that I was picking up where my crew left off, so we run Charlotte now. If you're not in the streets like you say, we shouldn't have a problem then," Nose said.

Diamond fought the urge to snap on him. Here he was talking to her and Gwen like they were nobodies, or as if MHB wasn't still the most violent group of women Charlotte had ever seen. Maybe the time Nose had spent in prison had made him forget, and if it weren't for Gwen grabbing a hold of Diamond's shooting hand, he would've been reminded before he and his boys had the chance to depart.

Though it was easy for Gwen to have Nose and his crew erased off the face of the earth with a single phone call, that wasn't the direction she wanted to take MHB. The legal route was the only way to keep the crew from the radar of the feds. They were only one brick or murder away from being indicted, and had that happened, every female member of MHB was going to jail. That was the route Gwen was trying to avoid the most.

Philadelphia was taking a lot of getting used to, but after a few months, Niya was starting to adjust somewhat. She hated being away from home, but it was necessary, since she had come home to a full-out war in Charlotte.

Even though they had neutralized that threat, the feds had made MHB its top priority again. Niya was on parole, and she couldn't take the chance of getting caught up in some bullshit. The feds would have loved to get her a second time around. Niya also had a lot of heat coming from the street niggas she had set up to keep the rest of MHB free. A lot of those guys were coming home, and most would be looking to even the score with her.

Eagle's aunt had lived in Germantown for years, and he still had some distant relatives up that way, along with a few connections Jedi had set him up with. For Niya, it was a no-brainer, because her ex-cell mate, Melissa, was also from there. Niya had looked forward to them hanging tough on the outside like they had when they were in prison, but the week before she and Eagle had arrived, Melissa got her parole revoked for jumping on her baby daddy's new girlfriend.

"Yo, did you call the twins today?" Eagle asked when he walked into the bedroom.

Niya was sitting on the bed Indian-style, examining the diamonds she had taken from Contez. Ever since she had them, she hadn't been able to take her eyes off of the gems. She pictured all the things she could do with the stones, none of which had anything to do with selling them. Niya wanted the diamonds for herself, and not even Eagle could convince her to get rid of them.

"Yo, did you hear me?" Eagle yelled, seeing that Niya wasn't paying him any attention. "Call ya kids today," he said with an attitude.

"Yeah, I hear you, Eagle. And you don't have to tell me to call my kids," Niya shot back.

Moving out of Charlotte had been one of the hardest things Niya had ever done. Not being able to bring her twins along with her only made matters worse. She missed them, and there wasn't a day that went by that she didn't think about them, but she knew it was too dangerous to have them along with her and Eagle. Besides the constant danger, she didn't want them to have to relocate. Gwen had built a nice, stable environment for them, as far as school and home life was concerned, and now with her and Terrence's relationship blossoming, it gave the twins the family atmosphere they desperately needed after the death of their father. Niya knew that it would have been selfish for her to pull them on the road and the run with her.

"You should just let me take you to go see them. I don't give a fuck about none of those fuck-boys in the city," Eagle said as he continued to get dressed.

"I know, babe, but it's just too risky. I don't wanna take any chances of somebody finding out that I'm back in town," she said, scooting up to the edge of the bed where he was sitting.

"Look, love, Gwen said that she was taking care of everything. It won't be much longer until I can go back," she assured him while wrapping her arms around his waist.

Eagle didn't like the sound of Niya not being allowed back into the city. The only reason he moved her to Philly was to ensure her safety until things cooled down. She was still the head of MHB and had the power to eliminate anybody who posed a threat to her life. All Niya had to do was say "go" and the shit would hit the fan. The only reason why she hadn't pushed the button was because she knew that it would start another war that would claim many lives on both sides. Niya didn't want MHB blood on her hands, especially since she'd be the reason for it all. She had already lost two of her best friends to the streets in Prada and Tiffany.

Niya knew the people opposed to her return were willing and able to kill in order to protect the street laws.

Although they were a major concern, the feds were still the greatest threat. They were worse than the streets, because they had the real law on their side, and they never played fair.

"Fuck these niggas, Gwen." Diamond spazzed. "We need to kill all these muthafuckas and be done with it. It will solve two problems: it will keep our respect and bring our girl back home," she said, pacing back and forth in the trailer.

Gwen knew she had to sit there and listen to Diamond vent. She understood very well how she felt and shared the same frustration behind Niya's temporary abolishment.

"D, I need you to sit down for a minute," Gwen said, closing her laptop.

"I can't sit down right now. I'm so fucking—"

"D, have a seat," Gwen insisted, pointing to the couch up against the wall.

Diamond could see the serious look Gwen had in her eyes, so she took a seat. Gwen got up from her desk, walked over, and joined Diamond and Alexus on the couch.

"I need you to listen to me," she said, nudging Diamond.

"Niya made a sacrifice for all of us, and when she did it, she was well aware of the backlash she would face," Gwen spoke.

"I know, but damn, sis." Diamond sighed. "We got the power to wipe every last one of these niggas off the face of this earth."

"Yeah, but at what cost? Do you know how many of us will die if we went to war with every thug in Charlotte? Not to mention what type of law enforcement that will be knocking down our doors?"

"Yeah, and that's a sacrifice I'm willing to make," Diamond responded, giving Gwen a serious look.

"Me too!" Alexus chimed in. Niya was like a big sister or a mother to Alexus, and she missed her just as much, if not more, than Gwen and Diamond.

Gwen knew that Diamond and Alexus weren't the type of women anybody could push over. They were about their business, and when it came down to Niya, each was willing to go the distance. Gwen felt the same way, but she was now a little more mature. She'd lost a lot, including a child and a baby father. She knew that a war wasn't a smart move right now, and the best thing to do at this point was to let things die down. MHB was still strong in numbers, but it was going to take a lot more than that if they wanted to regain control of the city and stay legit.

"I know what y'all need," Gwen said, patting both ladies on the leg. "How about we put together a trip to go see our girl!" She smiled, getting up from the couch and heading for the door.

Looking down at her phone, Niya pushed the call button and waited as it began to ring. It had been nearly a week since she'd spoken to Gwen and the twins, and after the harsh reminder from Eagle this morning, guilt began to settle in.

"Yo," Terrence answered, startling Niya, who had drifted off into her own thoughts.

"Hey. How's everything going, Terrence?" Niya asked in a soft voice as she walked over and took a seat at the kitchen table. "Is my girl around?"

"Yeah, she right here. Hold on for a sec . . . and tell my nigga E I said what's up!" Terrence screamed as he handed Gwen the phone.

Gwen had to take a deep breath. She was frustrated and happy at the same time, hearing Niya's voice. She had never waited this long to call.

"Bitch, what you been up to? You know I was worried about your ass, and I got Diamond down here spazzing the fuck out."

"Come on, sis. You know the situation. I told—"

"Girl, I'm just fucking with you. Trust me, I already know how hard this is on you, but just know everything down here is fine, and the twins are doing good in their new private school. They be coming home using all these big words. It's a good thing Terrence is here to translate," Gwen said while laughing.

"Yeah, I know your ass going to have my children all bougie and shit!" Niya laughed back.

"Did you get the pictures I texted you of their field trip?" Gwen asked.

"Got them and cried for two hours straight. They both getting so big. I had to make it my screen saver to remind me why I'm stuck up here in Philadelphia."

"Trust. I'm trying to get everything situated, so when you come back, we will all be flying as straight as some Catholic school girls. . . . Wait, that might not be a good reference." Both of the girls laughed. It had been some time since either had shared a good giggle, and it felt wonderful. They talked for about another thirty minutes on some MHB business, and before Gwen was about to hand the twins the phone, Niya made sure she asked about Ms. Blank.

"Are you still making sure someone goes by Prada's grandmother house at least once a week?" she questioned.

"No, because I'm the one going by there! Either me or Diamond, you know we not leaving Mama in anyone else's hand." Gwen's response made Niya feel even better, and now all that was left was to hear her children's voices.

Chapter 19

Eagle pulled up to the block in a BMW M6 looking like a bag of money. Twenty-third and Diamond Street had changed in its outer appearance, since the time he spent there during summer vacations when he was young, but Eagle knew inside the new projects, old wolves still resided. Today he was going to holla at his man, Flame, a well-known gunner in the neighborhood, who was respected by everybody. If Eagle had any chance of moving fifty AK-47s in one or two purchases, his man Flame would be the person who could do it, so that's what Eagle was hoping for.

"Nigga, where da hell did you get fifty K's from?" Flame asked in shock. "And grenades!"

"Damn, nigga, keep it down," Eagle shot back, looking around to see who had heard him.

"Man, I thought you had some coke or somethin'. How da fuck did you come up on some choppas?"

"Long story, my nigga," Eagle answered, shaking his head as he followed Flame up the sidewalk and into Flame's house.

Eagle thought about Niya killing Contez without warning, and by the way that it was done, he knew that it was a last minute choice on her behalf. It was crazy, but even though he was mad at her for doing what she did, Eagle was going to ride with her until the casket closed.

"Look, homie, there's no way in hell you gon' be able to pitch these kinds of guns one at a time," Flame said, pulling out his phone. "These li'l niggas around here will buy one from you then turn around and rob you with the same gun and take everything you got." Flame chuckled.

It had indeed been a while since Eagle had been in the hood, but not much had changed. It was wild fifteen years ago when he lived in Philly for a short time. The main difference now was that the youth used too many drugs. Not just any drugs, but the kind of drugs that made them do stupid stuff, and killing for no reason was one of them.

"A'ight, I just got off the phone with my man. We gon' go over there and see what he's talking about," Flame said after hanging up his iPhone. "Are you strapped?"

"Do a bear shit in the woods?" Eagle joked, lifting his shirt up to show the .50-caliber on his hip.

"Good. We goin' to see my man, but you know niggas get stupid around here. I fucks wit' you more than I fuck wit' him, so if he get crazy, I'ma let the flame go," Flame said, flashing the black Glock .40 on his waist.

"No doubt," Eagle responded, leaning in for a dap.

As they headed for the door, Eagle's phone went off. He initially thought that it was Niya calling, but when he looked down at the screen the number was UNAVAILABLE. Being as though he had so many homies in the penitentiary calling him on the regular, he answered.

"This is a prepaid call. You will not be charged for this call. This call is from . . . Jedi!"

Winter and Jade strutted into the breakfast diner looking like a set of runway models. Jade was half black/half Puerto Rican, pretty as they come, with a fat ass and some cute B-cup breasts that complemented her five foot six, 145-pound frame. Her hair reached the length of her shoulders, and her golden brown eyes were covered in a pair of Ray Ban shades.

Winter was 100 percent black, but light brown–skinned. She was short, five foot two, weighing 135 pounds with a set of 34-D breasts. She was also a show horse.

"I know you not gon' eat all of that food," Winter said, walking over to the table where Niya was sitting.

"Yeah, you look like you're eating for two," Jade added.

Niya spit out the food she had in her mouth onto the plate. Their comments made her lose her appetite instantly. Niya wasn't in a position to be pregnant right now, and although Eagle was fucking her like he was trying to accomplish just that, Niya made sure she was at the doctor's office bright and early for her routine Depo shots.

"Y'all bitches better be ready for tonight," Niya said, cleaning the corners of her mouth with the napkin.

"Yeah, we good, Niya. Cool out," Winter assured.

When Niya first moved to Philly, Melissa had put her in touch with her two little cousins, Jade and Winter. Niya took a liking to both of them off the bat. Winter reminded her of Prada. She was sharp as a knife for her tender age of twenty-one, and just like Prada, she knew how to use her looks to get what she wanted. Jade, on the other hand, was a little more serious and business- minded. She had the qualities of a leader, just like Gwen. For that and the fact that they were Melissa's peeps, Niya kept them both close.

"So, look, I don't wanna draw too much attention to us right away, so only get the attention of a few good dudes," Niya instructed.

"We know, we know. Just give us a chance, Niya, and you'll be surprised at what we can do out here in these streets," Jade spoke.

After being in Philly for over four months, Niya thought it was time to set up shop. It took weeks for her to come up with this idea, but after seeing how dead it was, cocaine-wise, it was like second nature for her to chase a dollar. The coke supply in Philly was dryer than Sudan, and with that, the prices of cocaine had shot through the roof. What tilted the scale in her coming to her final conclusion to get back in the game was when she found out that the price for a kilo was forty grand.

Inga, Niya's old connect, was still on speed dial, and all it took was one phone call and a cosign from her cousin Van to have some product delivered to the city. Niya wasn't at the point where she was about to go as hard as she used to go in Charlotte, but she definitely wanted to see what the streets of Philly had to offer.

Eagle and Flame pulled into what used to be Richard Island projects and parked on the block of Tenth and Popular. Flame jumped on the phone to let Monster know that they were outside. Eagle got out of the car with his gun in his hand, letting the young thugs posted up on the corner know that he was strapped, with a big gun nonetheless. It caused a bit of a stir, because one or two of the young cats walked off to retrieve their guns, which were stashed close by.

"Watch those li'l niggas down the street," Flame said, noticing the movement. It was a tense moment, but once Monster came out of the house and showed love with his greetings, everything calmed down. Seeing that, Eagle tucked the large gun back into his waist.

"Damn, playboy, you must got something good for me," Monster said, giving Flame dap.

"Yeah, my boy got heavy artillery," Flame responded, nodding his head toward Eagle.

"So what you got?" Monster asked Eagle.

"I got AK-47s, .45s, and grenades. I'm tryin' to let dis shit go in bulk, so I can't sell you ones and twos," Eagle explained.

He broke down the prices to Monster, charging seven hundred dollars per AK-47, with a minimum purchase of ten. The .45 automatics were going for three hundred dollars each, but with a minimum purchase of fifteen. Eagle only had twelve grenades total, and being as though they were a delicacy in Philly, he was selling them for a thousand dollars each.

"Damn, you really got grenades, homie?" Monster asked with his face turned up in awe.

"Yeah, shit's real in the field," Eagle answered. "So what's ya order? I'm not holding on to this shit."

Monster leaned up against the car and started to scratch his head. He did the math in his head of how much money he could make from a bulk purchase. Getting rid of the guns wouldn't be a problem at all. The youth in Philly bought guns as a hobby. Monster could easily sell the AK's for twelve hundred and the handguns for five or six hundred dollars. Monster wasn't sure how he was going to price the grenades, but what he did know was that he had to purchase a couple of them for himself.

At the end of the day, Monster purchased the minimums on both the AK's and the handguns. He was spending his last on the guns, but he was sure to get his money back. Within the hour of Flame and Eagle leaving, the order was covered, and a brand new batch of guns was out on the streets.

"I wonder who she's talking to," Winter said.

"I don't know, but whoever it is, it must be somebody important," Jade responded, watching the all-black Tahoe Niya had climbed into about ten minutes ago.

While Winter and Jade sat there waiting, another black SUV drove past their car and pulled right behind the Tahoe. They both looked confused as a well-dressed woman got out of the Dodge Durango then hopped into the Tahoe.

"What in da hell?" Winter said with a confused look on her face.

Moments later, Niya got out of the Tahoe and walked back toward the car with Winter and Jade. The Tahoe pulled off, but the Durango stayed. Niya walked up to the driver's side and tapped on the window, all the while keeping her eyes on the speeding cars passing by.

"I want y'all to follow me back to Philly. Follow me, but put some distance between us. The state troopers got an eye for drug runners," Niya said. "In the event I get pulled over, I want you to run into the back of the cop car once I pull over. Can y'all handle that?" Niya asked, bending down to look both of them in their eyes.

Neither one of them had the chance to say anything before Niya tapped the driver's side door then walked off down the road toward the Durango. It was exciting for Winter and Jade to see Niya making moves, but for Niya, it was back to business, and the only thing she had on her mind was getting the twenty bricks of cocaine back to the city safe and sound.

The whole ride back home, all Eagle could do was think about the phone call he'd gotten from Jedi, Contez's little brother, earlier that day. Eagle thought that Jedi was calling him to let him know that he was going to kill him, but to Eagle's surprise, Jedi didn't know who had killed his brother. The African worker that got away at the garage only saw faces. He didn't know any names, and he could barely speak English for that matter, so for the time being, Eagle and Niya were in the clear.

For Eagle, the news came as a relief, but at the same time, he still had to be on point, 'cause there was still somebody out there that could identify him and Niya as the culprits behind the shooting. If that was to happen, Eagle would have a huge problem on his hands, a problem he wasn't sure if he could handle. Them Africans ran deep, especially in Philly, and when it came to family, they went harder than them Arabs in Afghanistan.

Chapter 20

Diamond walked through the front door of her home, and the first thing she had to do was come out of her heels. Her feet were hurting like hell from making tours of the many properties on her maintenance list. She had to make sure all of her tenants were good, because come that weekend, she would be in the City of Brotherly Love visiting her best friend.

The flights were already booked, and the only thing Diamond had to do for the rest of the week was pack, but before she could do that, she needed to get a couple hours of sleep.

"Messages!" Diamond yelled out to her automated voice mail box that was hooked up to the house phone.

Listening to her messages blaring through the surround sound, she headed to the kitchen to get something to drink. Before she got to the refrigerator, a light scent of cigarettes caught her attention. It was extremely odd, because Diamond didn't smoke, nor did anybody in her immediate circle. As she got closer to the kitchen, the scent got a little stronger.

Diamond pulled the chrome .380 from her back pocket and gripped it tightly in both hands. When she crossed the threshold into the kitchen, she was shocked to see Nose standing there leaning up against her sink.

"Don't shoot." Nose chuckled, holding both his hands in the air like this was some type of joke.

Diamond wasn't laughing, and at that moment, she was about to raise her gun, until she felt something hard press against the back of her head. She froze, thinking this was her final moment.

"Put da gun up, shawty. I don't wanna see you go out like this, beautiful," Nose teased, while motioning his hand for his boy to lower the gun.

Reluctant to cooperate, Diamond loosened the grip she had on her pistol, but she kept it down by her side instead of putting it back in her pocket.

"See, that's why I like you so much, Diamond—"

"Don't say my name like you know me," she snapped, cutting him off. "Why da fuck are you in my house?"

"Mmmm, you still got some fight in you. For a minute, y'all bitches had me fooled, thinking y'all was out of the game. Come to find out, y'all still taxing niggas in the hood," Nose said, leaning off the sink and walking toward Diamond. "See, the problem lies where you think MHB still controls the city."

"We do, nigga," Diamond shot back. "The only reason why y'all niggas is back out on the block is because we let you. Don't ever get that misconstrued."

Nose walked up on Diamond and stood within a foot from her. She could see the hatred and the anger in his eyes as he towered over her. He wasn't threatened at all by the gun Diamond had clutched in her hand, nor was he going to bite his tongue.

"The west side and the south side is off limits to y'all hoes. If y'all bitches tax another corner in my hood again, I'ma make sure I give you everything you lookin' for, you dig? If y'all want a war, we can go to war whenever you see fit. They'll make a brand new line of designer body bags just for y'all. Think it's a game? Then try me," Nose threatened then walked off, bumping her in the process of leaving.

Diamond wanted to set it off right then and there, but when she turned around, Nose's boy was backing out of the house with his gun aimed at her. To try to do anything other than to let them leave would have been a huge mistake on Diamond's behalf. She did the smart thing and let the two men walk out of the front door without further confrontation, knowing she would live to fight another day.

To talk about selling cocaine was one thing, but for Winter to actually see it with her own two eyes was another. She, Jade, and Niya sat at the dining room table looking at twenty bricks of pure white cocaine heavily wrapped in Saran Wrap. Jade had witnessed her brother bagging up crack cocaine before, but never did he do it on this level.

"We're going to need some help with this shit," Jade said, grabbing one of the bricks and holding it in the air.

"You should ask ya brother to help us," Winter suggested, also picking up one of the bricks.

"No!" Niya bassed. "We don't need any help from no niggas. No offense to ya brother," she said, pointing to Jade.

Niya had another idea, one that she was familiar with, and she knew beyond a shadow of a doubt that if done right, everybody sitting at that table could become rich. Niya wanted to put Philly chicks on the map and have them known for more than just rapping and modeling.

"I think we should start our own crew," Niya said, getting their attention.

"You mean like a gang?" Winter asked with a curious look on her face.

"No, not a gang. I'm talking about something way better than a gang. I'm talking about a sisterhood."

"Look I'm all about woman power, but . . ."

"But what?" Niya said after Jade got quiet.

Jade looked at Winter and then at Niya. She was born and raised in the heart of North Philly, where it was either kill or be killed. The one thing that she did value was her life, and she knew that messing around in these mean streets could have her dressed up nice inside of a state-of-the-art casket.

"Niya, I don't know if you've been paying attention to what's going on out here in these streets, but people get murdered for less," Jade said, looking over at the cocaine.

Winter nodded her head in agreement, understanding Jade's concern. On that note, Niya got up from the table and walked into the other room. Jade and Winter looked at each other, not sure what to think. Before they could say anything, Niya walked back into the room with two small black boxes in her hand. She placed one on the table in front of Jade and the other in front of Winter.

"Oh, shit," Winter gasped, opening the box to see a black compact .45 automatic.

Jade pulled hers out of the box as well, checking the clip to see if it was loaded. Not only were the guns loaded, but they had hollow point bullets in them. Holding that gun in her hand gave Jade an instant feeling of power. It seemed as though all of her concerns about the niggas on the streets had diminished.

"If we play our cards right, we can take over the whole city," Niya said, removing the gun from her waist and placing it on the table in front of her.

The room became silent as all three women went into deep thought. Winter was pretty much down with whatever and had felt that way the moment she laid eyes on the twenty bricks of cocaine sitting on the table. Jade was more of a thinking person; she had to weigh the pros and cons with everything that she did.

"I promise I won't let anything happen to you, Jade." Niya spoke sincerely. "That's my word."

Jade sat there for a few more seconds in silence before she spoke. She took in a deep breath then exhaled. "You better not get us killed." Jade smiled as she shook her head. "I'm in."

Eagle sat at a table for two on the upper level of Miss Tootsies, a soul food restaurant on South Street. He and Niya were supposed to be having dinner there that night, but she was running late. By the time she made it there, Eagle had already started eating.

"Baby, I'm sorry. I had to drop Winter off, and then I had to park like six blocks away," Niya said as she leaned in and kissed his BBQ-sauced lips. "Let me get some," she said playfully, moving her chair next to his and taking a seat.

Normally, Eagle couldn't stay mad at Niya for long, but today he wasn't about to let her off the hook that easy, "You know da nigga Jedi wants me to go to his brother's funeral," Eagle said.

"Who's Jedi?" Niya asked, reaching over and grabbing a bread stick from Eagle's plate.

He looked at her and shook his head. He couldn't believe she had no idea who he was talking about.

"He's Contez's little brother," Eagle answered.

"Ohh! So why would he want you to go to his brother's funeral?"

"Because he doesn't know I had something to do with the murder. All he knows is that Contez was killed in North Philly. The worker that got away don't know us."

"Wow! So what are you going to do? You know you can't risk that, right?" Niya said, concerned for Eagle's safety.

If the Africans found out that Eagle had something to do with Contez's death, they wouldn't hesitate to kill him—and it wouldn't stop there. The African community in Philly was ruthless. They would kill everybody in Eagle's immediate family, and that included Niya.

"Don't worry about it. I'll take care of it," Eagle assured her, shoving another forkful of food in his mouth, "Let me ask you something. What's going on with you, Ni?" Eagle asked as he continued to chew his food.

"What do you mean, babe? I'm good."

"Come on, shawty. Ever since we've been in Philly, you've been riding reckless. Ya whole attitude changed. You drink damn near every night, you smoking weed now, not calling ya kids daily, and now you catching unnecessary bodies. What's going on?"

"Let's not ruin dinner," Niya replied.

Niya didn't want to talk about it then, but it was obvious to Eagle she had something on her mind. He wasn't going to let it go until she got it off of her chest. If she continued down this path of destruction, things were only going to get worse. Eagle wanted to nip it in the bud before that happened.

"We're not leaving here until you tell me what's going on," Eagle said, tossing the napkin onto the table.

Niya sat there in silence for a moment; that was, until Eagle snapped his fingers in front of her face to bring her out of the trance she was in. "Talk!" he demanded.

She looked at him and was about to say something but paused. She had so much bottled up that she didn't know where to begin. Just thinking about her situation made her frustrated. As bad as Eagle wanted her to talk, it wasn't going to happen that day.

"Enjoy the rest of your dinner," Niya said, leaning in and kissing his cheek before getting up and departing from the table.

Eagle thought about stopping her, but knowing Niya the way he did, she was at her shutdown phase. No matter what he said or did, she wasn't going to say anything, and if he pushed any harder, it would only make her do something stupid. Letting her calm down and giving her some space was the best thing to do.

Chapter 21

Jedi was surprised when the corrections officer told him that he had a social visit. He was only one week away from being sent to a halfway house, so for someone to come see him now, it had to be important.

When he got to the visiting room, his sister was sitting there with a huge smile on her face. Jedi was now the only one of her three brothers still alive, so to see him brought joy to her heart.

“Farrah, what are you doing here?” Jedi said, walking up to his sister and giving her a hug.

“I missed you, little brother.” She smiled.

“Come on, Farrah, what is it? Is everything all right?”

Farrah couldn’t hide anything from her little brother. The real reason why she came was because there was a message to be delivered to him.

“The elders wanted me to come tell you that they are looking into Contez’s murder, and for you not to get involved when you come home,” she explained.

“That’s what they wanted you to tell me?”

“Yes, Jedi. Everyone here and back home wants you to stay out of trouble. Father feels like he may lose you.”

Jedi sat and listened, but most of what Farrah said went in one ear and right out of the other. Finding out who was responsible for Contez’s death was Jedi’s number one priority once he hit the streets. If he had to burn the city down in order to find out what he wanted to know, then that was the route he was willing to take, even if it meant him getting killed in the process.

"Tell the elders I'll stay out of it," Jedi lied. "I'm sure they got their ears to the streets," he said sarcastically.

For the rest of the visit, Jedi and Farrah talked about the family and what was going on back home in Africa. Farrah made sure that she stayed off the topic of Contez's funeral as much as possible. Jedi didn't show it, but Farrah knew that he was hot under the collar 'bout the whole situation. Bringing up the funeral would be like pouring gasoline on fire, something Farrah desperately wanted to avoid.

Gwen tried her best to calm Diamond down, but she wasn't listening, walking around the house, yelling through the phone. She called Alexus, Kea, Rose, and a couple other MHB members, summoning them to her house immediately. She didn't care how Gwen felt about the possible casualties if it was a war. Nose had crossed the line when he came into her home and made the threats he did. As far as she was concerned, the peace treaty had been broken.

Dollaz walked into the house with the help of his cane. He had just come from physical therapy, and although he was drained, he wanted to share the good news of being able to walk nearly a mile without the use of his cane earlier. Instead, when he looked at Diamond screaming into the phone while walking up the steps, he almost turned around and walked right back out the door. Gwen jumped up off the couch before he could.

"Dollaz, can you please talk to your wife?" Gwen pleaded, walking over to him. "She's about to start a war, and she's not listening to me."

Gwen didn't even have time to explain the situation to him before Diamond came charging back down the steps. She went straight at Dollaz.

"Dis muthafucka had the nerve to break into our house and make a bunch of threats," she snapped. "If dis nigga wants a fuckin' war, we will give him one."

"I told you, Diamond, we're not in the streets anymore. If he wants his neighborhood back, then let him have it."

"No, you're not on the streets anymore. I'm out there every day," Diamond barked at Gwen.

Gwen got so frustrated with Diamond she rolled her eyes, turned around, and walked out of the house. As she was leaving, Kea and Porsha were pulling up to the house, and by the look of things, Alexus couldn't have been that far behind.

"What's going on?" Porsha asked while getting out of the car. "Diamond just called my phone and told me to get over here ASAP."

Diamond could be heard screaming at the top of her lungs, all the way from the driveway.

"She's losing it," Gwen said, leaning up against Porsha's car. "Y'all need to talk to her, 'cause shit's about to get real ugly," Gwen said then headed for her car. "We're not in the streets anymore!" Gwen yelled before getting into the car.

Gwen didn't want to stick around for the foolishness that Diamond was on. Everything that happened from this point on would weigh heavily on Diamond's shoulders. Gwen was getting to the end of her rope with this trying to keep everyone in line shit. She had the twins at home, and those were the only children she was responsible for.

Eagle had been driving around all day, trying to figure out what he was going to do about Contez's funeral, and more importantly, what he was going to do about Jedi when he came home from prison. Jedi was his cellmate for a little over a year, and Eagle knew his mentality and how hard he was going to go when he touched down home. Contez had meant everything to him, and sooner or later he was going to find out who killed his brother.

"Wait a muthafuckin' minute," Eagle mumbled to himself as he pulled into the driveway.

Stressed out to the max, all Eagle wanted to do was lay back for the rest of the day. Seeing Niya's car parked in the driveway beside a second car, he didn't think relaxing was in his future. Niya had never brought anyone to their home, as far as he knew.

"NiNi!" Eagle yelled out when he entered the house. She didn't answer, so he shot upstairs and headed for the bedroom. When he got there, Niya wasn't in sight. He yelled out her name again, and still no answer. It was silent throughout the whole house, and just when Eagle was about to leave the room, the playful Niya jumped out of the closet, scaring the shit out of him.

"Yooo!" he yelled, jumping back and putting one hand up for defense and gripping the Desert Eagle that rested on his waist with the other hand. Niya was cracking up, throwing a few playful punches at him. "You were scared to death." Niya smiled, walking up to him and wrapping her arms around his neck.

"You know I don't get scared. I was wondering whose car that was in the driveway, that's all."

"That's Winter's car. She couldn't get it started, so she rode with Jade. I told her she could have it towed later. And for the record, you was scared and I got you!" Niya teased.

"Yeah, what you almost got is shot," he replied, reaching up and grabbing a fistful of her hair. He pulled her head back and looked into her eyes. He couldn't help but to laugh at her childish act. Eagle had to acknowledge that it had been a minute since he saw her this playful.

***

Instead of taking the rest of the day off, like Terrence had suggested, Gwen decided to head back to the office and do some work. Despite Diamond's antics, there was still plenty of shit to be done, and at the top of the agenda was closing a deal on an apartment complex that Gwen had been trying to lease.

A car driving up the dirt road caught Gwen's attention, making her lift her head up from all the mounds of paperwork. When she saw Diamond's car, she shook her head and let out a deep breath. Surprisingly, when Diamond walked into the trailer, she was calm and somewhat humbled.

"I come in peace." Diamond smiled, holding her hands in the air.

"Diamond, do you know why I'm moving MHB in another direction?" Gwen asked, crossing her hands on her desk. "I mean, really?"

Diamond walked over and took a seat in the chair sitting in front of the desk. Diamond really didn't have an answer for the question, mainly because she was stuck in her ways and didn't want to let go of how things used to be.

"There comes a time in every drug dealer's life where he or she has this epiphany. They look up and realize that the game ain't a game. Even still, he or she thinks one more time, sell everything, and get out of the game," Gwen spoke. "Every last one of them say that, and most of the time they either get locked up or put six feet under. I don't want us to be like that. I don't want us to be the ones who had a chance to leave this shit and didn't do it," Gwen explained, speaking to Diamond in all seriousness.

Diamond felt like a young girl all over again, being schooled by a vet. Even if she wanted to protest, there wasn't anything she could say that would make sense. She just continued to listen.

"Do you have any idea how much property and land we own in this city?"

Before Diamond could say anything, Gwen answered.

"A lot!" she said proudly. "MHB has the potential to be larger than life. We're better than the rest, but we'll never be able to see our full potential if we're locked up behind bars or pushing up daisies. Let these niggas have that game," Gwen pleaded. "While they run around in the streets killing each other and filling up the county jails, we can be out here indulging in the corporate world. We're street smart and educated. With well over three hundred MHB members in the city, a position of power is within our reach. You have to make a choice, Diamond. You have to choose whether you wanna be caught up in the system, or if you wanna control the system. The choice is yours."

Eagle lay behind Niya with his arm draped over her side and his chin resting up against the back of her head. Neither one of them were asleep yet, and that came from them both having so much on their minds.

"I feel like I don't belong here," Niya said, breaking the silence in the room. "I'm losing my mind being out here."

"It takes time to get used to," Eagle said.

"That's the thing. This really ya thing, babe? I wanna go home," Niya said, almost sounding like she wanted to cry. "I miss my kids. I miss my family and friends," she went on.

"I know, babe. Just let things cool down for another year or so, then we can revisit the idea of moving back." It was funny to Eagle how now he was the one trying to convince Niya on why it was better to lay low than go back to Charlotte. He didn't want to lose Niya to the streets or prison.

"How about in the meantime, we try to start our own little family?" Eagle said, nudging her from behind. "I would love to have a baby with you," he whispered softly.

"Did you take care of that situation with going to Contez's funeral?" Niya asked, trying to change the conversation as quickly as possible.

The throw-off had worked, too, causing Eagle to bury his face into Niya's hair as he thought about what he was going to do. There was only one person in the world that could identify him and Niya as the ones who killed Contez, and the only way he could guarantee he wouldn't get pointed out by the worker in the future was if Eagle found him and killed him. It was either kill him or kill Jedi whenever he got home. Either way, something had to be done immediately, because Eagle and Niya wouldn't be able to live comfortably in the city as long as somebody else knew their secret. Just thinking about it made him get up out of the bed, get dressed, and head for the door. He was on a mission right now.

Chapter 22

"Wake up, nigga!" Winter yelled, kicking the side of the couch to wake Monster.

"What da hell," he snapped, turning over to see his little stepsister standing over top of him with a gun in her hand. "That better not be mine."

"Nah, nigga, it's mine." She chuckled, tucking it away into her back pocket. "Get up, nigga. I got a sweet come-up for you."

"What? You got another dope boyfriend for me to rob?" Monster asked, lighting up a cigarette.

"Nah, nigga, I got dat work in. Quarters, ounces, points—might even be able to get you a brick for thirty grand," Winter told him.

Anytime Winter had a lick or some type of scheme to pull off, the first person she went to was her big brother. Although she really hadn't grown up with him, he was her blood because they shared the same sorry father. He had not spent much time in either child's life, and both were sure they probably had even more stepsisters and stepbrothers around Philly.

"How much of it you got?" Monster asked, taking a pull of the cigarette.

"Enough! Now how much do you wanna spend?" Winter shot back, taking a seat on the coffee table.

Monster shot high just to see if she could cover the order. He had a feeling that she wouldn't be able to, which she wasn't. Winter had to jump on the phone to clear it with Niya.

"My people said that she can do it," Winter said.

"I'll call you in a couple of hours to set up a time," she said, getting up to leave. "And no funny shit. I hate to be the one who has to pop you, but I will if you try to play any games wit' dat fuckin' money," Winter said jokingly, although she was dead serious. One thing Winter didn't do was play with her money. "And clean ya house up. It looks like a tornado hit it."

You would have thought that Jedi was Prince Hakeem the way the crowd of Africans stood around him on the small street in Southwest Philly. Family and friends had anticipated this moment, praying that he would come home and stay out of trouble. Those prayers weren't answered, because Jedi was already violating his parole. He was scheduled to have arrived at the halfway house at three o'clock in the afternoon the day before, which he had failed to do. Not only that, but Jedi managed to obtain a gun, smoke some weed, and drive around the city drunk without a license, all in less than forty-eight hours of his release.

"Please stay out of trouble," Fanta, Jedi's mother told him as she sat next to him on the porch. "I don't wanna bury the last of my boys," she said, grabbing his hand and holding it tight.

"You ought to listen to your mother," Jedi's father added, walking out to the porch. "Your brother was killed out there in those streets, and if you're thinking of following in his footsteps, you'll end up the same way."

Jedi knew that this speech was coming, but it really didn't matter, because he already had his mind made up on what he was about to do. He sat there, tuning out his parents, who were giving him an earful.

"Father, I can't stay long. I have to check into the halfway house, but I'll be back in a couple of days," Jedi said, excusing himself from their presence.

It was all smiles, hugs, and kisses before Jedi left, but as soon as he got off of the porch, his smile turned hard. Codi was waiting at the other end of the block for him, and when Jedi walked up to him, he lowered his head in humility. He began to explain to Jedi everything that had happened in the garage and how the deal went bad. He was ashamed that he had run once the shooting started. It was something he regretted and would have to live with for the rest of his life, which could be short.

The only good thing that came from Codi's cowardly act was that he got a good look at the people who were responsible for Contez's death. Had he not been of some value in that regard, Jedi would have killed him right then and there. Instead, he had other plans for Codi, plans that included him helping Jedi find the people responsible for killing his brother.

Niya and Jade sat in her dining room with latex gloves on, cutting up the cocaine. It was pure, so Niya was able to turn two into three with no problem. She was like a chemist when it came to cutting and cooking coke.

The doorbell rang, almost giving Niya a heart attack, as she was elbow deep into the process. Even though she had on gloves, some of the coke still managed to get into her pores, causing her to feel some of the effects, most specifically, paranoia.

"I got it. Just keep mixing it," Niya instructed as she headed for the door.

She removed her gloves then took a peek out of the side window to see Winter and two other females standing on her porch.

"Damn, bitch, it took you long enough," Niya greeted when she opened the door. "Hurry up!" She motioned with her hand, trying to get everybody inside.

"No offense, but could you turn around?" Niya told the first female, placing her up against the door.

She began patting Tamika down for weapons, then gave her a thorough sweep for a wire. She checked Tamika's handbag and made her empty out her pockets to see the contents in them. Tamika went along with it, mainly because she saw that Niya had a big gun on her hip.

As soon as she was done searching Tamika, she turned around to see the other female standing there holding a gun by the nose. "Here. My name is Monica," she greeted, holding the gun out for Niya to take it.

Niya appreciated the gesture but still searched Monica for wires, which she didn't mind at all.

"You want me to trust y'all, you're gonna have to earn that," Niya said, nodding for them to follow her into the other room. "You get ya gun back later."

The whole dining room table was covered with coke, and from the moment Monica laid her eyes on it, she knew this was where she wanted to be. While everybody else saw coke, Monica saw money.

"I want y'all to get familiar with one word, because without it, you're nothing," Niya said as they all gathered around the table.

"And what's that?" Tamika asked, looking Niya in her eyes.

"Loyalty!" Niya shot back. "So if you're not ready for this life, you're free to leave." Nobody moved. "Okay, so now grab some gloves and help mix this coke up. We gotta start moving it."

Jedi walked into Shakira's, an African club on Fifty-eighth Street, only to be surprised by more of his friends. He walked through the crowd of people, shaking hands and being kissed by several hood rats who couldn't wait to give him some pussy. He was really feeling the love, but he had something else on his mind.

Ojay, the owner of the club, was like family, so any time Jedi needed to have a power meeting, the club was accessible for him. Jedi didn't even stop to take time out to have a drink with his friends. He wanted to get straight to the business.

"Are they here?" Jedi leaned in and asked Ojay, who was standing by the bar.

Ojay nodded then pointed to the back. Shakira's wasn't just a club; it was also a place where a group of elders sat and discussed business. They were like the shot callers for the African community in Philly, and pretty much nothing happened without their consent. Before Jedi did anything, it had to go through them.

He walked into the room and was greeted with a hug from his uncle, who just so happened to be one of the elders. There were three other elders in the room who only nodded when Jedi spoke.

"I know why you're here, nephew," his uncle said, taking a seat at the table with the rest of the elders.

"It's tragic, what happened to Contez, but we assure you that everything possible is being done to find the person who did this."

"I don't mean any disrespect to the elders, but this is my brother. I think I should—"

"Now wait a minute, Jedi. Don't forget where you're at," his uncle had to remind him.

When speaking to the elders of the community, it was obligatory to have respect. Questioning their judgment or trying to tell them what to do could easily get you killed. It didn't matter who you were, and Jedi wasn't any exception to the rules. The one thing they didn't realize was that Jedi didn't give a fuck. He had lost a family member, and he wanted revenge.

"Look. No disrespect, but I lost my brother. If it was your brother, would you stand around and do nothing? Wouldn't you want to know what was going on?" he asked.

Jedi had to fight to hold back his tears. He knew that the elders had some information about what happened to Contez, or probably even knew who did it. They were old, but they had their ears to the streets and could find out about anything. Fortunately for Jedi, the elders felt his pain. Jedi's uncle looked over at the elders, who nodded their heads, giving Jedi's uncle the okay to tell him what they knew.

"Your brother was running guns from the motherland. When he was murdered, fifty AK-47s, along with some .45s and hand grenades were taken from him. We got guns in North Philly a couple of days ago. We even had somebody buy one, and it was confirmed that they were the same type of guns taken from your brother. We took Codi down to the place, and he said that the guy wasn't the shooter. So far, this is all we got, but we're still trying to figure out where the guy got the guns. It's taking some time but we're piecing everything together," Jedi's uncle explained.

With that being said, Jedi was more grateful for the update. Before he left, the elders gave him strict orders not to get involved, and he gave them his word that he wouldn't. On his way out of the club, he grabbed Codi by his collar and pushed him out the door.

Niya and the girls stood around the table repackaging the cocaine. Some of the bricks were broken down into ounces, but none for nickels and dimes. The only thing Niya wanted to do was sell weight. It would move faster that way given the current market for cocaine in Philly.

Niya was so caught up in what she was doing that she didn't hear Eagle's car pull up into the driveway. All she heard was his car door slam, but by then it was too late for her to do anything. There was too much coke on the table for her to try to move it, and trying to divert his attention away from the dining room would be impossible.

The smell of cocaine smacked him in the face as soon as he opened the door, and his face frowned up immediately.

"Keep working, y'all," Niya instructed, excusing herself from the table. She stopped Eagle in the living room, but he could see clearly what was going on.

"Don't be mad at me," Niya pleaded, taking off her latex gloves.

"I thought we agreed not to fuck with coke," Eagle snapped. "You fuckin' hardheaded?"

"Can we go upstairs and talk?" Niya asked, not wanting her new crew to hear Eagle yell at her.

Instead of going upstairs, he walked into the dining room so he could see exactly what was going on at the table. There was coke everywhere, and his presence didn't stop the packaging process the least bit. The girls just kept working. Eagle wanted to flip the whole table over. He knew all too well the kinds of problems that came along with selling coke, especially in a city where robbery was prevalent.

Mad as hell, Eagle walked out of the room and headed upstairs. Niya followed right behind him, now feeling a little guilty for not telling him.

"So this is low key to you?" Eagle asked once they got to the bedroom. "You think you about to be under the radar fucking around wit' dis shit?" he snapped. "I don't understand you, Ni."

"We can use the money." She tried to convince him.

We don't need no fuckin' money, Niya. You doin' dis shit because you want to. You think dis shit sweet out here? Dis ain't North Carolina, Niya. These niggas will kill you out here . . . for nothing!" he yelled.

Eagle was right. They didn't need any money. It was the game. Niya was addicted to the drug game, and just like most niggas, the hustle was what kept her going. She missed her old life, riding around the city making money, watching workers pitch rocks to the fiends, and having a crew that was so sick that niggas didn't have any other choice but to respect them. She always felt like she was a part of something. She felt like she had a purpose in life and a responsibility to look after the people that she loved. Niya felt like a boss, a feeling that she so desperately wanted back. Eagle just didn't understand, and Niya really didn't feel like trying to explain it to him.

"Just let me do me. I know what I'm doing," Niya said, turning around and walking out of the bedroom.

Jedi sat on his California love seat with his feet up, looking around at the faces of his crew. His girlfriend, Audria, had gotten everybody together at the house for a welcome home dinner. The whole evening was going good. Lots of food, music, weed, and drinks had everybody feeling right. It was at that point when everyone was sitting in the living room telling old stories that Jedi was ready to get down to other business.

It was all crew love, so talking about the situation concerning Contez wouldn't leave the room. It was something that didn't need to be said, but it was understood by all. Web, Knock, Ike, T-Boy, Alisa, and Precious all sat in silence, waiting for Jedi to speak. Audria walked into the room from the kitchen and took her seat on Jedi's lap in the love seat.

"If anybody heard anything that happened with my brother, now is the time to say something," Jedi said, looking around the room. "'Cause when I find out who murdered him, not only am I going to kill the person who did it, I'm rocking any and everybody who had something to do with it. Not only that, if you knew something and decided not to tell me and I find out that you was withholding information from me, I'ma kill you too. So like I said before, now is the time to talk."

"All I know is that ya brotha was selling AKs out of a truck. I bought two of them myself," Knock explained. "He had two workers with him when he came through the block, but I don't know who they were," Knock continued.

Jedi had tapped Audria twice on her thigh. She got up and walked back into the kitchen, returning moments later with Codi by her side. Codi stood there with his head down, not wanting to look at anybody.

"Is this the coward that you saw?" Jedi asked.

"I know dat mu'fucka," Web chimed in. "He be cleaning the restaurant on Sixty-seventh Street. The elders be having him doing a lot of errands."

Jedi looked up at Codi. "Oh, you do errands for the elders, huh? What else do you do around here?" Jedi barked.

Codi sat there looking scared to death. Jedi looked at Audria then rolled his eyes toward Codi. She walked to Jedi, leaned over, and pulled Jedi's gun out of the cushions of the love seat. Rising back up with the gun in her hand, she pointed it at Codi's face.

"Answer the question," she demanded, pressing the gun up against his lips.

"I don't do nothing else around here," he answered with a little too much bass in his voice.

Audria didn't like that, and everybody in the room knew that she was crazy, especially when it came down to

Jedi. She was fine as a bottle of wine, young, dark chocolate, flawless skin, and a pretty face. She was country thick, too, and had large, 38-DD breasts. Through all her beauty, she just didn't have her wiring right upstairs.

"Open ya mouth," she told Codi, pushing the gun against his mouth. "I'm not gonna ask you twice."

Reluctantly, Codi opened his mouth and Audria pushed the .40-caliber into his mouth, almost breaking his teeth in the process.

"Yeaaah, that's what I'm talking about," Jedi said, getting up from his seat. "Take a good look at dis shit right here. This is what it's gonna take to get some results around here."

Everybody looked at Audria staring Codi down. "I don't give a fuck if y'all gotta put a gun in everybody's mouth you question. If that's what needs to be done, then do it. I would do the same for you if it was your brother or sister," Jedi said, looking around the room at each person.

Nobody could deny that if the shoe was on the other foot, Jedi would go hard for everyone in the room. That was part of the reason why his crew loved him so much.

"It's cool, Bun-Bun. Let him go," Jedi said, walking over to her.

She kept staring him down with hatred in her eyes. "I still need him, Bun-Bun," Jedi continued, tapping her on the ass and reaching up to grab the gun out of Codi's mouth.

It was a good thing that he did, because Audria was two seconds away from pulling the trigger. Her actions were only a reminder to Jedi that he was dealing with a problem, and at the right time and in the right place, Jedi was going to let Audria off the leash to do what she did best, and that was kill.

***

Aunt Debby was Eagle's only living aunt on his mom's side of the family. Growing up, she was the only family Eagle really knew on his mother's side. Aunt Debby babysat him seven days of the week when his mom and Cowboy ran the streets.

"Aunt D, you did ya thing today," Eagle said, walking into the kitchen where she was.

When Aunt Debby had a BBQ, she did it big. She cooked burgers, hot dogs, chicken, and colossal shrimp, all on the grill. She had potato salad, macaroni salad, fried fish, baked fish, king crab legs, regular crabs, and every kind of snack you could think of. Family members were there that Eagle had never seen before.

"I see you really must like this girl," Aunt Debby said as she ran dish water.

"Aw, Auntie, I love this girl. She's my baby." Eagle blushed, looking back at Niya sitting in the living room, laughing with his cousin. "When I was young, I don't remember my mom and my dad being in love like that."

"Your mom and dad was a relationship made of need. They both were there when the other was in need of someone. Although, over time, your mom became crazy about ya father. They were like the Bonnie and Clyde of the neighborhood."

"Oh, Ms. Debby, I got the dishes. You've done enough already," Niya said, coming into the kitchen and rolling up her sleeves.

"Little girl, please. I can do my own dishes. Now, if you wanna help, that's a different story."

Niya didn't know it, but Eagle was well aware that his aunt wanted to have a woman-to-woman talk with Niya. Aunt Debby knew Niya but never really got a chance to sit down and talk to her. Although it had been nearly ten years since Aunt Debby had seen Eagle, she was still a little overprotective of her favorite nephew.

"I'll let you two talk," Eagle said, excusing himself from the kitchen.

When he did that, Niya finally peeped the blitz and realized what Aunt Debby was up to. It was too late for her to do anything other than stay there and take the third degree. She looked at Eagle and balled her fist up, playfully punching both of her eyes to let him know they were going to fight later. Eagle smiled and walked off, knowing Aunt Debby was about to be the only person throwing the punches.

"What's done is done. We can't go back and change it," Lasan explained to Katah.

"He's my nephew, and retribution is in order," Katah replied, banging his fist on the table.

Sana, Katah, and Lasan had been discussing the events that took place with Contez. It was only two months ago the elders had gotten the word that Contez was dealing in illegal activities under the African banner, and without paying taxes to the elders. That was his first violation. His second and most concerning violation came when he decided to sell rare diamonds straight from the motherland.

Diamonds from Sierra Leone were considered to be a delicacy among the elders, and if anybody should get first dibs on the stones, it should have been them, instead of the elders' worst enemy, the white man. They tried to summon Contez in an attempt to purchase the diamonds, but he refused and declined to entertain them. Contez was the rebellious type and didn't care much about the elders and what they stood for. His lack of respect for them was what ultimately cost him his life.

"Katah, we understand how you feel, brother, but if you seek retribution now, everything we have done thus far will have been in vain. Let us get the diamonds back and then you'll get your retribution," Lasan pleaded.

Not wanting his nephew's death to be for no reason, Katah agreed to the elders' request. Once they got what they wanted, he could do as he pleased.

After the BBQ, Niya went to pick up Jade so they could talk about some news that had been circulating on the streets. As soon as Jade got in the car, she began informing Niya of the situation and how there were some older Africans trying to purchase some recently stolen diamonds. They had made it quite clear that there would be no questions asked about how the stones were received; they just wanted them and were willing to pay top dollar. Jade had gotten the phone number of one of the top dogs, and she passed it over to Niya. Niya didn't trust the Africans for anything, but she also knew that Contez was acting on his own. Being a boss herself, she understood how the death of soldiers was looked at when they were acting for their own selfish reasons. Niya also understood that no team could just let someone take from one of them without some type of recourse, even if it wasn't direct.

"Hold on. I'll be right back," Niya said, pulling over on Fifty-second and Baltimore Avenue to use the payphone.

She got out of the car and darted across the busy street, placing her arms across her chest to stop her breasts from bouncing everywhere. She looked around and wondered why the people at the trolley stop and the people standing in front of the deli were staring at her. Then she turned around and remembered that she was driving a $100,000 luxury car.

"I gotta get rid of that car," she mumbled to herself, dialing the numbers.

After a couple of rings, an African with a deep accent picked up. He told Niya to stay by the phone then hung up, only to call her right back from a payphone himself.

"I hear you guys looking for some ice for your drink, is that correct?" Niya asked.

"Yes, we are, but the ice must be very cold and made from the best water on earth," the man responded.

"Well, this water is from the motherland and is as pure as you can find," Niya said. The gentleman on the other end explained to Niya that he was indeed interested, but that he would need to talk it over with his family first.

"You got forty-eight hours. After that, the diamonds are off the market." Niya then hung up the phone in the man's ear.

Niya was becoming very impatient and frustrated. She was far from broke, but having an extra million and a half in cash lying around wouldn't be a bad thing. The diamonds were said to be worth two million dollars, but to get them sold faster, Niya was willing to let them go for a half million less; that was, if the Africans weren't playing around. They had forty-eight hours to come up with the money, and if they couldn't, Niya was going to just add the stones to her own personal diamond collection.

Jedi stood on his back porch with only a pair of sweatpants on, looking up at the moon and the stars, hoping he could get some type of sign. It was eating at him that he couldn't put the pieces of the puzzle together. He couldn't stop thinking that Contez was rolling over in his grave in disappointment.

"What are you out here thinking about?" Audria said, walking out to the back porch and wrapping her arms around his waist.

"I'm just trying to make sense of all this shit. I know I'm on the right track. It's just . . . it's just . . ."

"Come on, babe, don't stress yourself out. You'll put it together. I'm sure of it."

Jedi was sure of it too. He just needed a little more to work with. Once that happened, everything else would fall like dominos.

"Now I need you to do me a favor," Audria said, kissing the center of his back.

"And what's that, Bun-Bun?" He smiled, already knowing what she was up to.

"I need you to come in this house and beat dis pussy. You been gone for three years, seven months, and six days. Mama need you to eat dis pudding box," she said, grabbing Jedi by his hand and pulling him into the house with a seductive look on her face.

Jedi wasn't really in the mood for sex, but he knew beyond a shadow of a doubt Audria wasn't going to go another day without getting some dick. He could understand how she felt, and for that reason alone, tonight, and only tonight, Jedi was going to focus on something else besides Contez's killer. Tonight it was all about Audria.

Chapter 23

Club Lust was turned up to the max tonight. Just about everybody who was somebody came out to party.

MHB still held down VIP, doing it big as they always did. It was Gwen's idea for the girls to go out that night due to all the drama they'd had that week. She and Diamond were looking forward to heading out to Philly to visit Niya on Saturday, but it was time to unwind, so bottle after bottle was brought to their VIP section. MHB even sent bottles to other VIP tables to show that they still had it.

"Heads up!" Diamond leaned over and warned Gwen, who had a bottle of Ace tilted to her mouth.

She looked over and saw about five men walking into the VIP section. Nose, Kid, and a couple more niggas from his crew walked right into the MHB section. Diamond's hand went straight in her bag, and so did Kea's. Alexus clutched the bottle of Champagne tightly in her hand, just in case she had to start swinging it.

"I see y'all broads still got money," Nose yelled over the music, while everyone looked at him like he was crazy.

"Did you get my message?" he said, looking at Gwen. "I said y'all can't collect . . ."

"Yeah, I heard something like that. I'm still reviewing it and taking it under consideration," Gwen yelled back.

"Well, consider this: Y'all bitches can't collect shit from any hood. This whole city is mine now," Nose yelled back with a serious look on his face.

Gwen laughed while Diamond clutched the 9 mm in her bag a little bit tighter.

"I don't think you wanna push too hard. Shit can still get dark for you," Gwen replied, looking toward the dance floor behind him.

When Nose turned around, just about every female that was out on the dance floor had stopped dancing and was looking at him and his boys. The music even got lower, courtesy of the female DJ, who was also an MHB member. Nose looked back at Gwen, who had a smile on her face.

"We still here, and we still go hard," she told him.

Nose didn't see that coming, and at the same time, he didn't want to look like a sucker. He managed to crack a smile then saluted Gwen before he turned around and walked out of the VIP section with his boys. Now Gwen saw exactly what Diamond was talking about.

"Meeting at my house tomorrow," Gwen leaned over and told Diamond, then went right back to her bottle.

Monster had a trap house on Eighth and Norris Street, where he did most of his dirt. It wasn't Richard Island, but he still had some goons in the vicinity, in case things got crazy. Winter was his little stepsister, but when it came down to the street life, Biggie Smalls said it the best: "Keep ya family and business completely separated."

Niya didn't want to draw any negative attention to herself, pulling up in an Aston Martin, so she opted to ride shotgun in Winter's car, a blue 2007 Buick Park Avenue. Jade and Monica drove behind them in Jade's white Dodge Charger. Since this was her first deal in the city, Niya wanted to make sure her presence was known. It needed to be established that she wasn't to be messed with.

"Call ya brother and tell him we're pulling up now," Niya told Winter as she crossed Broad and Norris.

As soon as Niya got to the block, she noticed a few cats scattered about throughout the street. They looked as though they were trying to be unnoticed, but Niya was on point. "I know this is my brother, but I don't fuck wit' these grimy niggas around here," Winter said, pulling the black .45 from under the passenger's seat. Niya grabbed her gun from the center console, checking to make sure that the safety was on. Both of them got out of the car, along with Jade and Monica. Everybody knew their role, so as Niya and Winter walked toward the house, Jade and Monica stood by the cars with guns in their hands. They had orders to shoot anything moving if things got out of hand.

"Damn, li'l sis. You coming heavy," Monster said when he opened the door and saw that she had a gun in her hand.

"Come on. Let's get on with it." Niya rushed, wanting to get straight down to business.

Monster stood to the side and let Niya and Winter inside. Though the house appeared to be empty, it wasn't. Niya didn't waste time digging into her Coach bag and pulling out a kilo. She tossed it onto the glass table sitting in the middle of the living room.

"Damn, sis, you weren't playin'," Monster said, looking down at the coke. "That's crazy, 'cause I thought you was bullshittin'," he said, pulling a large, chrome automatic from his waist.

The deal had gone sour in a matter of seconds, and in even less time, one of Monster's boys came out of the kitchen with a 12-gauge pump in his hand. All Niya could think about was Eagle warning her of how niggas would kill her out here in these streets. She just shook her head and looked over at Monster.

"What da fuck is you doin', Monster?" Winter sounded, taking the safety off of her gun and pointing it at him.

When Monster turned to look at Winter, Niya dropped her bag and reached for the gun in her back pocket. By the time the man with the shotgun raised it to shoot, Niya was in the process of letting bullets fly.

Pop! Pop! Pop! Pop!

Before Monster could get a shot off at Niya, Winter closed her eyes and squeezed. The bullets tore through his back, but Monster didn't feel a thing. However, his body went limp from the waist down. He fell to the ground but was determined to get a shot off. Niya was only a few feet away from him, and as soon as he was about to pull the trigger, Winter kicked his arm.

Pop!

He got the shot off, but it didn't hit anybody. Winter kept stomping Monster's arm until he let the gun go. Niya wanted to kill him, but when she spun around to hit him, multiple shotgun blasts rang out from the dining room. Niya and Winter had to return fire if they planned on making it out of the house.

"Go! Go! Go!" Winter yelled, pushing Niya out the door while she continued to shoot at the dining room.

"Keep ya head down!" Jedi yelled out to Codi, trying to avoid being hit by a stray bullet that could have easily come crashing through his car window.

Jedi had no idea that he was about to be driving right into a shootout. He almost crashed his car, swerving out of the way. His car sat smack dab in the middle of Jade and Monica firing down on two of Monster's boys, who were across the street. After both parties heard shots being fired in the house, they began shooting it out with each other. Jade and Monica stood their ground the whole time.

"Get us out of here, Jedi," Codi whined.

It made Jedi mad, thinking that was the same coward attitude that got his brother killed. It was a break in the gunfire that gave Jedi the opportunity to make his move and get the hell out of there. When he picked his head up, Jedi could see two women running across the street. Codi could see the women also, and for a second he thought he was seeing things.

Niya stopped at the driver's side door, spun around, and fired several more shots at the front door of the house to make sure nobody would try to come out and shoot her while she was pulling off. Codi could see her clear as day and became so excited that his words could hardly come out.

"Dat's her. . . . That's her right there!" Codi yelled out.

"What are you talkin' about?" Jedi inquired.

"That's the girl from the garage," he yelled.

Jedi looked over as Niya was getting in the car. He grabbed his .40-caliber from under the seat then exited the vehicle. Police sirens blared in the near distance, but Jedi didn't care. As Niya was pulling off, he let off several rounds in her direction. The bullets crashed through the back window and knocked out a taillight.

He started to fire again, but Jade pulled out of the parking space right behind Niya, blocking Jedi's view. He shot at Jade's car just because, blowing out her back window.

"Fuck!" he yelled, running back to his car.

He took off down the street behind the two cars but didn't get far before noticing one of his tires was flat, probably shot during the shootout. He simply watched as the two cars got smaller and smaller, and once they had finally vanished into the night, Jedi realized he might have missed his chance.

Eagle sat at the kitchen table, putting bills through the money machine, tallying up everything he and Niya had made that month off the gun sales. He had plans on moving back down South, just not North Carolina for the time being, so he wanted to make sure that his money was right before he made the move. In the midst of him writing down some numbers on his notepad, Eagle's phone started ringing. The number that popped up was unfamiliar to him, but he answered it anyway.

"Yo, E, I need you to come get me, bro," Jedi said as he leaned up against the phone booth.

"Damn, homie, where you at?"

"I'm on Broad and Girard, bro. Da police is out here real heavy, and I'm dirty," Jedi said, looking over at Codi standing on the corner.

"You by yourself?" Eagle asked, not really sure if he could trust him.

Jedi looked over at Codi again. "Yeah, bro, I'm by myself," he answered. "Just come and get me, bro. I need you."

"A'ight, fam, I'm on my way."

Jedi hung up the phone then walked over to Codi. The cool night breeze made it a little chilly out, and now that Codi's adrenaline had subsided, he was starting to feel cold.

"Come on and walk with me," Jedi told him.

It was late at night, and there weren't many people out on the streets, but Jedi wanted to get off Broad Street anyhow, especially since he still had his gun on him.

"Are you okay?" Jedi asked, seeing that Codi was a little shook up. "It's almost over. Just hang in there."

Codi kept his head lowered but continued walking in shame. "I know I never told you this, but I'm sorry about what happened to Contez. It all happened so fast, and when I heard the shots, I panicked. When I saw his body on the ground . . . man, I just ran," Codi said, shaking his head. Jedi just listened to him explain his side and why he did what he did. It sounded pathetic, and Jedi was done listening to him speak.

"Remember when I told you it was almost over?" Jedi said, stopping so that he could face Codi.

Codi picked his head up and looked around. He saw nothing but darkness, no streetlights, no cars driving by, and not a sign of human life for blocks. When he looked up at Jedi and saw the gun in his hand and the empty stare he was giving him, Codi knew that this was going to be his final resting place.

"I'm sorry," Codi said, dropping to his knees. "Do what you have to do."

Jedi pressed the .40-caliber up against his head and felt nothing when he pulled the trigger. *Pop!* The bullet entered deep into his skull, killing Codi instantly. Jedi took the gun, wiped it down with his T-shirt, then tossed the gun next to Codi's dead body before walking off back toward Broad Street.

Chapter 24

"Can you just tell me his condition?" Winter spoke into the phone.

The nurse at the front desk did not want to give that type of information out over the phone. For security purposes, nurses were forbidden to give a patient's status, even if the person requesting was his family.

"They're not telling me shit," Winter said, walking back into the room with Niya and Jade.

Everybody was still trying to process everything that had happened that night. Surprisingly, Niya wasn't even mad at Winter for what her brother did. In fact, she was even more surprised that Winter shot her own brother for her. If the shoe was on the other foot, Niya didn't know what she would have done. All in all, she appreciated what Winter had done.

"So now what are we gonna do?" Jade asked, curious as to whether they were going to continue trying to move the cocaine.

"Oh, don't get it fucked up. That robbery shit comes with the game," Niya said, getting up off the couch. "We down a brick, but niggas is gonna know not to fuck with us."

"Yeah, I'm sure the word is out there by now," Winter added. "I'ma go visit my brother later on and try to dead this situation."

"Well, we're gonna chill for a couple of days and let it cool down a li'l bit. It's the weekend, so I think we should hit the mall, do some shopping, and go out tonight," Niya suggested. "We can get right back to the grind on Monday."

Niya was interrupted by her phone vibrating on the table. It was Diamond, so she excused herself and answered it. "Hey, bitch," she greeted, walking off into the next room.

"I see you don't know how to call anybody," Diamond said, looking at Dollaz, cooking on the grill in the backyard.

"I'm sorry, girl. I've been so busy out here. I thought y'all were bringing the twins down this weekend anyway."

"Yeah, we was, but something came up. I can't get into the details, but we working on getting you home. I missed da hell out of you, sis," Diamond confessed. "I need you out here with me."

"I know, D," Niya said as she started to tear up.

Niya missed everybody back home, and there had been many sleepless nights when she felt like saying to hell with it and going back. The thought of losing so many of her sisters in a senseless war was the only thing that kept her from doing so.

"Don't worry, D. Everything's going to work out for the best. You just make sure you stay out of trouble and let everybody know that I miss them and love them so much."

Niya had to end the call on that note. Too many feelings were starting to come back at once. The more Niya talked about Charlotte, the more she wanted to go back home. Right now, Philly was her home, and until things changed down South, she had to make the best out of it and keep Charlotte in her rearview.

Jedi walked into Shakira's and went straight to the back. The elders weren't expecting him, but Jedi didn't care. He was about to go on a warpath and, out of respect for his people, he wanted to get the elders' permission to move out. Jedi didn't even knock on the door. He just walked right in, catching everybody off guard.

"You wrong, Jedi," Ojay said, grabbing him by the arm to pull him back out of the room.

He didn't even notice what Jedi had done until it was too late. "Ojay, let me go," Jedi demanded, looking down at the firm grip Ojay had on him.

Jedi's uncle looked at him then waved off Ojay. Since there were three out of the four elders there, they were able to deal with the situation if it needed to come down to a vote. Jedi's rude entrance would be dealt with on a later date.

"Look, I know y'all told me to stay out of it, but I believe I found the people responsible for my brother's death," Jedi spoke.

He explained everything that had transpired the night before, and how Niya had gotten away before he could kill her. The elders didn't take too kindly to Jedi not doing what they told him to do, but they continued to listen to him anyway, hoping to gather information from him.

"And what is it that you want from us, nephew?" his uncle asked after hearing everything.

"In order for me to find this female and whoever her companions were, I need to put in some work. Out of respect for you and my family, I'm asking for your permission to do what needs to be done."

The elders became silent. They didn't even have to have a conversation amongst themselves to come up with the answer. Jedi's uncle spoke for all.

"As we told you before, Jedi, we want you to stay out of this. The elders will handle it; I assure you of that. You have provided more than enough information for us to bring this to closure."

"You can't be serious," Jedi responded, displeased with the order.

"Any further actions taken by you concerning your brother will not end well for you, son," Jedi's uncle warned. "Do I make myself clear?"

Frustrated and wanting to get as far away from the elders as he could, Jedi agreed with a simple nod of the head. He turned and was on his way out of the door when Mansini, one of the elders, called out Jedi's name.

"*Ma turi,* Codi?" he asked in Mandingo.

The nerve of him inquiring about the coward that ran out on my brother, Jedi thought, making him even angrier and more determined to go hard.

"I'm sure y'all will find out," Jedi said then walked out of the room.

Niya and Jade were on their way out of the door when Eagle's car pulled into the driveway. There hadn't been much conversation between the two ever since Eagle confronted her about the table full of cocaine he walked in on. Niya hated that they weren't communicating and wished that Eagle could truly understand what she was going through. Coming to Philly was his idea, and now all Niya was trying to do was reinvent herself.

"I'ma wait in the car," Jade said, giving them a little space.

"Are you going to be home for dinner?" Niya asked, making small talk.

Eagle stopped and took a seat on the hood of her car. He missed Niya, and not the one who was standing in front of him. He missed the old Niya.

"Can I ask you something?" Eagle asked, looking Niya in her eyes. "Do you still love me?" he asked with a confused look on his face.

From the way things were, he was starting to think that the love was gone. The question hit Niya so hard she had to sit down herself.

"Do you really have to ask me that question?" Niya responded. "Have I really been that much of a bitch that you would feel like I don't love you?"

Eagle just put his head down.

"Besides my kids, I love you more than anything else in this world. Look at me, Eagle," Niya said, getting up and standing in front of him. "I never want you to feel like this. Just tell me what to do and I'll do it, babe."

"I need you to leave this coke game alone while we're in Philly," Eagle requested.

Niya let out a sigh but then caught herself.

"All right, babe. Can we make a deal? I got about twenty-five more bricks to move. You let me get rid of it and I'll do anything. We can move, we can get married, have a baby, and I'll just fall back and let you take care of me until we get old," Niya proposed. "You can even help me move the coke to speed up the process." She smiled.

Niya knew what she was doing. She made him an offer he couldn't refuse, and with marriage and a baby on the table, Eagle didn't even have to think about his answer. He agreed and made her pinky swear on it, which she did with no problem. The next question Eagle asked was the most important.

"Where's the coke?"

"Get da fuck out of my room," Monster growled through clenched teeth.

He had a look on his face that could kill. The bullet had hit him in his spine, paralyzing him from the waist down. He couldn't believe his own sister had shot him, over a brick, no less. Winter felt bad, but it was Monster's fucked-up decision that had him lying up in a hospital bed with no feeling in his legs. What Monster had failed to realize was that it could have been worse. He could have easily been killed by Niya, who intended on doing just that, had it not been for Winter rushing her out the door.

"I'll let your mother know where you're at," Winter told him then walked out of the room.

"Fuck you, Winter! Fuck you!" he yelled as he watched her leave.

Winter could hear him screaming the whole time she walked down the hallway. She wanted to get as far away as she could, knowing Monster had unwanted authorities lingering around, waiting for a statement. She didn't want them trying to ask her any questions.

"Yo, I'm leaving the hospital now," Winter spoke into the phone to Niya. "He can't feel his legs, but he's still alive," she told her.

She stood in the hallway waiting for the elevator. She was so caught up in her conversation with Niya she didn't pay any attention to Jedi, who had walked up and was waiting too. Jedi had a memory like an elephant, and after seeing Winter run across the street with Niya during the shootout, he would never forget her face, nor Niya's. He was at the hospital hoping to question Monster about the AK-47s, but then he saw Winter, which was even better.

They got onto the elevator and Winter still didn't know who he was. She had no idea what was about to happen to her, but Jedi knew, and as soon as the opportunity presented itself, he was going to make the best of it.

Chapter 25

Alexus sat at the desk looking for some paperwork Gwen had asked her to drop off at the notary the following morning. When the office phone began to ring, she threw back her head and let out a loud sigh. She wanted to get out of there, and more than likely that phone call was going to prevent her from doing so. After a while, it stopped ringing, but then her cell went off.

"Damn!" she said, reaching over and grabbing her phone. "Yes, Gwen," she answered, seeing who it was.

"Damn, bitch. Watch ya tone when you answer this phone," Gwen joked. "I was just making sure you didn't forget to pick up them contracts for the notary."

"Yeah, I'm here. Now, where exactly are they?" Alexus asked, leaning back in her chair.

"I figured you had forgot. I told you they was in the file cabinet in the unsigned contract folder." Gwen giggled.

"Don't get smart." Alexus laughed back. "What are you and Terrence up to anyway? It sounds like the kids are asleep. Hold on!" Alexus noticed a car coming up the dirt road, so she got up to see who it was. Gwen could be heard yelling on the other end of the phone at Terrence to stop playing. He was tickling her and wanted her to get off the phone so they could take advantage of the free time.

"I wonder what these niggas want," Alexus said, seeing that it was Nose's car. "There's two of them," she told Gwen.

Gwen could hear a little concern in Alexus's voice, which made her worry. "Lex, you good?" Gwen asked, getting up from the bed.

"Yeah, they don't want shit. Hold on for a second."

Alexus locked the door then walked back over to her desk to retrieve the gun that she had in her pocketbook. It wasn't there, and she remembered she had placed it in the center console of her car. She hurried over to Gwen's desk to retrieve the key for the gun box that sat underneath. As she was placing the key in the drawer to unlock it, Nose kicked in the door. It almost came off the hinges from the force he used.

"Whoa, whoa, shawty. Come up from there," he said, pointing his gun at Alexus.

"You got some balls coming up in here like this," she snapped.

"Yeah, I know. That's what they tell me. But anyway, I'm here on the account that ya people came through this morning collecting. I don't know if you remembered the conversation me and your boss had at the club, but let me reiterate it for you. Y'all bitches are finished in Charlotte," he snapped.

"I don't remember that, but I do remember her asking you if you were sure you wanna go down this road, nigga," Alexus threatened.

Nose was no longer impressed with these ladies' words. In fact, he was fed up with MHB and didn't think they should have the power they had or the influence over the streets the way that they did. He was at the end of his rope, and it was time to send a message.

"Yeah, I'm sure," he said, raising the gun up and pointing it at her face.

Alexus looked into his eyes to show that she wasn't afraid to die. She knew for sure that he wasn't stupid enough to pull the trigger, knowing the repercussions behind it.

"Squeeze!" Alexus yelled, taunting him.

Pop!

The bullet hit her in the center of her forehead, knocking Alexus out of the chair. He walked over and stood over top of her body and let it go.

Pop! Pop! Pop! Pop! Pop! Pop! Pop!

"A'ight, no need to cry now. You weren't crying the other night when you and ya girlfriend were shootin' shit up like some wild cowboys," Jedi said, waving his gun in Winter's face. "Now I'ma ask you again: Where does she live?"

"I swear I don't know where she live. Don't nobody know where she lives," Winter lied.

She was trying to stay alive, but at the same time, she was willing to die before she told Jedi where Niya, or anybody else in her crew, lived. Even if she did, Winter knew that as soon as she told him what he wanted to know, he was going to blow her head off anyway.

"I admire the fact that you don't wanna give up ya girl, and in another life, I probably would have tried to wife you . . . but listen to me," Jedi said, grabbing her by the cheek and turning her face toward his. "If you don't tell me where I can find your friend, I'm going to kill you. Not the easy way either. I'm going to do so many horrible things to you that it's gonna make you wanna kill yourself," Jedi threatened, smacking the side of her cheek.

His demeanor was calm, and looking into Jedi's eyes, she knew that what he had in store for her was going to be vicious. All she could think about was him beating and raping her until she was dead. Winter didn't mind dying, but she didn't want to go out like that. She had to think about it for a minute.

"I don't know where she lives, but I can take you to the place where we be chillin' at," she offered.

Jedi walked over and grabbed her bag off of the floor. He rambled through it until he came across her phone, and then he passed it to her. "Call her," he demanded, looking down at Winter.

She looked at Jedi like he was crazy. She wasn't that stupid. "I'll call when you get me out of this house. We take my car, you can lay me down in the back seat and I'll show you where she's at. After you do what you do, you leave me alone. Deal?" Winter asked.

Jedi looked at her then tapped her forehead with the gun. "Deal," he responded.

"No, no," Winter shot back, not feeling comfortable with the response time on his answer. "You a Muslim, right?" she said, noticing the prostration mark on his forehead.

Jedi nodded his head, acknowledging his religion.

"I want you to swear by Allah that you're going to let me go," Winter told him.

Winter knew a little bit about the religion of Islam, and she knew that for somebody like Jedi, who prayed as hard as his forehead showed, the last person he wanted to play with was Allah. Having him swear by his Lord was Winter's only chance.

"I swear by Allah that I'm going to let you go. . . . Now get up," Jedi said, grabbing Winter by her arm and heading for the door.

Gwen sat on the bed frozen after hearing everything that had just transpired at the trailer. Alexus had put her on hold and never hung up, so Gwen heard everything, even the fatal shots that ended Alexus's life. She was sick. It was if all her energy had been drained from her, and the only things left were the tears that continued falling down her face. This was by far the closest loss to losing

Zion that Gwen had ever experienced, and it wasted no time eating at her, something she couldn't afford right now.

As hard as it was, Gwen needed to pull it together. This was like an act of terrorism on MHB soil, and since she was the second in command, she needed to get the troops together, because Nose had surely just declared war. There was no negotiating, no waving the white flag or nothing of the sort. One or two things were going to happen, and that was either MHB was going to kill everybody in Nose's crew, or his crew was going to kill every member of MHB. No matter how things turned out, the beef was definitely on now.

"Gwen, babe, what happened?" Terrence was unsure what had changed her mood so quickly. Gwen hadn't even noticed him going into the bathroom and now returning. He lay beside her and began wiping the tears from her face. He could tell that something bad had happened.

"I need you to watch the kids. I have to—"

Gwen couldn't even get it out without her throat knotting up. She just shook her head, grabbed her keys and cell phone off the table, and was trying to walk out the door. Her legs were trembling so hard and the tears were coming down her face like raindrops now.

Jedi pulled up and parked on Woodland Avenue right across the street from the African restaurant. Winter was lying down in the back seat with her hands zip-tied to the front of her. "Sit up and make the call," Jedi said, tossing Winter's cell phone back to her.

She took a good look around, scoping the area before she made the call. Instead of calling Niya's phone, Winter called Jade, who picked up almost immediately.

"Damn, bitch, where you at?" Jade sounded off.

"Girl, you know me. I got my son with me right now, so you know I'm tied up."

"Oh, you got ya son wit' you. Is he being good or bad?" Jade asked, stopping in midstride as she and Niya were walking back toward her car.

"Yeah, you know he always be acting up after spending some time with his daddy. I need you to come pick us up. My car broke down on the Avenue by Fifty-fourth Street," Winter said. "And bring some diapers. I think he needs to be changed."

"A'ight, I'll be there in a few minutes," Jade told her then hung up the phone.

Jedi reached back and grabbed the phone from Winter then made her lay back down in the back seat, right where she wanted to be when everything hit the fan.

"Yo, we got a problem. Winter is in some kind of trouble," Jade looked over and told Niya as they were about to get in the car.

Winter and Jade had known each other since they were kids, and growing up, they developed their own code words and phrases to communicate both a good and bad situation. Jade knew it was a problem when Winter started talking about her son. Winter didn't even have kids. Jade basically translated the rest of the conversation to mean that Winter had a nigga in her car that she didn't want there. Asking Jade to bring the diapers actually meant bringing guns, and if guns needed to be brought, then it really must have been a problem.

Gwen didn't call the police right away. She didn't want them to be the first to see Alexus's body. Instead, she called Porsha, Rose, and Kea, all who met up at the trailers around the same time. Alexus's body belonged to MHB, and that was who would see her first.

"Where is she?" Rose asked, walking up to Gwen, who was still standing outside of the trailers when everybody pulled up. Porsha and Kea pulled up, jumped out, and ran up to Gwen. They all looked to her with pain in their eyes.

"I didn't go inside yet, but I know she's in there," Gwen said, putting her head down. "I just couldn't bring myself to . . ."

She couldn't hold back the tears. Knowing how she felt, nobody wanted to go inside. They all sat there for a minute or two before Rose volunteered to go in. Alexus was like everybody's little sister, and Rose was no different. She wiped the tears from her eyes, walked up the wooden steps, and opened the door. She wasn't in there for two seconds before her loud cries pierced everyone's ears.

"Nooooo, nooooo, oh God, noooo," Rose cried out.

Everybody outside began crying even harder. Kea turned around and vomited all over the side of the building, while Porsha had to walk off. Gwen got up enough strength to walk up the steps and enter the trailer. She looked down at Alexus's bullet-riddled body and fell to her knees, covering her mouth to muffle her cries. It was one thing hearing it happen over the phone, but to actually see her sister lying there in a puddle of blood was the most horrific thing she'd ever seen in her life, and the image would forever be ingrained in her mind.

"Are you sure this is where she's at?" Niya asked pulling up on Woodland Avenue, a block away from the African restaurant.

"Yeah, there goes Winter's car right there." Jade pointed down the street.

"A'ight, y'all two stay put. I'ma go check it out," Eagle said, cocking a bullet into the chamber of his Desert Eagle.

He got out of the car, tucked the gun in his waist, and then proceeded down the street. Eagle didn't want to just walk right up on the car not knowing what to expect, or who was in the car, for that matter. The windows were tinted so he couldn't see anything. Going into the restaurant was his best option, and from there, he would wait until something happened before he did anything.

Winter convinced Jedi to allow her to get on the floor in case bullets started flying and she accidentally got shot sitting in the back seat. Winter was at an angle lying on that floor. She tried so desperately to reach her gun, which sat snug under the driver's seat. Her arm reach was off by a couple of inches, and she was afraid that if she made too much movement back there, Jedi would become suspicious. Little did she know, Jedi's mind was somewhere else.

"Nigga, what you doin' down here?" Jedi mumbled to himself, seeing Eagle go into the restaurant.

He looked down the street to see where Eagle had come from, but there was too much traffic to tell.

"Fuck it. Are you ready?" Niya asked, cocking her gun back slightly to make sure she had a bullet in the chamber.

"Yeah, I'm ready," Jade responded, pulling a .45 from her bag and taking the safety off.

They both exited the vehicle and started walking down the street. Jade walked on the same side of the road as Winter's car, while Niya walked on the other side by the restaurant. Though their weapons were concealed under their shirts, they were easily accessible for gunplay.

The closer Jade got to Winter's car, the faster her heart beat. She stopped about four cars away and waited for Niya to move. Eagle walked out of the restaurant when he saw Jade getting in position.

"We can't just run down on the car, 'cause we don't know if Winter is inside or not," Niya said, walking up to Eagle.

"We really don't have a choice. As soon as this cop car drive by, we movin'," Eagle instructed.

"What the fuck?" Jedi said, seeing Niya and Eagle standing together talking.

It made sense to him immediately. The elders, along with Codi, told him that it was a man and woman together who murdered Contez. With Eagle standing there talking to Niya, Jedi realized that he had his two culprits.

"You gon' die too," Jedi said, grabbing the AK-47 off the passenger's seat.

When the cop car drove by then turned down Fifty-fourth Street, Niya, and Eagle started walking across the street toward Winter's car. Jedi got out of the car with the large assault rifle, and without hesitation, without any questions being asked, opened fire on Eagle and Niya.

"Oh, shit!" Eagle yelled, pulling Niya behind a parked car.

Pop! Pop! Pop! Pop! Pop! Pop! Pop! Pop! Pop! Pop!

The large projectiles ripped into the car they had ducked behind with ease. Shattered glass fell over the tops of their heads as the loud roar of the fully automatic weapon sounded throughout the street. Jade had a clear shot at Jedi but froze when he began shooting. Just hearing the AK-47 had her shook to the point where she, too, got down behind a parked car. She could hear people screaming and running past her in an attempt to get out of the way.

"Come on!" Winter yelled out, stretching her arms as far as she could, finally grabbing a hold of her gun under the seat.

Jedi was shooting in short bursts, walking down on the car Eagle and Niya were behind. Winter lifted her head up in the back seat to see where Jedi was. He was about fifteen yards out, with his back turned toward her. With her hands still zip-tied in front of her, Winter emerged from the car and fired her weapon.

Pop! Pop! Pop!

She didn't hit Jedi with any of the rounds, but it definitely got his attention. He spun around and let it go, sending multiple bullets Winter's way, causing her to get low.

"Stay down!" Eagle yelled out to Niya then jumped up from behind the car.

He had a clear shot with his weapon. He looked to his right and saw a cop car racing down the street. Jedi spun around and let the cop car have it too, bringing the car to a screeching halt. The two officers rolled out of the car and took cover, being no match for the heavily armed Jedi.

Jedi opened fire on everything moving, and while everyone took cover and tried to stay out of the line of fire, the thundering sound of the AK-47 went mute.

Everyone was hesitant to rise from their respective places of cover, but it was the screams of an innocent bystander that made the two officers come from behind their cruiser, guns aimed and ready to be discharged. Thinking that they were about to engage in a gun battle, the cops, and just about everybody else, were relieved that Jedi was gone. It was like he had just vanished into thin air, and the only thing left was the AK-47 lying in the middle of the street.

Chapter 26

Terrence walked into the bedroom and couldn't see anything. Despite it being one o'clock in the afternoon, Gwen had the whole room blacked out, while she lay still but awake in their bed.

"Babe, you gotta get up," Terrence said, walking over and pulling apart the blinds.

The sunshine lit up the room, and its brightness caused Gwen to duck her head under the covers.

"Porsha and Kea are downstairs waiting, so you gotta get up," he spoke, taking a seat on the bed right next to her.

Gwen was sick about Alexus's death, especially since she was the one who sent her to retrieve the paperwork from the office. She felt like she was always the cause of someone's death, even when she was trying to do the right thing as far as the new direction she was moving MHB in. All she wanted to do was lie in the bed with her thoughts and not be bothered.

"Gwen, I understand what you're going through, but lying in the bed ain't gonna help. You're a leader, and you got a bunch of females waiting for you to lead them."

Gwen came up from under the covers and slowly sat up on the bed. Her face had a depressed look, and the dried tears, along with the bags under her eyes, made it obvious she had been up all night crying.

"She's dead because of me," Gwen said, shaking her head. "That was supposed to be me. They thought that I was going to be at the office," Gwen said, wiping the tear that began falling down her face.

This was the first time Terrence had seen Gwen this upset, and as bad as he wanted to try to convince her that this wasn't her fault, he knew that now wasn't the right time.

"Gwen, you gotta get out of that bed, girl," Kea announced as her and Porsha walked into the bedroom.

"Yeah, G, we ain't got time for this," Porsha added, heading for the bathroom.

Terrence leaned in and kissed Gwen then got up and excused himself so they could talk. He didn't like to get involved with MHB business, and he wasn't going to start now.

"Did you call Niya yet?" Kea asked, taking a seat next to Gwen on the bed.

"No, not yet. I know once I call her, all hell is about to break loose."

Porsha walked out of the bathroom, drying water from her hands. "I think it's a little too late for that," Porsha said, flopping down on the bed.

Gwen looked at Kea and then back over at Porsha with a curious look on her face. "What makes you say that?" she asked, seeing that something was up with the two of them.

It wasn't Porsha or Kea that Gwen needed to be worried about. Diamond was the one who had been missing in action ever since yesterday. Nobody could seem to get in touch with her, not even Dollaz. Kea and Porsha both felt like Diamond was out for blood, and if that were true, there wasn't anything or anybody that could stop her.

Once Kea explained the situation to Gwen, she knew that it was time to get out of bed and get a hold on the situation before it got any uglier.

***

"We're not packing big bags. Just get all the important documents and one or two changes of clothes," Eagle instructed Niya while he cleaned out the safe.

"I don't understand, Eagle. Why do we have to leave?" Niya asked, walking across the bedroom.

If they stayed in Philly, they were as good as dead. Now that Jedi knew that Eagle was responsible for Contez's death, he wasn't going to stop until Eagle and Niya took the same dirt nap as his brother had. Knowing Jedi for as long as he did and witnessing what he was capable of doing, Eagle made the cautious decision to leave the city, rather than staying and going to war with the Africans.

"And where da hell are we going now?" Niya asked with an attitude. "I'm tired of running away every time a li'l drama goes on."

Eagle looked over his shoulder at Niya, who was standing right behind him. He grabbed the rest of the contents inside of the safe then turned around to face Niya. He'd pretty much had enough of her mouth, "You said you're tired of running, right?" Eagle looked down to her and spoke angrily. "How about you stop doing dumb shit and then we won't have to blow every city we move to?"

"Oh, so this is my fault? You blaming me for all of this?" Niya snapped.

Eagle reached into the little black bag he had and pulled out the diamonds Niya had taken from Contez. Niya looked at them before he balled them up into his hand.

"If you weren't so fucking worried about these dumbass diamonds, we wouldn't have to leave the city!" Eagle yelled, throwing the diamonds across the room.

Niya's reaction was that of a dog whose master just threw a tennis ball in a game of fetch. Eagle shook his head, watching as she scurried over and began picking up the diamonds.

"Look at you," he said, walking over to her. "You look pathetic," he spoke, looking down on her.

It was more hurtful than anything for Niya to hear Eagle talk to her in the manner in which he was. This was the first time he'd said or done something like this to her. It not only hurt her feelings, but it also made her mad. She grabbed as many diamonds as she could find then stood up.

"You know what, Eagle? Fuck you. You were talking all that gangsta shit when we were in Charlotte, but now you up here shook. You scared to death of these niggas in this city. You wanna know what's pathetic? Yo' weak ass."

"Watch ya fuckin' mouth."

"Yeah, the truth must hurt, you fuckin' pussy."

Eagle wanted to knock every tooth she had down her throat. When it came to talking shit, Niya had a mouth on her, but so did Eagle.

"At least I'm not a fuckin' rat," he said then walked off, bumping her with force in the process.

Niya's whole face dropped to the floor. He'd hit her with a low blow this time, one that made her take a seat on the bed and reflect on the events that took place back at home. She was sick, and as she sat there on the bed in deep thought, the sound of the front door slamming rang throughout the house.

Winter wasn't under arrest, but the detectives had plenty of questions for her down at the station. They wanted to know who Jedi was and why was he on Woodland Avenue firing an AK-47 in broad daylight. With that question, she didn't even have to try to lie about it, because she didn't know Jedi or why he wanted to kill Niya so bad.

According to her story, Winter was kidnapped and thrown into the back seat of her car. She made it look like a simple carjacking. She said that the guy had to be either African or Jamaican due to his accent. Her story was more than believable, given the history of the Africans in Southwest Philly, who were known for stealing and shipping cars and guns back overseas. When the detectives asked her about the gun that was found in the vicinity of where she was at, Winter knew she had to be smart about the answer that she gave. Knowing that they would do ballistics on the gun and test her hand for signs of gunpowder, Winter told them that the gunman left the gun in her car right before he got out and started shooting. She told the detectives she gained access to the guns and began shooting at him in an attempt to get away from him.

Winter was in the police station working her magic, and not once did she slip up or make it seem like she was lying or hiding anything. In the eyes of the detectives, she was purely a victim, and after about an hour or two, she was taken out of the police station uncharged.

"Did you hear about what happened with your nephew the other day?" Lasan, an elder, asked Jedi's uncle. "He made a big mess."

The shooting happened right in front of an African restaurant owned by Sana, another elder, so the word got back relatively quick. Jedi's uncle was unaware of what took place and was embarrassed that he found out about it like this.

"He openly defied us and disobeyed our ruling on the matter," Sana added as he took a sip of cocoa wine.

Disobeying a direct instruction was one of the highest forms of disrespect to an African elder, and the punishment for doing so could be fatal. It didn't matter that Jedi was of blood relation to an elder. When it came down to it, he would eventually have to answer for his actions.

"I will speak to my brother about Jedi. In the meantime, I will do everything I can to get him off the streets. The last thing we need is him finding out what really happened to Contez. If that happens, none of us will be safe," Jedi's uncle said before getting up from his chair and leaving the room.

Eagle walked back into the house after sitting outside on the porch for about an hour. Niya was still sitting on the bed in the same spot she was in when he left. A lot of foul things were said on both sides, but at the end of the day, Eagle loved Niya with everything he had.

"Can we talk?" he asked, standing at the bedroom door with two bottles of water in his hands.

Niya didn't say anything. She just sat there with a sad look on her face. Taking her silence as a yes, Eagle walked over and sat next to her on the bed, passing Niya one of the waters.

"You know, growing up in this city, I never had anybody. My dad was murdered during a home invasion when I was three. I don't remember, but my mom told me that I was lying in the bed with him when it happened," Eagle began. "Ten years later my older brother got shot in his head by his best friend over an ounce of coke. That actually hurt more than when my pop died, because me and my brother were somewhat close."

Niya sat there, listening to Eagle dig into his past, wondering why he'd never told her this before.

"A year after my brother was killed, I lost my mom to a heroin overdose."

The more Eagle talked about it, the more some of his old feelings started to come back, all the way to the point where tears filled his eyes.

"Niya, this city took away everybody that I loved. I swear I don't wanna lose you too," Eagle said, getting off the bed and dropping to his knees right in front of Niya. "Look at me, Niya."

She picked up her head, wiping the tears that fell down her cheek. Eagle needed her to look him in his eyes for what he was about to say. Her reaction to it was going to determine their survival in the mean streets of Philly.

"Babe, we gotta leave, and we gotta leave now," he said with a sincere look in his eyes. "He's not gonna stop until both of us are dead, and we don't have enough manpower to go to war with him. I wanna die by your side, but not this early in the game," he said, lifting his hand up to wipe the tears from her face.

Niya wasn't ready to die yet either. She had a little time to reflect on her life and all the reckless behavior Eagle was telling her about. Even she had to admit that some of the things she did put both her and Eagle, along with Winter and Jade, in danger. Now all she wanted to do was fix it. She looked into Eagle's eyes and said the words he wanted to hear.

"Let's get out of here!"

Chapter 27

Gwen knew just where to find Diamond. Even long after Prada's death, she always was the ideal person to talk to when things went wrong. That was part of the amazing bond Gwen, Niya, Alexus, and Diamond had.

"I remember when I first met her," Gwen said, walking up behind Diamond, who was kneeling down in front of Prada's tombstone.

"I never seen anyone that could dance as nasty as she could." Gwen chuckled, kneeling down next to Diamond.

Diamond cracked a smile, thinking about how true that statement was. Her train of thought quickly went back to what she was thinking about moments ago, and the smile she had on her face disappeared.

"You know it's about to be a war, right?" Diamond asked, not taking her eyes off Prada's tombstone.

"Yeah, I know," Gwen answered in a depressed tone.

Gwen wanted to, and even tried to avoid it, but they drew first blood. No apologies and no amount of money could make this go away. Gwen was holding Nose, and everybody else that rallied behind him when he came home, responsible.

"Is she coming back?" Diamond asked, concerning Niya. "You know it doesn't matter at this point."

"I'm sure she will once I can get in touch with her. I've been trying to call her phone, but it goes straight to voice mail every time. I regret not getting Eagle's number after all this time," Gwen said, shaking her head. "If she doesn't call me by the end of the day, I'll drive over to Beatties Ford Road and get Eagle's number from his people."

"Yeah, do that, because after Alexus's funeral, Charlotte is gonna be a war zone, and I don't have any picks," Diamond said as she rose to her feet.

"Listen, D, I know how ya feel, but at the same time, we gotta be smart about it," Gwen cut in.

"Alexus's funeral is the only funeral I'm trying to attend. In order for that to happen, I need you to follow my lead on this one. . . . A'ight? We good?" Gwen asked, reaching out and grabbing Diamond's arm.

Diamond nodded her head. She already knew how Gwen was thinking. Preserving the lives of fellow MHB members was priority, and if anybody could put together a perfect war strategy, it was sure to be Gwen.

"I'm wit' you," Diamond said as both of them turned around to leave the cemetery.

"There they are." Niya pointed as Eagle pulled into the Fresh Grocer parking lot on Fifty-sixth Street.

Winter and Jade were sitting inside of Jade's car with the doors open, drinking fruit smoothies. Niya didn't want to leave without saying her good-byes, so Eagle afforded her that much. Seeing as how Jade and Winter had no idea what was going on, Eagle prepared for it to take a minute. He got out of the car and stayed on guard while Niya did her thing.

"What are you looking so sad for?" Jade asked as Niya approached with her arms crossed over her chest.

There was no easy way to break the news, nor did she have all day, so Niya just came out with it.

"I'm going to Atlanta," she said, reaching out for Winter's smoothie.

"I knew it was something," Jade said, slamming her smoothie in her cup holder. "I can bet anything you're about to leave today," Jade spoke.

"Dat bitch ain't going anywhere." Winter smiled, looking over at Niya. "Right?"

Niya took another sip of the smoothie then passed it back to Winter. The sad look Niya had on her face gave Winter the answer to her question. She got out of the car and tossed what was left of her smoothie across the parking lot. This was going to be a little more difficult than Niya had expected. Being around Jade and Winter every day over the past seven months formulated more than just a friendship. They became a sisterhood, much like the one Niya left behind in Charlotte.

"If you're moving to Atlanta, then so am I," Winter said, grabbing her bag from Jade's car.

Niya didn't know how to respond to the notion, but what she did know was that Winter was serious.

"Come on, Winter, you don't have to do that," Niya tried to tell her. "Ima come back and visit—"

"I know I don't have to do anything," Winter said, cutting Niya off, "but we made a pact that no matter what happened, we were gonna stick together. Wherever you go, I'm rocking out wit' you," Winter said, throwing her bag over her shoulder and walking off toward Niya's car.

Niya smiled, watching Winter storm off like she was a little kid. She looked over at Jade for her response, but Jade felt the same way. They were a crew now, and from her perspective, the only thing that was going to separate them from one another was a bullet.

"I'm riding 'til the wheels fall off, baby girl," Jade said, extending her arms for a hug. "Now tell that crazy-ass girl to get over here before Eagle ends up killing her." Jade laughed, looking over at Winter sitting in the back seat and not paying any attention to Eagle, who was tapping on the window in an attempt to get her out of his car.

Niya looked over and laughed too. Being honest with herself, Niya was glad that she didn't have to leave her friends behind this time. In fact, Jade and Winter's willingness to drop everything and hit the road with her only made Niya's love for them even stronger. Nobody ever went this hard for Niya, not even anybody from MHB.

"Just a minute," Aunt Debby yelled out from the kitchen after hearing the doorbell ring.

She slowly made her way to the front door, and when she opened it, Jedi was standing there in a Philadelphia Gas Work uniform. He had a pleasant smile on his face and a fake chart in his hand, showing no signs of being a threat. Aunt Debby was still a little unsure, so she inquired.

"Are you here to check the meter in the back?" she asked, knowing that it was already checked two days ago.

Jedi was on point as well. "No, ma'am. We had a gas leak in one of the houses down the street, and we're going door to door to check the rest of the homes on the street. If you step outside, you can see the police sitting there on the corner," Jedi said, pointing to the end of the street. "It'll only take a minute."

Aunt Debby peeked out the door and saw the officer at the end of the street with the lights on. Having seen that, she was more comfortable letting Jedi in.

"You can't be too careful nowadays. People are crazy out here," she said as she led Jedi to the back of the house.

Jedi followed behind her, pulling the .38 special from his back pocket and cocking the hammer back. Thinking about the cop on the corner who was actually doing a traffic stop, Jedi opted to try and kill Aunt Debby a little quieter.

As they passed through the dining room, Jedi looked around for something he could use. A ballpoint hammer sitting in an open tool chest became his weapon of choice, and just as Aunt Debby was about to cross into the kitchen, Jedi struck the back of her head with the hammer. The blow cracked her head wide open, sending her to the ground. The single blow almost killed her instantly, but it was when Jedi rolled her over and repeatedly hit her in the face that Aunt Debby checked out. Blood splattered everywhere, including all over Jedi.

He knew that she was already dead, but his reason for disfiguring her face was to send a message that Eagle had messed with the wrong one. He wasn't playing any games with Eagle, and if he'd thought about leaving the city, it was going to be a mistake on his part. Jedi was going to kill everybody Eagle loved until he got to him.

Everybody had to do their last minute running around before they blew that city. Jade and Niya rode together, while Eagle and Winter took care of their business. The idea of them splitting up started as a joke, but Niya took full advantage of it, since she didn't want Eagle around for what she was about to do. Riding along with Jade was perfect.

The rendezvous point was Thirtieth Street train station at eight o'clock in the morning. The train heading for Atlanta was departing at 8:45, and whoever didn't show up was getting left behind.

"I got one more run to make, and then I'm done for the night," Niya said, jumping back into the car.

She reached into her Burberry bag and pulled out a small black satchel containing the diamonds.

"What's that?" Jade looked over and asked before she started up the car.

"It's a li'l something I came across."

Niya opened the satchel and poured a few of the diamonds into the palm of her hand. Jade looked at the pink stones and was amazed by their beauty. The money that she was about to get for them was going to be start-up money for when they got to Atlanta. All Niya had to do was get them to their destination.

"Take me to Sixty-seventh and Woodland," Niya told Jade, only wanting to get this day over with.

Winter really didn't have much to do. The only thing she was worried about was getting her ID, birth certificate, and social security card. She did have a little bit of money she wanted to leave behind for her brother Monster once he got out of the hospital. Nothing was going to be able to fix what had happened, but the least she could do was help out with his medical bills. What she had saved up rounded out to about sixty grand.

Eagle sat in the car on Tenth and Poplar waiting for Winter to come out of the house. He kept his eyes peeled open and his hand on his gun the whole time. The silence in the car was broken once his phone began to ring. He looked down at the screen and saw that it wasn't a number he recognized. Thinking it might be Niya calling with her new cell number, he answered.

"Yo, what up?" he said, watching as Winter walked out of the house.

"Well, if it ain't my good friend Eagle."

Jedi's voice sent a chill down Eagle's spine. He looked around suspiciously, wondering if Jedi was somewhere in the vicinity. Nobody was outside except a couple of drug dealers on the corner.

"Wassup, Jedi? What was all that about, homie?" Eagle asked.

"At first I didn't know who shawty was, but then when I saw you with her, it hit me."

Jedi remembered looking at thousands of pictures of Niya while being Eagle's celly.

"Nigga, I just didn't think you would come home and rock my brother. If I would have known that, I would have killed you in the joint, my nigga," Jedi spoke.

"Killed me in the joint? Nigga—" Eagle caught himself about to get into a word fight with Jedi. He wasn't about to do that. "You looked good out there the other day. I think the AK was a little too big for you, but who am I to judge?" Eagle chuckled in a taunting way.

"Yeah, my nigga, I tried to take ya muthafuckin' head off," Jedi replied, smiling at the thought of opening up the AK at Eagle. "Next time I'll make sure I use something a li'l smaller so I can hit you. I wouldn't want you and ya bitch getting away from me again."

"Yo, Jedi, on some real shit . . ." Eagle couldn't even explain the situation that happened with Contez. He felt bad about it, but it didn't matter how he put it or how he tried to explain. What happened at the garage was going to be put on him. Besides, he wasn't about to blame everything on Niya anyway.

"You don't gotta explain, my nigga. The only thing that matters is that I'm going to kill you and ya bitch when I catch y'all."

"I don't think that's gonna happen," Eagle said, unlocking the door so Winter could get back in the car.

"I hope you don't think I'm about to let you leave the city. You know I can't let that happen. I'll kill every last family member you have living."

"Oh, yeah? Nigga, you touch anybody in my bloodline and it'll never be safe for any of y'all African muthafuckas to walk the streets. I'll down every last one of y'all," Eagle snapped.

Eagle didn't play when it came down to his family, especially since he only had a few members left in it. Jedi felt the same way about his. Both men knew one thing for sure: if they said they would do something, that's what they meant. Jedi had already got it poppin', though.

"I hear you, my nigga. I guess I'll be seeing you in traffic. Oh, and just to let you know, ya Aunt Debby was only the first," Jedi said then hung up the phone.

Eagle dropped his phone, slammed his car into gear, and peeled off down the street, heading straight for his auntie's house.

Niya instructed Jade to park on Sixty-ninth Street, two blocks away from Le Mandee's restaurant, where she was supposed to meet up with the buyers of the diamonds. They both got out of the car and stood by the trunk, going over all the scenarios that could happen inside. Niya always wanted to be prepared for the foolishness in case it occurred.

"How do I look?" Niya asked, stepping back so Jade could get a good look at her.

"Like the bomb."

From the moment Niya and Jade entered the establishment, things became awkward. The loud conversations that were going on before they walked in ceased, and it was as if the whole restaurant became silent.

The man at the counter waved both of them over, and out of nowhere, a tall, black, heavyset man walked up on them. All eyes were on them, some because they couldn't stop looking at Niya's fat ass protruding out of her jeans. Jade's sexy self was getting a lot of attention too.

"What can I get you ladies?" the man asked with a deep African accent.

"Yeah, can you tell Sana that Niya is here?" she said, resting her hands on the counter.

The man's facial expression changed and immediately he nodded for his boy to give them a pat down. Niya already knew what it was, reaching into her bag and pulling out her .45 by the side and passing it to him. Jade followed suit, handing her weapon over as well.

They were escorted to another section of the restaurant, where Sana, Lasan, and Jedi's uncle, Katah, were sitting. Niya didn't bother taking a seat, because she planned on getting in and out.

"Do you have them?" Sana asked, sipping his coconut wine.

"Yeah, I got them. Where's the money?" Niya shot back, unwilling to pass off the diamonds so fast.

Sana waved for one of his men. He walked over with a duffle bag, placing it at Niya's feet. When Niya reached down to grab the bag, the man stopped her. "Where's the diamonds?" Sana asked again.

"You think I'm about to give you these diamonds without seeing the money? Don't be stupid," Niya told him.

She reached back for the bag and was stopped again. That's when she felt a bad vibe. She looked at Lasan, who kept his hand under the table. She knew she couldn't trust these Africans.

"If y'all ain't got the money, we can come back tomorrow," Niya said, adjusting her bag over her shoulder.

"I'm sorry Niya, but I can't let you leave here with those diamonds," Sana said.

"So what are you going to do, kill me?" Niya asked.

"If you make us," Lasan spoke.

Niya put her head down and shook it. They were serious, and Niya knew it. She then reached into her bag as though she was about to grab the diamonds, but instead of pulling out the diamonds, she pulled out a grenade, immediately pulling the pin to let the elders know she wasn't playing.

Seeing the kind of grenade Niya had in her hand, the elders didn't want to take a chance with her. Had it detonated, it would have killed everybody standing within fifteen feet. Sana waved off the African who had walked over, hoping it would have eased some of the tension in the room. Niya wasn't impressed at all.

"Look, if you want the diamonds, you need to come up with the money. I'll be in the city for another twelve hours and then I'm gone. My number didn't change, so call me when you're ready," Niya said, backing up slowly toward the front entrance.

Nobody even thought about doing anything stupid. Web looked on, watching as Niya walked past him. He couldn't believe what he was seeing.

The grenade couldn't kill everybody if it exploded, but there wasn't a soul in the place willing to sacrifice their life in order to stop her. They were even courteous enough to hand Niya and Jade back their guns on their way out the door.

Something didn't feel right, but Niya wasn't going to stick around and find out what it was. Once she and Jade made it outside, Niya gave the only advice suitable in this situation: "Run!"

Every African that was in the restaurant stood still, waiting for one of three elders to say something. They all looked on as Sana slowly walked across the floor. He stopped, looked around the room at all the dark faces, and said two words that would have everybody riled up like angry bees.

"Kill them," Sana said then walked back across the room to his table.

Four or five Africans immediately took off out the door behind them, and just like ticks on a bull in the wild, they were on Niya and Jade's ass.

Chapter 28

"Jade's not answering her phone either," Winter walked back into the room and told Eagle.

Aunt Debby's house was swarming with police, homicide detectives, and the forensic unit. After processing the scene and collecting as much evidence as they could, the detectives allowed the coroner to take Aunt Debby's body out of the house. Eagle sat on the couch watching as his aunt's body passed by him. A detective tried to ask him questions, but Eagle wasn't answering any of them. The only thing he told the authorities was that he found her like this.

"The sun is starting to come up. You think we should wait at the train station for the girls?" Winter asked, taking a seat next to Eagle on the couch. "We still have a couple hours if you need time."

Eagle was zoned out, sitting there staring into space. All he could think about right now was killing Jedi in the worst way possible. It was one thing to kill Aunt Debby, but to do it in the fashion in which it was done was heinous. It was a closed casket situation for sure.

"I'ma go change my clothes," Eagle said, getting up from the couch and walking upstairs.

Winter didn't know what to do except keep trying to get in contact with Niya and Jade. Departure time was a mere three hours away, and with the new chain of events, Winter wasn't sure if she and Eagle were going to make it there on time.

"Come on, Jade. Pick up the phone," she mumbled to herself, looking up the stairs.

"You think it's cool for us to go out there?" Jade asked Niya, who was peeking out the front window.

The Africans had chased Niya and Jade all around Southwest Philly the night before. They stopped several times to engage in shootouts, but every time Niya and Jade got back into the car and pulled off, the Africans were back on their tail. They were relentless in carrying out the order from Sana.

Fortunately for Niya, she was able to put some distance between her and the Africans, giving her the opportunity to ditch her car on a side street. She and Jade ran on foot for what seemed like forever, until several blocks in, where they sought refuge in an abandoned house near Fifty-sixth and Greenway. There they stayed for hours, while the Africans canvassed the area.

"Yeah, we should be good," Niya said as she walked to the back of the house.

Niya climbed down out of the back of the house then looked around thoroughly to make sure that the coast was clear. They both looked tired and dirty from sitting in the abandoned house, but the important thing was that they were alive.

"We only got a couple of hours to make it to the train station before we miss our ride. I'm so not feeling this phone right now," Niya said, looking at the low battery sign on the screen.

"My phone is still in the car," Jade hissed.

Niya stopped on the corner of Fifty-sixth and Chester, hoping that a cab would come rolling down the street. She sat there for a couple of minutes before she realized she wasn't being smart. They were still in Southwest Philly, where the majority of the African community in

Philly lived. It was only a matter of time before she got the attention of the wrong people.

"We gotta get outta here. Come on, girl. Let's go," Niya said, darting across the street to catch an oncoming trolley.

It wasn't Niya's ideal way of getting downtown to the train station, but at this point, it was her safest option.

Jedi lay across the couch with Audria crouched in-between his legs, sucking his dick. He took deep pulls of the marijuana stick as he watched her head bob up and down at a fast pace. Audria's mouth was super wet and soft, a combination she knew how to use very well.

"You miss Jedi?" he asked, reaching down and grabbing the back of her head.

She took his dick out of her mouth then began licking and kissing up and down his shaft. "Mmmmm, baby, you know I missed this dick." She moaned, slowly jerking his member while kissing his balls.

Jedi took another pull of the weed then threw his head back in pleasure. Audria was going crazy on his dick, sucking and slurping away, and just when she took the whole of his dick back into her mouth, Jedi's phone began to ring. He put the weed stick in the ashtray and grabbed his phone off the coffee table.

"It better be important," Jedi answered, looking down at Audria continuing to deep-throat his dick.

"What's good, bruh? You wanna go holla at ol' boy?" Web asked, still trying to catch a body this year. "You know da nigga might up and try to leave the city. We should go handle that."

"Nah, bruh. He's not going anywhere anytime soon. He can't leave now. I'm sure of that," Jedi assured.

Jedi knew Eagle just as well as Eagle knew him. One thing about being in prison: one could really learn a lot about someone over a long period of time. In Eagle and Jedi's case, they had been cell buddies for close to two years. Being cellmates that long meant that they pretty much knew the other's daily routine. One would know what time his celly eats, sleeps, uses the bathroom, and if time permitted, he could know how his celly would think.

"Yo, it's seven o'clock now. Go grab the homies and meet me at the spot in an hour," Jedi spoke, looking to the sky. I got some other work I need y'all to take care of," he said then hung up the phone.

He grabbed the back of Audria's head, pushing her face down on his member. Just thinking about what he planned on doing to his uncle and the rest of the elders made him want to bust a nut. Audria could see it in his eye that he was at his point, and once his eyes rolled to the back of his head, he shot his load off in her mouth. Audria didn't waste one drop, swallowing every last morsel.

Thirtieth Street station was relatively packed when Eagle and Winter showed up. They were the first to be there, and since it was ten minutes before eight, Eagle expected for Niya and Jade to show up any minute now.

"You still didn't get an answer?" Eagle asked when Winter walked back over with her head down.

"Dis shit crazy. Both of their phones are off. . . . Oh, shit! There they go right there!" Winter yelled, seeing Niya and Jade coming through the front doors. Winter ran over with open arms, hugging both of them. She was happy they had made it.

Eagle didn't even get up, opting to stay seated on the bench, and waited for Niya to walk over. She could tell that something was wrong the moment she laid eyes on him.

"Babe what's going on?" Niya asked, taking a seat next to him on the bench. "Come on, babe. Talk to me," she said, lightly scratching the back of his head.

"He murdered my Aunt Debby," Eagle got out before burying his head in his hands.

Niya was in total shock. She had a lot of love and respect for Aunt Debby, so for her to have gotten caught up in this mess with the Africans was like a shotgun blast to the chest. It made Niya want to leave Philly now just as bad as Eagle did. She looked down at her watch and saw that the train was leaving in about twenty minutes.

"Babe, let's board the train and get the hell out of here," Niya said, getting up and pulling Eagle by the arm.

Eagle didn't budge. He pulled his arm away from her then reached in his pocket and passed Niya the tickets.

"Babe, we can come back for the funeral. Let's just get to Atlanta and get settled in."

"Niya, I'm not leaving," Eagle said in a calm but stern voice.

"Well, I'm not going anywhere either," Niya shot back, sitting down next to him.

Eagle was about to say something, but his phone started ringing in his pocket. To his surprise, a Charlotte area code popped up on the screen.

"Yo, what up?" Eagle answered, looking over at Niya. "Oh, wassup, Diamond? . . . Yeah, she's right here," he said, passing Niya the phone.

"I know. I know. I know. I just bought this phone last night, and it's a piece of shit," Niya spoke into the phone.

"I guess that's the reason why you're not answering ya phone," Diamond replied.

"So, wassup? What's going on?" Niya asked.

"I got some bad news, and I think if you're standing up, you might wanna sit down."

"Come on, D. What's going on?" Niya asked again.

The first thing that came to Niya's mind was that something had happened to her kids.

"They killed Alexus," Diamond informed, fighting back the tears.

Niya sat there in silence, having to remove the phone from her ear. She was relieved that it wasn't her kids, but it being Alexus was just as bad. She was just as important to Niya, and it crushed her to hear of her death.

"Are you still there?" Diamond asked, thinking Niya had hung up the phone.

"Yeah, I'm here."

"The war is on anyway, so you might as well come back home. We need you here with us right now," Diamond said.

Niya wiped the tears from her eyes then took a moment to get herself together. Alexus had done something that she never thought could be done, and that was replace the loss of Prada in her life. Alexus was like her oldest daughter. Niya thought about the day they first met, and how Alexus looked sitting up in that car, scared to death of Niya killing her. *And if it had not been for Prada, I probably would have,* Niya thought, laughing to herself. She also remembered how Alexus was the first person to jump up, ready to die with her just a year later. Niya had promised Alexus that she and MHB would always protect her. The failure of that made Niya hurt even more. She took a couple of deep breaths, trying to get her words straight. Eagle, Winter, and Jade all looked at her, wondering what was going on.

"Say no more. I'll be there," Niya told Diamond before hanging up the phone.

"Yo, wassup?" Eagle asked with a concerned look on his face.

Niya stood there spaced out for a second, thinking about what her next move should be. She wanted to stay in Philly with Eagle and take care of the Jedi problem, but then MHB needed her for what was about to go down in Charlotte.

Niya wished that she could be in two places at one time, but that was impossible. She had to make a choice, and as Niya looked up at the train schedule then back down at her watch, she realized that she only had a few minutes to make up her mind whether she was going to stay in Philly with Eagle or hop on the next train smoking to Charlotte, North Carolina.

To Be Continued . . .

ORDER FORM
URBAN BOOKS, LLC
97 N18th Street
Wyandanch, NY 11798

Name (please print):________________________________

Address: ________________________________

City/State: ________________________________

Zip: ________________________________

QTY	TITLES	PRICE

Shipping and handling: add $3.50 for 1st book, then $1.75 for each additional book.

Please send a check payable to:

Urban Books, LLC

Please allow 4-6 weeks for delivery